Adrift in the Cemetery  /  Martin Campbell

GW00673137

# ADRIFT IN THE CEMETERY

## Martin Campbell

*A story about surviving among the dead*

First published in 2024
By Martin Campbell

ISBN: 978-1-3999-7086-0

A CIP catalogue record is available for this title
from the British Library

Typesetting by Lumphanan Press
www.lumphananpress.co.uk

# – 1 –

## PERSON OF INTEREST

The *Greenock Reporter* front page was accurate and might have been amusing, except to the friends and family of Scott Birrell and the tragic circumstances behind the headline.

*"Dead Body Found in Cemetery."*

There had been a police investigation, arrests and the trial of Iain Black and Steven Barnett. When the jury returned a *not proven* verdict, the *Greenock Reporter* further reported that Mr. Birrell, 39, an unemployed construction worker, had been found just inside the cemetery gates, twenty yards off the road, behind bushes. He was face down in the grass, with an injury to his left temple. The cause of death was a temporal bone fracture and a resultant bleed on the brain. Blood from his head wound had been found on a flat rock beside his head.

It was the first rock killing in Greenock since two boys were convicted four years previously of dropping breeze blocks onto a passing car from a pedestrian bridge over the M8. But hitting cars with builders' blocks as they sped past and battering someone up close with a hand-held lump of sandstone were different.

The details that came out in the court case were shocking,

and juicy enough to keep readers hooked, speculating about what had happened at a spot most people in Greenock had passed at some time in their life. Did the murderer hold the rock in his hands when he cracked the victim's skull, or did he lift it over his head and throw it down after he'd knocked his victim to the ground? It was stone-age-primitive nature of the act, like a caveman killing for a slab of meat or a chance to mate, that kept so many people following the court reports.

The jury heard that Mr. Birrell's injury was first thought to have been as the result of a fall; a theory supported by the initial investigation. Scott Birrell had been admitted to A&E at the Inverclyde Royal Hospital six times in a period of eighteen months leading up to his death, each admission following a drunken fall in the street.

It was only when the site of Mr. Birrell's death was checked more carefully that police discovered the bloody rock by his head had been removed and then returned to its original muddy depression, embedded in grass. Suspicion then fell on Black and Barnett, who had discovered the body and reported it.

Iain Black, from Port Glasgow, said in his evidence that he had found Mr. Birrell lying unconscious when he had been, *"caught short"* and gone into the cemetery to do the toilet. Barnett confirmed this account from the witness box, adding that he had, *"nearly boaked"* when Black had shouted him over to have a look at Mr. Birrell's head wound. Two passers-by also gave evidence to say that they had met Black and Barnett, running out of the cemetery. Black had asked the couple to phone the police, claiming that neither Black nor Burnett had charge on their phones.

Black had been charged with murdering Birrell after luring him to the cemetery to rob him, and the charge against Burnett was one of attempting to pervert the course of justice by providing false testimony in support of his friend.

After four hours and further instruction from the judge, the jury decided that there was not enough evidence to convict Iain Black of beating Scott Birrell with the rock, despite more than half the fifteen jurors believing that he probably did it. Black walked free from court with the *not proven* verdict and the charges against Burnett were subsequently dropped. Case closed.

Except it left both the Police and the Procurator Fiscal Service with another unsolved murder on their books. They were consequently recipients of absolute pelters in the real news media and on the new social media, *Friendster*, where they were accused variously of wasting public money, falsely accusing innocent men, failing to find a murderer, targeting Catholics/Protestants/people who had posted messages slagging off the police/people minding their own business/homosexual men.

Between them, Glasgow and Greenock had accounted for two thirds of all homicides in Scotland the previous year, 2002, and there was political and public pressure on those tasked with finding and convicting murderers to up their game.

And that was when Davie Perdue became a person of interest in the case.

* * *

Weeks after the trial, the verdict and the public hullaballoo, witnesses came forward. Several gave matching descriptions of a man seen entering or leaving the cemetery. Davie was not named in the information that police put out. Police knew only from the witnesses where he had been seen, and vaguely what he looked like.

*"Tall guy with a beard and a woolly hat, pulled doon over his ears. His coat was thick, like an old-fashioned thing your granny would wear, but he didnae look that old."*

*"I remember he had heavy boots, like he was a miner or a farmer maybe. He walked with his chin tucked in, not looking at anybody. Could have been an alky, but I wasn't close enough to smell him."*

*"Didnae see his face, but he had wild hair, bits sticking out from under that hat. He walked like he had somewhere to go. I said hello because we were the only two people there in the cemetery, but he just totally blanked me, walked right past. Ignorant bastard. I remember he was wearing an old coat and trousers that flapped about his legs."*

Most of the reported sightings were recent, and none of them pre-dated Scott Birrell's murder or the trial. These inconsistencies in the timeline were ignored by police and the public, in the excitement of the scent of a suspect.

Davie tried to read the papers each day, even although it was yesterday's news by the time he found it stuffed in a bin or left on a bench at the bus station. He knew that he had to act fast on the second morning, when he was described in detail to readers of the *Greenock Reporter*. Experience told him that a few curious looks at the homeless guy walking the streets would change to a game of spot-the-murderer very soon.

On his first week back in Greenock, Davie had done a nervous tour of the town's charity shops, new and old. Nervous, because he feared being recognised in the civvies he had worn to travel back on the train, or in any of the clothes that he had in his kit bag. The last thing he wanted at that time was to be spotted by anybody who remembered him and drawn back into his old life, or a new old life.

*"Oh, hello Davie! Hivnie seen you for ages. How you been? Back for a holiday in the old town, is it? Have you moved back? Still with the police? Where are you staying?*

*Want to meet up for a pint and a catch up?"*

Too many questions that would require too many lies.

So, he decided that he needed to look less like Davie Perdue. The hat, pulled low, helped. He considered some wild hair colouring or shaving his head, then dismissed those ideas as drawing more attention, not less. Instead, he would stick with the hat and hide behind even more facial hair. But that took time.

A new wardrobe might work; bright gear that the Davie Perdue who people remembered would never have worn. He had the funds. But anything eye catching would say look-at-me, when what he wanted was look-through-me.

Although Greenock was a big place, there were enough regulars, homeless and otherwise, who would spot a stranger in their midst, especially one without transport, walking the same streets each day. It wouldn't be too many days before the curious locals started nodding to him. Then the friendly nods would become, *"Morning."* Then there would be more nosey enquiries.

Davie concluded that his main problem was being homeless without looking homeless. That's what raised suspicions. Maybe it was the cop training. To him, somebody seen walking about the same places again and again without apparent purpose was either lost, mentally ill or casing joints as targets for future crimes.

Walking between the charity shops, he kept his head down, looking as if he was busy, no time to stop, on his way to something that wouldn't wait. While he walked, he tried with difficulty to draw on memories of London streets, driving or walking past rows of shop doorways with begging or sleeping bodies, trying to picture how they looked. He was ashamed to realise that the reason he couldn't remember what the London homeless were wearing wasn't because of their nondescript clothes; it was because within weeks on the job they became invisible to him.

In that first week back in Greenock, he looked at clothes sizes in two competing cancer charity shops, picked out what he could carry in two large bags and headed back to the cemetery.

Weeks later, in preparing for his getaway from publicity, he reluctantly abandoned the coat he had bought, leaving it in the cellar. It was the warmest thing he owned, but also the most obvious give-away in the newspaper descriptions of the person of interest. *"There's a man wearing a granny coat there."* He could hear people say it as they pointed at him as he walked through town.

Tying his hair back as tight as elastic bands would hold it, he pulled on both his jumpers and both pairs of trouser and headed out. Time to get out of town, for a while at least.

As he stood waiting in the queue at the bus station ticket office, Davie caught his reflection in a framed panel showing the timetable. Beside it was an A4 poster with a Strathclyde Police E-fit showing a person of interest. His reflection in the panel wasn't the image he carried in his head, of smart Davie Perdue, officer of the law, keeper of the peace. The resemblance between the rough looking man in the reflection and the adjacent police E-fit was as if he'd modelled for the police artist.

It scared him. He froze for an instant then turned away, leaving his place in the queue. Trying not to hurry, he headed to the toilets. He dodged the entry fee by pulling the bar of the toilet turnstile towards him and slipped through. In a toilet cubicle he pulled one of his jumpers out from his waistband and rolled up both his sleeves to mid-forearm. Coming out of the cubicle, he stood at the sink. He smeared hot water onto his hair to flatten it further. Combing his fingers through the beginnings of his raggy beard did nothing to get it under control.

He was trying to blend in as best he could, going for a carefully-put-together-grizzled-hipster look. If he'd had a pair of thick rimmed glasses, he might have pulled it off. In the scratched toilet mirror, what he saw was a werewolf-who-got-dressed-in-the-dark look.

Loup-garou, rather than Davie Perdue.

\* \* \*

Keeping his head down to avoid the bus station CCTV, he went back to the ticket office and bought a single to Buchanan Street, Glasgow. He was being over cautious, he knew, but better to be safe than arrested. His experience told him that at this stage in an enquiry nobody was scanning hours of CCTV footage looking for him. He was just a person of interest, not yet a local police resource priority or the subject of any nationwide manhunt.

*"Are ye no cold, son?"*

The voice made him jump. The woman behind him in the queue for the bus voiced what everybody else in the queue was thinking. His fears about being recognised as a wanted man were unfounded. It wasn't as a fugitive from justice or as a potential werewolf that he stood out, but as a man without a coat in Greenock on a windy day in March.

He went for the back bench seat on the bus, where nobody would pass him as they got on or off, and where he'd be more difficult to see if the bus had the new onboard CCTV. Ten minutes after the bus pulled out of Greenock, he was asleep, the tension of the last few hours catching up.

# – 2 –

## LIVING WITH THE DEAD

There had never been an offer for the Gatekeeper's House. Interest from anyone naïve enough to believe that a house that size, with that number of rooms could be had for such a price evaporated as soon as the location was revealed.

There had been half-hearted attempts to attract buyers or developers, as enthusiastic estates staff came and went. After ten years of trying, it was conceded that selling the house was a lost cause. The house deeds were duly archived and forgotten in a filing cabinet in the bowels of the Inverclyde Council property office.

According to graveyard tradition, the gatekeeper was the spirit of the first person to be buried in a new cemetery. This person was tasked as a spiritual caretaker, to forever protect the graves of the dead from desecration by the living. Marion Russell had been buried on 15th May 1846 in Greenock Cemetery, the day after it opened. Her small gravestone was marked in section P on the Cemetery Walk Leaflet. It was difficult to find, hidden behind a holly tree that had grown to an enormous height.

In the spirit world, the cemetery gatekeepers dwelt in a tree or in a gravestone near the cemetery entrance. In real life, the cemetery gatekeepers had lived in a solid built house, rent free.

In the largest municipal cemetery in Europe, the address of the Gatekeeper's House was Number 2, Bow Road, Greenock. This confused satnavs, for anyone trying to find the house. Although you could see the roof and top floor windows when you were driving on the long straight that was Bow Road, most of the granite building was hidden behind a mass of trees and an eight-foot boundary wall that ran for half a mile without a break.

If you slowed as you drove past, and looked carefully, you could just see where the old entrance to the cemetery had been bricked up. Two faded, straight lines of mortar marked where the gate piers had stood, supporting the massive, cast-iron gates. Each gate had been over fifteen hundredweight; a measure, like the gates themselves, long forgotten.

From 1846, when it first opened, the cemetery had expanded to over 320 roods, or 80 acres. Funeral carts, drays and wagons turned off Bow Road through the gates and passed the Gatekeeper's House until the 1920s. The cemetery entrance was moved when driving the dead became a dangerous occupation.

After a few near misses, an accident at the entrance led to three more funerals, when a hearse, powered by four horses was in collision with a 20-horsepower Austin.

The new entrance was created at the end of Bow Road. From there, a long driveway now snaked its way past the ornate obelisks and pillars marking the burial places of the rich, through a patch in the southwest corner given over to paupers' graves, and up to the new crematorium at the top of the hill.

The last available lair in the cemetery, sold in September

1994, was a grassy space against a wall near the top of the cemetery. The funerals in the cemetery after that date were predominantly cremations. The only exceptions were pre-paid lairs. These were either side-by-side plots or existing, single lairs that were opened to allow relatives to be piled on top of one another, up to a maximum of six deep.

Well, not directly on top of each other. When it was known that there were more family members to be added, the first set of gravediggers would construct a kind of bunkbed framing to put in the hole and the added coffins would then be rested on slots in the framing.

Built on a hill, there was little flat land in the cemetery, other than the graves themselves.

\* \* \*

The Gatekeeper's House had been occupied first by a cemetery superintendent, then by two generations of undertakers who were also tradesmen. They built sized coffins to order and stored bodies in the basement of the house before funerals.

An outbreak of bubonic plague in nearby Glasgow in 1900 panicked local officials, and as a result the new tenants of the Gatekeeper's House became a pest control man and his large family, brought in to exterminate the black rat population in the cemetery.

The scavenging rodents had worked their way up the hill from ships at Greenock Docks, feeding on scraps from over-flowing bins, then sleeping under gravestones that had collapsed. They also nested in large numbers in the big box tombs, where they could stay dry and hidden from view.

Later still, the house had been shared by the families of workmen employed to tend graves, clean tombstones, and keep in check the acres of sloping woodland. The shrubs and trees, originally laid out to tastefully frame views of distant hills for the deceased had, over many years, grown to claim all available space, with roots creeping through coffins and overhanging branches obscuring headstones.

When the ground maintenance work in the cemetery became a job for a dozen men rather than two or three, the work was farmed out by the local council, and the Gatekeeper's House fell vacant. It had remained unoccupied but kept wind and waterproof since the 1960s. When it was first put up for sale, more in hope than in expectation, the euphemistic language of the estate agent told no lies, but hid a few truths.

*"Spacious, well-proportioned detached property, with neo-Gothic façade. Rooms are spread over three floors and feature a vaulted cellar. Four bedrooms, two reception rooms, kitchen, scullery, bathroom, washroom/laundry room. Many notable original features, including a fine period fireplace. In need of modernisation and offered with no onward chain."*

Nowhere in the brief particulars did it say that the house was in a cemetery, or that prospective buyers would need a team of lawyers to negotiate with various departments in Inverclyde Council for permission to construct a private entrance near the original entrance to get in and out, as the main entrance to the cemetery was closed each day at dusk.

It was long after the property was boarded up that the Gatekeeper's House was renamed by locals as the Goalkeeper's House. A sharp-eyed journalist noted that the house had eleven rooms in total, the same number as made up a football team. The *Greenock*

*Reporter* got the idea for the new name from an earlier piece in the *Glasgow Herald* about Cathcart Cemetery on the south side of the city. It had become a graveyard pilgrimage for Glasgow Rangers and Glasgow Celtic fans, paying homage to team managers from both clubs who were buried there, in an era when managers wore waistcoats rather than tracksuits.

The humorous obituary piece in the *Greenock Reporter* lamented the decline of Scottish football in general and the departure, from the field at least, of eleven great Scottish footballers, linking each of the players to a room in the Goalkeeper's House.

Goalkeeper Andy Goram was in the basement room of the house because he was the solid foundation of the team. He was also in the basement to avoid the light of publicity from press accusations of fraud, extramarital affairs and his mental health problems.

Forty years before the infamous Duncan Ferguson was sent to jail for the same offence, Willie Woodburn, with twenty-four Scotland caps, had been suspended *sine die* for headbutting another player on the field of play. Willie's football skills and his surname in particular got him a place in the only 'reception room' in the house that had a fireplace.

Jim Baxter was in the bathroom for his renowned dribbling skills and Jimmy 'Jinky' Johnstone was in the washroom for his association with water, having been rescued from a rowboat in the River Clyde by the coastguard after a drunken night out, celebrating a victory by the Scottish national team.

The bedrooms in the house were filled, somewhat predictably, by a variety of Scottish players who all had reputations for scoring off the field rather than on it.

The piece in the *Greenock Reporter* was rounded off with an unresolved question about whether the kitchen should be occupied by the great Scottish winger Charlie Cooke, who couldn't cook, or by renowned chef Gordon Ramsay, who couldn't play football, despite claims in his autobiography to have played for Glasgow Rangers.

None of the players allocated to a room was buried in the cemetery. Despite this, the *Greenock Reporter* piece did the rounds in local pubs and the Goalkeeper's House name stuck and spread. In the years that followed, radio phone-ins would ask for names for a 'cemetery eleven' to populate the Goalkeeper's House with an alternative, fantasy football team. Listeners would come up with the same irreverent names each time; Jimmy Graves (Greaves), Dug (Doug) Rougvie, Scottie Tomb (Broon), Greenock Morton legend, Zombie (Andy) Ritchie, John 'Digger' Barnes, Jimmy Bone, etc. etc.

Davie Perdue lived in the basement of the Goalkeeper's House for three months in 2003. Like goalkeeper Andy Goram, Davie sought to avoid publicity at all costs.

# – 3 –

## EYES IN THE DARK

To say that Davie Perdue lived in the Goalkeeper's House wasn't strictly true. It wasn't his permanent residence or his holiday home. It was where he spent most nights when he slept under a roof.

When the empty Goalkeeper's House had been locked and boarded up, the entrance to the basement cellar, a sloping door, was lost in the undergrowth. Invasive Russian vine had crept from the cemetery wall onto two of the trees behind the house, suffocating them and pulling them to the ground near the door. Only by crawling over one tree trunk and under another was Davie able to reach the door, now a fused mass of the vines clinging to the original oakwood. He had broken through the vines so that the door could be lifted just enough for him to squeeze through. When the door was closed behind him, the vines were again a solid mat, with no outward sign of Davie's entrance.

The symbol of a door on gravestones in the cemetery signified the passage from this life to the next, and when Davie climbed into the cellar, it was his transition from one world to another. Inside the basement door, it was as black as lum.

The thick external walls of the house gave some insulation against the cold. No matter how chilly it got inside, it was always warmer sleeping in the basement than on the streets. Where some of the inside basement wall had crumbled, Davie could feel the lead sheeting behind. This primitive, Victorian damp proofing ensured that the room stayed dry for most of the year.

Davie remembered little of what happened during his first week there. Days vanished. He found a way of surviving by not thinking beyond the next hour. After he had lost the first few days reflecting on what might-have-beens, he was thinking more clearly. No more pondering, no lip chewing and ruminating, just practical doing, to make the basement habitable. What did he need? How and where could he get it? How would he get it back? Done. What was next?

The change happened without him being aware of it. There was no pivotal moment when he flipped from the Davie, couldn't-give-a-damn-what-happens-next he'd been on the train from London, to Davie, this-is-me-now-living-in-a-cemetery.

Builders' skips were good for free materials. Like a bird building a nest, he carried back discarded batts of loft insulation, one at a time, under his coat, shaping them in one corner of the basement and then lining the soft cavity he had made with cardboard and a soft blanket he'd found in one of the charity shops.

There was an ancient farmhouse sink in one corner in the basement with a single tap, still connected to Victorian pipes, gravity feeding water from the reservoir on the edge of town. The tap was clogged with at least twenty years of rust.

Davie sat at the stone sink for two hours solid, dripping Coca Cola from above onto the tap and rubbing the sticky liquid into the threads. He remembered shiny pennies from his boyhood, and stories of what Coca Cola did to your guts. It was mind numbing work, squatting in the dark, holding the plastic bottle and allowing one drip to go all the way through the threads on the tap before he released the next one. But he had nothing but time, and thoughts of how running water would make his life in the basement much easier.

When the Coke ran out and the phosphoric acid had done its job on the rust, Davie greased up the tap inside and out with discarded vegetable oil. Patiently yanking the tap left and right, again and again, it eventually gave in, spluttered and spat out the stagnant water sitting in the pipes, before settling into a feeble but steady flow. Success.

Davie suspected that the pipes carrying the water to the tap were made of the same lead that had been used to damp proof the walls, but he was happy to take the risk to his health for the short time he intended to be there. The alternative was spending hours filling plastic bottles from toilets or garage taps and humphing them back to the basement, drawing attention to himself in the process.

In those early days of simple priorities, before Scott Birrell's murder had brought him the unwanted attention, Davie thought of himself as an inconspicuous hunter-gatherer and the basement as his luxury cave. He had shelter and he had water, and he went out daily in search of food. Nobody was looking for him. He was alone but not lonely then and he did not seek the company of others until later.

The only modern indulgences to his caveman existence were a torch and a radio. The wind-up torch, spotted in the window of *Cash Generators,* was bright and compact. He gave up on it after a week however and settled for sitting in the dark for a while.

The brief cheeriness and pretence of normality the torch gave were not worth the pain of cramp in his hands from constant squeezing of the trigger to maintain the feeble light.

The radio was a Grundig *Concert Boy*, found at the same secondhand shop. The speaker had been knocked about, with the result that the sound was tinny, but it was fine for his purposes. It was quiet enough not to be heard outside, with good enough sound quality to keep him updated on the news, or to play for an hour on Radio 3 when he had trouble sleeping.

Having bought the batteries for the radio, he found a simple torch that didn't need the forearms and wrists of a weightlifter to operate. The batteries were a recurring expense, but Davie justified having light and sound in his cave by remembering the few nights he'd spent without either to distract him, sitting there huddled in the basement, in the dark with darker thoughts.

He was snuggling down one night, using his torch to try to read the frequencies on his Grundig *Concert Boy* before going to sleep. He'd been at it for ten minutes when he first noticed them.

He went back to the radio, trying to ignore what he'd seen, then deny it. Eventually, he couldn't blank it out any longer. When he shone the weak light from the torch at the foot of the opposite wall of his basement, two eyes were looking back.

At first Davie dismissed it as a reflection from his newly-cleaned water tap or from the plastic coke bottle. When he scanned back to the spot on the wall however, the eyes blinked. In the near darkness, Davie could see no form behind the eyes, just two glistening yellow orbs, suspended in a black background.

From a dozy state of near sleep, fiddling with the radio dial, Davie was jolted wide awake. Until then, he had felt secure in the basement, believing that the only entry and exit was through the vine covered door. He knew that this was still the case, but only for humans. Something smaller and more agile could find its way in from above or even below, through the rooms of the house, or maybe through the spaces in the floors and walls.

The smell of food may have been the attraction. He was surprised that it had taken so long. He'd been there two weeks at that point. Or had his visitors been there all along, living and moving silently in the dark while he slept?

He pulled his blanket bedding tighter, picturing rats gnawing at it, then at the food he'd dragged inside, then at his toes while he slept. Would they even wait for the light to go out? His imagination jumped from the two eyes on the wall to images of a pack, roaming the cemetery, burrowing, feeding on corpses. He forced himself to stay awake for the fear of being chewed by teeth that had fed on dead flesh. Propping himself awkwardly against the wall, in a position that he thought would make sleep impossible, he prepared for a long night.

He searched with his hand along the wall by his bedding. The eyes had disappeared by the time he'd found a lump of mortar to throw across the room. He continued flashing the torch on every few minutes and waving it about silently, like some cowboy with a lighted stick, warding off wolves from his campfire.

At dawn, some weak light leaked through the gaps in the cellar door where the planking and the frame had separated with age. Davie opened his eyes and realised that he had finally given in to exhaustion, despite his awkward position against the wall. His head was on his shoulder and when he tried to straighten up the muscles in his neck complained.

He felt like he had whiplash. It took him five minutes, slowly rocking his head from side to side before he had enough flexibility in his neck to turn and look around the basement without pain.

He shone his torch around the foot of this bedding first, checking for holes or teeth marks. There were none that he could see. He stretched, then emerged from his nest and began to explore the cellar systematically, using a combination of the faint shafts of daylight and the torch.

He found some raisin-sized beads here and there, that might have been rat shit, but Davie was no authority on whether the droppings had come from a rat, a mouse or a fox. They could just as well have been lumps of dirt, and he wasn't about to test them by touch or smell to find out.

\* \* \*

Although the gap between his expectations and his experience of living in London had worn him down, and ultimately dulled his enthusiasm for life there, Davie had learned much during his time in the city. This included seemingly useless information about the ever-present rats that lived under the streets in the capital city.

Many of London's homeless shared the same living space as the rodents. One of Davie's compulsory training days at Hendon Police College had covered *"dealing with"* the homeless; the risks they posed to the public, and the increased risks they themselves faced from hypothermia, abuse and diseases, including those transmitted by rats.

Davie remembered spending most of that training looking out a window of the baking hot room on a summer's day, wondering if he and his colleagues were going to get an early finish and time to soak up some rays.

As he scanned the floor of his airless basement home with his torch, details from that training session, where he thought he had been physically but not mentally present, came back to him, unexpectedly.

*"Hantavirus and Weil's disease, caused by rat faeces and urine..."; "Exposure to poorly ventilated areas..."; "Rare cases found in the homeless..."*

It spurred him to renew his efforts, searching the floor for other signs of the rats and checking for any obvious spaces in the ceiling or wall that he could block up.

He considered his other options. Buying rat poison looking like he did would draw more than questions and suspicious looks at the local hardware shop. A phone call to the local cops about a potential suicide or a mad homeless poisoner was possible.

He spent that next day walking around town, continuing his scavenging or buying bits and pieces to make the cellar more secure and comfortable, repeatedly going over the pros and cons of staying there or looking for somewhere else to sleep.

That night, the eyes were back.

Davie had laid in a pile of stones to throw, and a new set of batteries to avoid the nightmare of being huddled in the dark with no light, listening for tiny, scuttling feet approaching.

He'd been there an hour, switching the torch on every five minutes, when he picked out the eyes again. They were in a different spot this time, closer than before, on the wall adjacent to where he had set up his bed. He felt the hair on his neck rise as he watched the eyes float up the wall six inches, then slowly back down to their resting position.

By changing the angle of the torch along the wall, he was able to make out some form; a black hump behind the eyes that were still watching him. His first thought was that he was in the basement with the biggest rat he'd ever seen.

As he continued to stare down the eyes with his torch, now difficult to hold steady on one spot because of his shaking hand, he watched the eyes rise up again, and realised that the hump behind them was stretching, standing up, ready to attack. He fumbled for one of the stones from his pile, just as he heard the sound.

Not the hissing or growling of the rat he was expecting, but a quiet, *"miaow."*

In all the time that he was there, Davie never found out how Yashin got in and out of the basement, or why he preferred the basement to any of the other rooms in the house.

He was a sumo of a cat, the size of a small fox, solid black in colour with just a tip of white on his tail. Like Davie, he returned to the Goalkeeper's House only at night, usually well after Davie had settled down. Despite his bulk, the cat moved silently, which explained why Davie had not realised that they had been sharing the room until a fortnight after he moved in. Also like Davie, Yashin never peed or shat in the basement. That was just bad form, regardless of whether you were human or feline.

Davie assumed that Yashin had been living in the house for a while, feeding on mice and birds he could catch in the cemetery, food from rubbish bins or unattended cat bowls in local gardens, maybe even the occasional rat that Davie had mistaken him for. Davie could tell that Yashin was a good hunter or scavenger, because of his size and the fact that he turned his nose up at scraps of food Davie offered him as they got to know each other a bit better.

He named the cat Yashin after one of his boyhood heroes. The great Russian goalkeeper Lev Yashin, who played in four World Cups and was nicknamed *The Black Panther* or, for Scottish people who had never seen a panther, simply *The Cat.*

Growing up, playing football in parks, Davie and his mates would claim the identity of great teams of the day before they kicked off. Some days, it was, *"Right, you'll be Real Madrid and we'll be Rangers,"* or, *"We're Manchester United and you can be Celtic."*

Likewise, each boy took on the persona of one of his heroes for that game. The rules about which player could play for which team were flexible, so Real Madrid might have two Kenny Dalglishes playing for them, or Joe Jordan could be seen scoring a hat-trick for Bayern Munich. Davie was always Lev Yashin when he did his stint in goal. When he was *The Cat*, he could leap further and make more saves worthy of inclusion in the recorded highlights that he played back in his head later in the day.

And now the house had two goalkeepers in the basement: Andy Goram and Lev Yashin.

It was early Spring in Scotland, but that meant little. One night when the temperature outside had dropped close to zero, Davie woke in the morning to find Yashin curled up at his side. On rare occasions, Yashin would deign to have his ears scratched for a few minutes before moving off to take care of business for the day. So, Yashin tolerated sharing his room with Davie. For his part, Davie's quality of life, such as it was, had been improved by his feral pet. Any rats thinking about moving into the basement would reconsider if they met Yashin.

# – 4 –

## FAKE BEGGARS

Davie Perdue was homeless but not poor, not yet anyway. He had his stash, built up during his three years in London, when he was trying to make enough and save enough to make the jump onto the property ladder.

On his return to Scotland, he could have used his bank funds to bounce back, rent a flat in Glasgow, get a job, get back into the game. But he chose not to, not so soon. In the meantime, he wondered if he was Greenock's richest homeless person.

In a time long past, when the wandering homeless were tolerated as merely tramps, walking the country in search of harvest labour or other seasonal ways of making money, there was some grudging public respect for their efforts. Some of these nomadic men buried their earnings in secret locations – in a buried tin, in a dry spot in the woods – then returned periodically to the same place to withdraw or even deposit funds.

Davie didn't keep his cash in a hole in the ground, but in a hole in the wall.

He picked his times and places to withdraw enough cash to get by. Just enough to keep ticking over when he needed it.

He chose early mornings, and cash machines that couldn't be seen by passing foot or motor traffic. Members of the working public seeing a homeless man punching his PIN into an ATM perpetuated the myth of the fake homeless. Davie had learned more about those who lived on the Scottish streets in the few weeks he'd been back in Greenock than he ever did during all his time in London.

* * *

There was a caste system in the society of the fortunate and the homeless. Everyone understood it and most lived by the rules.

There were the low-level untouchables; homeless men and women, trying to get enough to eat and staying warm in doorways. They were a caste called lying, worthless scroungers, kicked, spat and peed on by passers-by from a higher caste, those who were the salaried settled. For this higher caste, those with a home to go to, the belief in the cause-and-effect association between being bone idle and becoming homeless had long been established and reinforced by listening to the right media sources and reading variations of the same story in the *Daily Star* and the *Sun*. If you could get money, get a lot of it and get it legally, you were a person of virtue. Money was the test of that virtue. If you couldn't get money legally, you were of little virtue or worth.

It was self-evident. According to headlines and editorials, if you were homeless and shiftless, it was a lifestyle choice. You had decided that anything was better than washing or working for a living. You had been a skiver all your life. You were probably getting too many benefits, paid for by the sweat of others, and spending this unearned money on fags, drink or drugs. Your time was spent begging, drinking and robbing when you got the chance. If you were living on the street, you were there because you had fucked up, and it was your own fault.

Don't give money to homeless beggars because they don't need it. They've already got a place to live, or they've been offered a place to live, or they've had a place to live and been chucked out because of drinking and drug taking.

So, there were the salaried suits at the top and the beggars at the bottom. That was the simple hierarchy of the caste system. Getting money, getting a lot of it, legally, put you at the top.

But there was another special caste, populated by the lowest of the low, at a level even beneath the untouchables. This was a group who the untouchables and the upper castes were united in loathing.

They were the fake homeless and the fake beggars. Despicable crooks, diddling the trusting public out of money. Christian hustlers, some called them. Able bodied, financially solvent, home renters and owners who would stoop so low as to wear a disguise to steal from those who earned less than they did.

They were like evil Robin Hoods, taking money intended for those with little from those who believed they were relieving misery. The public anger came not only from those who gave to beggars, but also from those who never would. It was a topic of breakfast table outrage that scammers were out there duping the gullible and making the more savvy look naïve.

Beggars with the cardboard signs reading, *"ex-services veteran"* were just the thin end of the wedge. They may or may not be homeless, but many had never worn a uniform. In this caste of cheating bastards, there were different levels of sophisticated deception.

There were the patter merchants, all men, moving on a strict shift system around carefully chosen street pitches, grooming then milking four or five people at a time, usually women. Their trick was convincing the trusting mark with whom they had developed a special friendship that her kindness was all that stood between the scumbag and his death by starvation or hypothermia. Disingenuous beggars and hustlers; something should be done about them, everyone agreed.

Then there were the worst of all. Far, far more unscrupulous in the eyes of the suspicious public were the smooth operators, the master fake beggars, proficient and ruthless. They parked up in shiny cars somewhere quiet before changing clothes and working one or more pitches. Some worked alone, some worked in gangs, pooling what they had conned at the end of the day.

Davie had seen a few slick operators during his time in London, and when he started visiting Glasgow. They were professional operators in prime spots who milked the kindness of strangers by day and then probably went back to their warm, two-bedroomed apartments by night. But in Greenock?

For one thing, the waterhole in Davie's hometown had been dry for some time and even the most desperate of the thirsty animals had moved on. The last of the sugar barons, shipbuilding magnates and other industrialists had left town over thirty years ago and with them any associated easy-touch wealth that could be tapped.

There were no prime begging spots where suited, powerhouse money men strode by during the day, salving their consciences by dropping a fiver or a tenner in a hat after a two-hour lunch, paid for by some other money vulture. Even at night, the drunken spare change in the pockets of the deserving rich went to taxi drivers as tips, rather than to the undeserving poor huddled outside pubs or nightclubs.

So the fake beggars of Greenock were probably a myth, Davie thought.

And there was also a secret line of defense against any who might try this lowest type of deception. The most hopeless of the real beggars, those scrounging money to fund cider, Buckfast habits or the contents of a needle might have lost all dignity, pride and in some cases bladder control, but they still had a sense of smell. They could sniff out any fakers with a full set of teeth and a healthy complexion infringing on their pitch and chase them off, like a murder of crows mobbing a hawk.

There was no *costume de rigueur* for the genuine homeless. There were no fashion police to caution on wearing clothes that were too big, too small, wearing socks with sandals, trousers with a camel toe, missing or added fastenings, colours that should never be worn together or clothes with added holes or food stains. For the street pretenders however, there were a few sartorial slips that could identify them as cuckoos in the nest of the homeless.

Davie had seen one guy, more of a chancer rather than a genuine fake beggar, set up his pitch near the bus station. He caught Davie's attention for two reasons. He was new, as new as the shoes he was slipping inside his sleeping bag as he got comfortable, and his ears were pierced. The clincher was the black and white, look-at-me puppy tethered to the roanpipe behind him.

In the time it took Davie to buy some supplies in the supermarket, three homeless worthies, each with his own pitch at the bus station, had gathered around the guy, nudging him with their shoes and asking to see his. The guy made a sack race exit down the street, dragging his dog, as a bigger crowd gathered.

But fake beggars were not the only homeless myth in town. During the years Davie was growing up, right through to when he joined the police, went to London and came back, mothers had been scaring their children into "being good" with stories of Greenock's very own bogeyman.

The Catman of Greenock was only ever seen crawling or dragging himself about, with two red eyes staring out from a face blackened by soot or oil. He was said to live among the town's feral cat population, feeding on rats in abandoned housing estates like Clune Park, "Scotland's Chernobyl", or in old hospital or factory buildings, depending on which mother was scaring her children, or whatever site of urban decay was her closest reference point.

The extended, adult version of the story told how the Catman was a Russian sailor who jumped ship or was left ashore when his ship left Greenock harbour in the 1970s. He then had a nervous breakdown, either from the stress of hiding from immigration authorities or from the horror of realising that he had been abandoned in Greenock. The breakdown had left him in his present unbalanced state, the story went.

Tales of the Catman written by outsiders described Greenock as a *"sleepy town on the Scottish west coast"* or a *"charming sea port"*; descriptions that were as fanciful as those of the Catman and instantly identified the writers as being from Edinburgh or England. Did the homeless Catman exist? Like stories of fake beggars, years of local lore had made it difficult to untangle what was real from what was not.

The number of fake beggars and foreign beggars in Scotland had been a problem in the past. That much was fact, not myth.

The problem had been solved by government-issue beggar badges, which could be flashed to passing pedestrians to verify a beggar's legitimacy, and his or her legal right to beg. But that had been in 1425.

The modern-day equivalent of the beggar badge was the *Big Issue* Vendor badge.

\* \* \*

Fake beggars in fancy shoes didn't have *Big Issue* badges, but after a month back from London, Davie did. He sold the magazine, traveling to Glasgow each time to avoid being recognised in his hometown. He did it more for the contact than for the cash. The need to be around other people became like a periodic thirst, living alone in the Goalkeeper's House.

The job suited him. No ID, address or bank account needed. After his first stint with the five free magazines, he would buy twenty at a time, sell them for twice the price as agreed and then go back to Greenock.

Stand while selling and be sober and clean; those were the only job requirements. He was able to pick his days, but not where he sold his magazines. The prime spots were earned and guarded by long termers, sellers who were out there in wind, rain and snow, year-round, building up a customer base, their resilience impressing regular commuters who bought the magazine, even if they never read it.

So, the pitches Davie got were just "off Broadway". These were streets with enough foot traffic to sell his stock of magazines, and on good days to have a bit of soul-sustaining banter with the buyers who had time to stop.

On the bad days, he got more unwelcome advice than sales from the passing punters.

*"Big Issue? Big Issue?"*

*"Get up off yer arse and get a job, pal."*

Lazy insults, since he wasn't on his arse, but standing, and selling magazines *was* the job. But poverty was a choice, a result of laziness, wasn't it? Davie had comebacks that he was itching to use.

*"Have a nice day pal, somewhere far away from here."*

*"If I wanted to hear an arsehole talking, I'd fart."*

But he never rose to the baiting. There was no point. He'd seen it. It just led to more backchat, fights or being reported as an "aggressive beggar". He knew that dispelling the centuries old, parasite-by-choice myth would take more than smart one-liners from him.

As well as the insults from potential buyers, there was also passing shouts from further off.

*"Piss off, ya scrounger bastard,"* or, *"Fuck off ya alky/ junkie/ waster/ dosser/ wanker/ minger,"* or Davie's favourite, *"Away back to your own country and beg."*

This scatter-gun abuse was mindless, mostly from young folk trying to impress other young folk in their company.

*Big Issue* sellers were tarred. The government-issued beggar badges of the 15th Century and the modern-day Vendor badges were intended to validate sellers' integrity as legitimate street traders in the eyes of the public. But instead, even after 600 years, the badges still marked them out as charity cases, with the ambivalence that brought.

The law said that you could sell newspapers and coal on the streets of Scotland without a street trading licence. But nobody selling newspapers or delivering coal was ever offered a sandwich or a half-eaten pizza instead of cash for goods. Even illegal street hawkers shouting about three pair of socks for a pound were never seen as anything other than authentic salesmen, despite the questionable quality and origin of the socks. That was the difference. The public didn't see *Big Issue* vendors as businesspeople.

*"Helping the homeless help themselves."* The *Big Issue* slogan said nothing about what was being sold or its value. The vendors weren't shouting about the showbiz or football celeb on the front cover, or the well written articles about Eastenders or Prince Charles inside. The *Big Issue* slogan was instead pleading, *"Please, please buy a Big Issue."* Which was not a great sales pitch.

So, selling the *Big Issue* was many hours slog for meagre returns and guaranteed abuse along the way. Despite all of that, Davie enjoyed it for other reasons and still came back for more. He liked meeting up with other vendors at the beginning of the day, exchanging stories and learning from them.

Vendors could sell between 7am and 8pm, must stand if able to do so, must always carry their badge and must not be intoxicated or use physical or verbal aggression. Those were the rules. Within those rules, there was some leeway for style, however. Davie was impressed and entertained by how some of the vendors used showmanship, a dying art, to sell their magazines.

Hammy was a forty-something man who looked sixty-something. His standout physical feature was his hair. It was unwashed, thick and matted at the back, the shape of a platypus' tail. When Davie first saw him working his pitch, his first impression was of a hyperactive squirrel. Hammy always took as many *Big Issues* as he could carry from the collection point, and he sold them all, every time. He had street charisma.

In another life, perhaps one he had lived, he'd have been convincing buyers to invest or donate cash to something they had never heard of. He had the killer persuasive technique of pulling at heartstrings and at the same time making the purchase of the *Big Issue* seem like it wasn't a choice.

*"It helps to know yer Greek for this game, son,"* was his enigmatic reply when Davie asked him directly about his technique. A reply that was more evidence of Hammy's previous life.

*"Ethos, pathos and logos. They're the three salesman's friends, see."*

Davie was too embarrassed by his own ignorance to ask more.

Hammy may have had an education in the Classics as a foundation for his salesmanship, but the singing helped too.

He had a rich, Johnny Cash baritone voice, the result of hammering his throat with 40-a-day smoking and hard drinking in the past. He would roar out the same dozen songs each day, the order random. They all shared the same, woke-up this-morning-blues-walking-like-a-man theme and familiar twelve-bar melodies. Could a white man sing the blues?

Hammy could.

Many of his songs had call-and-response patterns that allowed Hammy to invite, if not demand audience participation. There were tales about devil women, hoochie coochie men, trains coming down the tracks, and times when Hammy's good times had gone bad. He remembered most of the lyrics and adapted the rest to suit. Instead of being your hoochie coochie man, he became your *Big Issue* man, instead of being a bluesman who wanted to kiss-you, he became the man who wanted to sell you a

Big Iss-ue. Even the punters who had heard the songs many times before still smiled as they handed over their cash.

When he had sold all his magazines, his singing stopped, sometimes mid-verse. Back to business, Hammy headed off for another armful of *Big Issues* and started again. Rinse and repeat.

Like Hammy, many *Big Issue* vendors were not technically homeless. They had a place to stay with heating, hot water and a door that locked. With those benefits came strict tenancy conditions. Whether the majority of the people buying the *Big Issue* would consider these basic digs as a home however, was debatable.

At times, it struck Davie that he was deceiving those around him, and that he was no better than the fake beggars that everyone despised. Although he had a hard luck story like the others selling the *Big Issue*, he wasn't destitute, mentally ill or addicted. He was down on his luck like them, yes, but he really was homeless by choice. He had money in the bank that he could use to move up, or to give to others to relieve some of the misery that he saw. Instead, he chose to live on the street and in the basement, pretending. He was playing a role, a bit like someone at one of the "tramps' suppers" he'd seen advertised while he was in London.

Rich people would organise charity fundraisers to raise conscience money, with guests turning up in torn and worn rags in fancy rooms and being served up pseudo homeless food; mashed potatoes with gravy and sausages, liver and onions, or cremated pizza. An insult to the homeless, but what a laugh to dress up and pretend on a Saturday night.

* * *

Davie was living in a cemetery. It was the dead centre of Greenock. There were high walls because people were dying to get in. There were views from the hill to die for. There were more crosses than a football coupon. Davie had heard all the jokes as a boy.

He understood very well the strict conditions of his tenancy in the basement of the Goalkeeper's House. They were written on a plaque in raised cast-iron typeface on the cemetery entrance gate.

*"This gate will be closed at dusk. No person shall be in Greenock Cemetery after sunset or before sunrise. No person not being an officer or servant of the burial authority, or another person so authorised by or on behalf of the burial authority shall enter or remain in a cemetery at any hour when it is closed to the public without first having obtained permission from the Burial Grounds & Crematorium Supervisor. No persons may enter or leave the Cemetery except by the entrances and exits provided for that purpose."*

The rules were vigorously enforced by the crematorium supervisor and the ground staff.

The opening and closing of the cemetery each day was theatrical. The cast iron gates were over twenty feet high, decorated with carved wreaths and a St Andrews cross pattern. When all other cast iron gates and railings throughout Greenock were taken off to be melted down for use in World War II materials, an exception was made. The entry gates were left, hung on their massive square stone piers. When they creaked open with difficulty each morning, you half expected to see two-wheeled Greek chariots pulled by teams of horses race across the pavement from the cemetery.

Davie had arrived in March. As spring arrived, he had more time to be out. Up to Glasgow and back, thinking time on the bus or train, taking care of business, selling *Big Issues*, collecting what supplies he needed to bring back. Gates were open April to August, 8.00 a.m.- 9.00 p.m., dawn until dusk.

Timing was critical. If he missed the gate curfew, it was a choice between finding a hassle-free spot to sleep or climbing the massive front gates, or the wall that ran the length of the main road. Climbing the gates risked being spotted or breaking an ankle. The wall that ran the length of Bow Road, eight foot high but more vine than wall, could be scaled, but he would be spotted easily by motorists in the constant flow of traffic and either reported or remembered, neither of which was good.

* * *

Inside the cemetery, the lives of most people in the graves that Davie passed on his way to his basement were recorded with a bare statement of the dates on which they were alive. The basic birth and death dates said nothing about how any of these people had spent the days in between.

Saving on the costs of chiseling extra words, many headstones said simply, *"Died", "Passed Away"* or *"In Memory".* For a few, there was more detail about the way of passing. Family tragedies: *"After an illness bravely borne", "Drowned", "Accidently Killed".* Death was a question of perspective for others. Some inscriptions spoke of how others, still alive, viewed the life beyond. Members of the Free Church of Scotland buried in the cemetery had all been *"Taken Home",* and older graves spoke of greater faith also, *"Went Rejoicing Out of This World",* or *"Gone to Another Room".*

Two lines of barbed wire fencing ran on top of stretches of cemetery wall further up the hill where it abutted housing on the Bow Road and Ness Road. This was not to prevent spirits leaving the cemetery but to discourage those who lived in the housing estate from using the privacy of the graveyard for under-age drinking or sex on the tombstones.

On nights when he missed the curfew, Davie had spent nights in the Orangefield Tunnel. It was 150 yards of disused, overgrown railway, accessed by scrambling down a grassy bank just opposite the cemetery gates. There was a rail workers' safety alcove about fifty yards in, dry and sheltered from the wind. Davie could curl up there and get some sleep, undisturbed.

Missing the cemetery curfew reminded him of his childhood, staying out late, kicking a ball on summer nights, but having to be in by dark as the days shortened.

*"That door'll be locked at eight o'clock, mind, and if you're no back you'll no get in."*

His mother said it so many times, but never actually locked out her nine-year-old son.

By that age, Davie had forgotten what his father looked like.

# – 5 –

## INFAMY

Davie was four years old when the two policemen came for his father. They knocked on the door while Davie was racing his cars up and down the front lobby of his house. Recently tall enough to reach the handle, Davie opened the front door before either of his parents could respond.

His mother's hands flew to her mouth at the sight of the policemen. Police at the door meant somebody had died. But when the policemen didn't remove their hats, she was puzzled.

The taller of the two spoke first.

*"Is your husband at home, Mrs. Perdue?"*

When she didn't reply immediately, they stepped past her into the house. Isobel's mood changed quickly from confusion to anger.

*"Here, you two, you cannae just barge into folks' houses without being asked!*

*What's all this about? What are doing here?"*

Davie's father, alerted by the voices, stood at the end of the lobby in the entrance to the front room. As the two policemen moved towards him, his head dropped.

*"It's OK Isobel,"* he said, *"I think I know what this is about."*

Isobel pushed Davie behind her and looked from Donnie

back to the two policemen, struggling to understand what was happening.

"*Donnie, Donnie what do they want with you? Tell them to get out of our house.*"

The taller of the two spoke again.

"*Donald Perdue, I'm arresting you under the Marriage Scotland Act 1977...*"

His colleague produced a pair of handcuffs. He put them back on his belt, after a slight shake of the head from the arresting officer, and a nod towards Davie, peering from behind his mother, holding a toy car that the policemen had stood on, both axles broken.

"*Donnie, Donnie, what are they talking about?*"

Isobel had given up on trying to keep her voice down and avoid the attention of the neighbours. She was shouting, denying what was happening and trying to bar the policemen's way, one hand on her husband's chest, the other on the wall.

"*You've made a mistake here,*" she said, shaking her head again. "*Tell them Donnie, tell them!*"

"*I'll get this sorted out, Isobel,*" Donnie said quietly as he was led down the lobby and out the front door.

*I'll be back later, and we can talk about it then,*" he said, over his shoulder.

It was the contrast between his father's calmness and his mother's hysterics that told Davie something was very wrong in his young world. He registered that something bad was happening to his dad, but he couldn't understand why his mother was the only one upset about it. Afraid and confused, he started crying. He didn't know whether to join his mother in the fight with the policemen or do as his dad said and let them take him. Plus, his car was broken.

His dad said he'd be back, but he wasn't. When he phoned later that day, it was the last time his mother spoke to her husband. Davie never saw his dad again.

He had been taken to jail.

Davie was too young to understand why or for how long. Years later, at the Police College at Tulliallan, the Marriage (Scotland) Act 1977 didn't feature at all in the police recruits' legislation training, and bigamy was mentioned as an offence only in context of other, rarely prosecuted, "quaint" Scottish crimes, like hamesucken and plagium.

The sentence for his father was two years, but it was life for his mother. In the small street community where they lived, there was limited variety. What neighbours were known for and what they were known as was often the same thing. Being Jock the plumber or Janet the teacher's sister or Moira, one of Janet's bairns were all neutral terms of reference, used when people talked openly about others in the street. Being fat Betty or Gordie with the stutter or Kevin the alky were similar identifying labels, but only used selectively for gossip.

Davie's mother went, in a single day, from being Isobel the respected cook at the hospital to being, *"Isobel, who was married on the bigamist"*. Not married to, but married *on*, the same way that a woman who stepped outside the unspoken conventions of her neighbourhood might be known as being married *on* someone of a different religion or married *on* a black man. With the revelation of the bigamy, Isobel's marriage was legally void and her position in the local hierarchy became that of other unmarried mothers, reputation ruined.

Local memories might have faded and the whispering spotlight moved more quickly on, but the circumstances of Isobel's misfortune were so unusual, so exotic for a street where not much happened, that she might just as well have carried a sign around her neck.

Except for two real friends at work, everyone she knew treated her differently from the day of Donnie's arrest. It wasn't like an illness or a death in the family, where people she knew might offer concern, sympathy or condolences. There was no script, no playbook for someone who had been deceived by a bigamist. It was a juicy scandal that had it all; secrets, cheating, crime and of course sex.

People reacted by trying not to. It was an unspoken knowing. People she talked to in the shops, in the street, even at work would maintain a plastic smile and speak about anything except what was foremost on their mind, and Isobel's. As Davie grew, his likeness to Donnie was a constant reminder to Isobel of Donnie's deception and her shame.

Donnie had been brickie, and a good one. He'd come up from Newcastle for a big construction project on Greenock Quay. The contract was for three months. He found digs with a landlady, travelling back to Newcastle every weekend, at first. Then it was every second weekend after he met Isobel in a pub, when she was on a works night out.

Did Donnie reinvent himself as a single, eligible man on that first night? Was he so smitten with Isobel that he decided to abandon everything in his past life, including his wife in Newcastle, to be with Isobel? That was the best-case scenario in Davie's later thinking. It was an attraction so strong, so unstoppable that Donnie and Isobel were drawn together like two magnets and Donnie was pulled from his life in Newcastle, regardless of what he believed to be right or wrong.

The worst-case, more likely scenario was that they both had too much to drink, Isobel fell pregnant, and his father decided that he had to marry her, despite already having a wife in Newcastle. It was a not a case of doing the right thing, more like avoiding what Donnie considered the greater of two wrongs.

Davie never found out what happened or when because his mother never spoke about it, ever, even when he was older. Any questioning was shut down. He was warned off by his mother's silences when he asked as a boy and by her angry embarrassment as he grew older.

Not knowing made his confusion worse.

Davie would never know. His mother avoided any relationships with men for the rest of her life and, as far as he knew, never spoke to anyone about Donnie.

His father wrote to her from prison. The young Davie remembered the letters only because of the strange, sludgy colour of the envelopes. Donnie wrote to say how sorry he was, asking for forgiveness, telling Isobel how much he loved her, maybe asking about Davie, how he was doing in school, how good it would be to see them both again. Those were Davie's guesses anyway. Every time a letter dropped through the door, it was ripped, unopened, into the smallest pieces, and thrown in the bin or the fire, depending on the time of year.

His father tried to contact Isobel when he was released after 20 months. There was a flurry of letters, one every day for over a week, then phone calls. Davie saw his mother pick up the phone without speaking and put it back down just as quickly, dismissing his questions with a cold look that said, *"Don't start."* Davie was too young to understand what was happening, but his mother's reaction told him it could only be his father, and told him just as clearly not to ask.

Just as his mother had gone from respected mother and hospital cook to fallen woman, Davie became, *"that poor wee laddie"* or *"the wee bastard boy"*, depending on which of the neighbours was talking.

When he started school at five, it was no big deal. There were plenty of other children in the school without fathers, being raised by widows or mothers who were divorced or separated. It was only as he got older, nine or ten, that he started to feel some of the betrayal and unwarranted guilt that his mother was still living with.

Boys, mostly boys, would ask him, *"Well, where is your father?"* and his unwillingness or inability to answer just made other children more curious and insistent. He tried telling them that his father was dead to shut them up, but Greenock was too small a place for that. Everybody knew everybody's business, and when there were some details missing, they could be made up.

*"My mother says that your dad isn't dead. She says he's living in Glasgow."*

*"My dad says that your dad ran away with another woman."*

When he got to High School, it was worse, even when he gave up trying to invent stories about his father and came clean, or as clean as a 14-year-old could with what he knew. But the other 14-year-olds, the nosey and the cruel, kept digging for more details that Davie didn't have. It would die down for a while, only to come back again when somebody else in his year at school would be dared by their mates to ask Davie about his father, while they watched on, tittering.

As he got to school leaving age, thinking about college or a job, it was his name that attracted the same round of questions.

When the marriage was declared void because of the bigamy, his mother had reverted to her maiden name, Isobel Murray. By that time her son had been registered and christened as David Perdue. At a time when she wanted to crawl in a hole and die, meeting with people at the Greenock Registrar Office and explaining her shame was the last thing his mother wanted to do. The long process of changing Davie's name or trying to get Donnie's name removed from Davie's birth certificate would have brought more attention to her and to Davie, so Isobel did the minimum necessary, which was nothing.

The day that Donnie was carted off in the back of the police car was the day that the best part of Davie's mother's life ended. Looking back, Davie thought it was also the day when, aged four, his interest in the police and the law truly began.

He struggled to understand what had happened and learned fast that asking his mother was not allowed. This made him more and more frustrated with curiosity. Every time there was an item about police operations or somebody being up in court on the TV news, he listened intently trying to take it all in, in the hope that he could amass enough information to understand reasons for his father's arrest. Later, when he could read, he'd scan the *Greenock Reporter* and the *Daily Record* for crime stories, anything about people being arrested. There were plenty of cases, but none about boys whose dads had been taken away without a reason.

By the time he found out what a bigamist was, he had absorbed more incidental learning about police and criminal procedures than anyone his age at school, and maybe it was that knowledge, later in his teen years, that made his application to the police an inevitable choice. He didn't know if he'd like it, he just knew that he'd be good at the job.

When he was seventeen, it was his grandad who got the job of telling him what his dad had done thirteen years before and answering most of the questions Davie had been bursting to ask for all that time. His mother knew that it couldn't be put it off any longer.

She also knew that she didn't want to relive the pain by doing it herself.

He was set to leave home to begin his police career. He would still be living with his mother during his training, except when he was doing residential blocks at the Police College.

On the day when the family secret was to be revealed, his grandad, never a man to rush a job, looked out a window and pointed at the Victoria Tower, an ornate 250-foot, rocket shaped building. It was the showpiece for Greenock's Council Offices and could be seen from most places in the town.

*"That's a bit like you, Davie,"* he said, pulling back the curtain so that they both had a good view. *"All set to launch on your mission."*

*"Aye, I suppose so, grandad,"* said Davie. *"Just hope that I can get further off the ground than a big pile of stones, eh?"*

*"Well, right enough, and I'm sure you will,"* his grandad chuckled.

*"Before you go, though, you'll need a final flight briefing from planet Greenock, so that you know as much as you should."*

\* \* \*

When his dad was taken by the police, Davie's grandad had become the man in his life. Ron Murray was too old to do all the running around, kicking a ball stuff that a dad did, but he'd been a good father, a long time ago, and he still remembered what was important. He didn't have a wife anymore and never had a son although he'd always wanted one. So he and Davie were a good match.

Isobel was still his mum, and she still took care of Davie, fussing about what he did and what he ate and how he looked and how he spoke and where he went, but after Donnie left Davie noticed that his mother was quieter, not speaking to other mums like before. She was most relaxed when Davie's grandad came to visit, or when she and Davie got the bus and went to his house across town.

When he was young, Davie's grandad spoke to him mostly in stories. Sometimes stories that he'd read about or made up, but more often things that had happened to him, moulded into longer stories, with the names changed. Davie couldn't tell whether a story was true until his grandad was halfway through it, and by that time he was hooked and didn't care.

Davie still enjoyed the stories his mum read with him from books, the ones with words and pictures. His grandad had a few books in his house with pictures. Well not pictures, but photographs of cars and planes and buildings mostly. They were old books with heavy covers that he'd lift down from a shelf and give to Davie to keep him occupied while his grandad and his mother chatted. The best stories however, the ones that Davie still remembered, were those that his grandad told without any books or pictures or photographs. They were the stories that had him beguiled from the first sentence.

Sometimes scary, sometimes funny, and always leaving the audience of one asking for more.

Royal Navy Petty Officer Ordnance Artificer Ron Murray, hair brown, eyes blue, complexion fresh, according to his Ministry of Defence record and the identity card that he showed Davie, served on two ships during World War II.

*"See, I was good at fixing all sorts of things on the big ships,"* is how he described what he did to Davie, and that was how he started most of his war stories.

There were some stories that never got finished and some that hardly got started. Davie's mum would hear the beginning and jump in when she remembered where the story was going.

*"No, dad, not that one. He's too young to hear about that,"* or, *"I think Davie would prefer that story that you told him last time dad,"* accompanied by a remonstrative frown.

Petty Officer Murray had sailed on the Arctic Convoys for the most terrifying six months of his life. Churchill had described the voyages as, *"the worst journey in the world."* How Churchill would know that, Ron never understood. The fear and the horror of what Ron Murray saw during that time aged him prematurely. Men, wounded, dead or in bits, lying on deck or floating by, were constant reminders of how close each sailor was to being next.

Ron went, in the space of months, from a bright-eyed teenager to an older, hardened stoic, learning to hide or simply ignore his emotions just to survive. When he came back from his time on the convoys, his own mother saw that it had changed him.

*"Ron's no the young boy he was,"* she told neighbours and anyone else who would listen, *"nobody could thole what he's been through and still be the same."*

He never spoke about what he'd seen, or God forbid felt, when he was on the convoys, then or later. A navy man, a real navy man, didn't. Being unaffected was expected. That was the Navy way. It was nothing that was taught specifically in training. It was learned instantly in that first shelling or torpedo attack; a crash course on being a man. You fought the enemy and your personal demons with a face that showed nothing, so that no one else could know how shit-scared you were.

*"What did you do in the war Daddy?"* It had originally been the caption on a war recruitment poster of 1915, shaming men to sign up. It was only all those years later when he became a father himself and Isobel was old enough to ask the same question that Ron Murray found a way of thinking about what he did do in the war, then talking about it.

To begin with, it was like opening a photo album filled with his worst memories. He could open the album at any page and there was a queue of horrors, jostling for attention in his memory. They came back, vivid and fresh, in full colour as soon as he thought about HMS *Perseus*. They were scenes that could never be shown to a child.

Isobel could be fobbed off when she was younger. *"Daddy sailed in the big boats,"* or, *"Daddy fought the bad men,"* but as she grew, she became, like her son Davie, a curious and determined child who came back with more questions and wouldn't be put off with being ignored or distracted. She forced her father Ron into answers.

When he read stories from his daughter's dog-eared library books, he'd simplify as he went along, paraphrasing and substituting words that were not in her vocabulary for those that were, and cutting out the experiences in the book that might keep her awake at nights. So, *Babar the Elephant* ran away from the jungle when he was hungry, rather than when his mother was shot by a hunter, and *Scruffy the Tugboat* wanted to go sailing, rather than look for 'bigger things', as he floated down a river, rather than a brook.

Ron did the same adaptive storytelling job on his Arctic Convoy memories, abridging the stories by flushing out the horrors, and creating amended high adventure and tall tales from what was left. Isobel liked hearing about the ice, whether it was the ships dodging icebergs and polar bears, someone slipping across the deck and almost falling in the sea, or her grandad hacking icicles off the ship's wires with axe and dropping them down the necks of his shipmates.

A generation later, it was those same stories from the Arctic Convoys that Davie always asked for. Grandad was allowed to tell them by a vigilant Isobel. Davie benefited from the passage of time for, by then, Ron had banished most of the demons that rose up when he had first prodded the stories in his memory and he had also sanitised and road tested the versions of the stories on Isobel, over many years.

The stories all started the same way, with one of his grandad's farfetched descriptions about the Arctic conditions on the ship.

*"Well Davie, I'm telling you, I'll never forget how cold it was that day. We had to break the frozen smoke off the ship's funnel."*

*"That day was one to remember Davie. I had to tie a scarf twice around my nose to stop it falling off."*

*"I remember when I was having my dinner on that day, Davie. My glass of milk turned to ice cream before I could drink it."*

Or Davie's favourite, *"It was the coldest day ever Davie. It was so cold that I was telling loads of lies, hoping that my pants would go on fire just to warm me up."*

Davie was old enough to know that not all these introductions could be true, which then got him to wondering what other parts of the story were made up. Then his grandad would get going on the incredible size of the waves and the icebergs and the bombers and submarines and by then what was true didn't matter. Davie was happy to believe all of it or none of it.

So, it fell to his grandad to tell the true story that Davie had wanted to hear since he was a boy. What happened to Davie's dad. In a well-choreographed visit by his grandad, Isobel spent an hour making the dinner next door while Davie got the full, everything-you-wanted-to-know-but-were-afraid-to-ask version of his father's betrayal, imprisonment and attempts to get in touch. His grandad was straight with him, answering all his questions as best he could, so that Isobel didn't have to. When he was finished, Davie knew everything except where his father was, and whether he ever wanted to see him again.

He still didn't know the answers to those questions, or to others that had come to him, years later. Would he have taken as much interest in the dry-as-a-bone subject of the law at school and would he have become a cop in Greenock, then Glasgow, then London if his father hadn't been arrested? Who knows?

\* \* \*

After he graduated from the Police College, he was still at home, looking around for a place of his own. It was then that his mother showed the first signs of the illness that was to end her life a year and a half later. Whether she had high blood pressure before she met Donnie or as a result of how her life had turned out was never known. The stroke that killed her was preceded by fainting spells, blurred vision and nose bleeds, all of which caused Davie to stay at home longer than he had intended, and to make him more determined to leave Greenock after his mother died.

When he left, he thought he would never be back. Bound for glory, rising up through the ranks, life in the big city, then in the big smoke, everything going for him. But there he was now, living in a basement in the cemetery with nothing going for him except his invisibility and a different view on what was ahead.

His mother had been a church goer before Donny was jailed. She had made Davie join the Greenock Boys Brigade, aged 6, against his wishes, perhaps hoping that he would be exposed to the missing male role model in his life or would gain knowledge and skills that a decent father might otherwise have taught him.

Five years in the Christian youth organisation had taught him how to march in cold gym halls, vault over wooden pummel horses for no reason he could understand, and the value of *Brasso* to polish his uniform's belt buckle. Obedience, discipline and all the other stuff that tended towards a true Christian manliness were served up in various forms at the weekly evening sessions and topped off on Sunday mornings from the pulpit with a helping of reverence and indecipherable sermons about an incomprehensible God.

Even if he didn't understand it, five years of the pummel horse and being pummelled with Bible verse had left its mark, and a line came back to him then, sitting in his dark basement.

Matthew 6:34. *Do not be anxious about tomorrow, for*

*tomorrow will be anxious for itself. Let the day's own trouble be sufficient for the day.*

That's how he was living, by the day. He dreaded the day when that would have to change.

\* \* \*

Going in or out of the cemetery gate in daylight hours was when he was most exposed, when a passer-by was most likely to wonder why somebody looking like him was in a graveyard or why he was there so often. But like a dog who had learned to cross a busy road safely to survive, Davie timed his entry and exit to be inconspicuous, avoiding the busiest visiting times and the paths most used.

When he was inside the gate, he had a safe route, away from the main paths, following the curve of the boundary wall, out of sight behind trees. This took him close to the house. His final twenty yards to the fallen trees and cellar door was a marshy straight line hidden only by low bushes.

The walling up of the original cemetery gate had unforeseen consequences. Years of rainfall that would have run off into Bow Road through the gates had dammed up against the new wall. When the problem became apparent, cemetery workers had punched four weep holes at the base of the new wall to bleed off the excess water onto Bow Road and into the main drains.

This worked well as a slow drain, with a trickle of the fetid pool that had built up over years continuously leaking out through the weep holes. However, whenever it rained with any intent, the reservoir of underground mud and sludge was replenished. Leaves swept downhill, clogging the weep holes, until council workmen on the other side of the wall cleared them when checking the road drains.

In the early days in the basement, Davie spent a lot of time worrying about two dangers: curious cemetery visitors investigating the hidden door, and his feet being sopping wet.

It rained a lot. The Scottish Gaelic word for Greenock was Grianaig. This translated into English roughly as, "sunny and hilly place". Greenock had been thus named either by someone who visited the town on a rare summer's day, or by someone with a sick sense of humour.

In his first two weeks, Davie lay awake at nights, worrying alternately about someone coming through the basement door, and his chances of contracting cholera or some century-old plague from the bacteria in the sludge flowing downhill from the graves and pooling outside that same door. But these irrational night fears were replaced each morning by the reality and misery of having to wear boots that were squelching most of the time and just damp at best.

Davie was sitting in the dark one night, listening to the water dripping from his boots onto the floor when he remembered Mr. Marshall and came up with a very old solution to his very new problem. It promised him both dry feet and a protected retreat.

# – 6 –

## THE CRANNOG

At school, Davie hated History, more than French, more even than a double period of Maths. Except for a few swots in his year, everybody he knew had one dread, above all others, of some forty-five-minute period in the timetable. For Davie, it was History.

Ancient, medieval or modern, but always pointless. Memorising stuff that dead people had done, sometimes centuries ago, for God knows what reason, just so you could regurgitate it in an exam? How could that be called education, and why did he have to waste any of his valuable teenage time thinking about it? Yet he was force fed the dead past for three and a half years. Then Mr. Marshall arrived.

There were teachers who came into the classroom, gave you what they were paid for and were just as thankful as you when the bell rang. You didn't care what they knew because you knew they didn't care. In Davie's experience, most teachers in the staffroom pack were better than that. Most were worthy and worn down but trying something close to their best.

Then there were a few, just a few, who blazed brightly, at least for a while. These rare shooting stars could come into a classroom and perform, leaving at the end of the period with the reluctant agreement of all present, even the class bampot, that the teacher had taught, and the students had learned. These select few men and women could make any class put in front of them at least curious, and that was halfway to wanting to know answers, or even asking questions.

Mr. Gordon Marshall, specialist subject Scottish History, teaching mission to make history one of the formative influences of intellect and character in young people, was one such teacher. After all these years, Davie was grateful that he had been in his class on that day all those years ago.

Quietening the class was the easy bit. Teachers could shout, bang something on a desk, clap hands or even stamp feet. It was keeping the peace long enough, creating a space in which learning might at least be a possibility, that was the trick. Noise would creep back like water rising. Whispering, murmuring, then talking over each other to be heard, then descending into chucking paper, pens and whatever else came to hand across the room as the dam burst and control was lost.

The period on Davie's crumpled timetable for that week said "*History: Technology in the European Neolithic Period*". Looking at what was on for that day, Davie felt tired just reading the title and had considered skiving off to read magazines in the school library for that period or maybe for the rest of the afternoon, so that he could also miss "*Maths: Factoring Quadratic Equations*".

Mr. Marshall never raised his voice or his foot to get attention. It helped that he was always sitting, waiting before students filed into the class and that he had written or drawn something on the whiteboard to get attention without having to ask for it.

The class that saved Davie from wet feet all those years later began with numbers on the board; $1.16699016 \times 10\text{-}8$ hertz. They were written in blue marker pen beside a sketch of a coloured, crescent moon with a smiley face.

*"What colour is this moon?"* was Mr. Marshall's opener, when everybody was seated, digging out pens or pencils. It was an easy one to start.

*"White,"* and *"Grey,"* came two voices at the same time.

*"And can anyone tell me what is meant by the expression, 'once in a blue moon'?"*

*"Is that when Greenock Morton beat Rangers and Celtic in the same season Sir?"* said Alec Cromley, last into the classroom, forced to sit at the front and now turning to soak up the approving laughs from his cronies behind.

*"Good example Cromley,"* said Mr. Marshall, praising him and taking some of the wind out of his disruptive sails.

*"As Mr. Cromley says, it is something that happens very rarely, and this equation here,"* Mr. Marshall said, standing and tapping the whiteboard, *"tells us just how rarely."*

Mr. Marshall did a quick scan of faces to check that everyone was still looking puzzled.

*"So just how often do we have a blue moon?"* he continued.

Then, after a pause, *"OK. Calculators out,"* to a chorus of groans.

*"No, just kidding. I'll tell you the answer to this one, and then ask you a more difficult one. The equation tells us that a blue moon happens about once every 990 days."*

Davie looked around to see a few of the class swots copying down the number from the white board, and the answer. He was wondering how the hell this could come up in a History exam, and already dreading the *Factoring Quadratic Equations* that he had since resigned himself to later in the afternoon.

*"Now here's the one for you to figure out,"* Mr. Marshall continued. *"I want you to write down your answer somewhere, and the person closest to the correct answer gets to clean the whiteboard later."*

This brought more groans.

*"OK. Some history, because if you check your timetable that's what this class is about, right?"* Mr. Marshall said, coming to stand at the front of the class.

*"Imagine for a moment that you are living in Scotland during the Neolithic Period, about 7000 years ago. Imagine you're walking about, hungry, trying to find things to eat, minding your own business. But during that time there were other things, bigger than you, also walking about looking for something to eat."*

He paused, to check that he had everyone's attention.

*"So, the question that I want you to answer is this. How often would you be chased by a sabre-toothed tiger or a nine-foot bear? Would it be once in a blue moon? More often than that? Less often?"*

Davie didn't remember his answer to the question, or the right answer, but he did remember finding out what the smarter Neolithic Scots did when they were being chased.

They ran home, fast. And that's what gave Davie the idea for how to solve his wet feet problem.

\* \* \*

It took almost a week of scavenging around the cemetery when it was quiet, finding flat stones, carrying them back and hiding them in the undergrowth near the Goalkeeper's House. He resisted the early temptation to use half-buried and forgotten gravestones nearby. They were flat and no one would miss them, but stealing gravestones was in Davie's head disrespectful, bordering on criminal.

There were some broken paving slabs that had been left by builders up by the crematorium. These were ideal for what he needed, but he could only carry one at a time and it was knackering. More than once he'd had to chuck what he was carrying into the undergrowth when he heard voices ahead.

Closer to the Goalkeeper's House there was an old hut where gravediggers had once kept tools, coversheets and boards. The roof timbers had long since collapsed under the weight of the stone roofing slabs, and what was left of the walls was covered in thick moss. The slabs, now lying inside the hut, were like slates from a giant's house. Davie first tried carrying one, gave up and resorted to tumbling each slab end-over-end until he had it in place. His laboured technique would never feature on *YouTube*, but it was effective, if you had a lot of time on your hands, as he did.

The ground along the cemetery wall leading to Davie's back door, where the water collected, was bog factor ten for most of the year. Anywhere you stood, you sank. There were pools of surface water in places to warn of what lay beneath, but elsewhere the first warning for Davie was when he felt mud creep over the ankle collar of his boot, urging him to move faster.

Each time his foot sank, it was not the fresh smell of earth after rain, or the forest floor odour of a garden centre that rose up; it was a fetid stench of something that had been there too long. Davie convinced himself that it was only fermenting leaves, grass and soil and not the smell of rotting flesh and organs from the body decomposition fluids flowing downhill from the graves.

The first snake of stepping stones that he laid sank, as he had expected. He marked the spots with sticks and laid another set on top. Some took three, and in one spot he needed eight – a combination of the paving and roofing slabs – before the slabs stopped disappearing too far beneath the surface. When he had one curling path to the basement doors established, he laid two more that led nowhere except into deeper mud.

\* \* \*

When Mr. Marshall had cleared the formula for the frequency of a blue moon from the white board, he sketched a conical hut on a small island, using his blue marker to indicate the water that surrounded it on all sides and a black marker to represent a nearby shoreline.

Underneath he wrote the word, *"crannog"*.

*"Now, imagine again that you are living in Neolithic times. This is your house. You have made it to the shoreline, chased by the hungry sabre-toothed tiger or the bear. What do you do next?"*

*"Swim faster than shit through a goose, Sir,"* said Cromley, happy to soak up the laughter behind him without turning around this time.

*"Well, that is one solution,"* said Mr. Marshal, nodding at Cromley, *"but what* else *might you do, to avoid soiling yourself or being caught and ending up as lunch?"*

Suggestions were shouted out and Mr. Marshall wrote them all on the whiteboard: Throw rocks, fight the bear, run along the shore, play dead, get the bear to fight the tiger while you ran away. He stopped writing at *"hypnotise the bear"*, another Cromley suggestion, and turned to face the class.

*"Now what if you could walk on water?"* he said quietly.

There was silence and a few slack jaws as he turned and started to add a random pattern of black circles between the shoreline and the thatched, conical hut on the island.

*"What the people living on this island did, and did very well, was protect what they had,"* he continued, as he joined up a series of the circles to make a zigzag line leading from the shore to the crannog.

*"They chopped down oak trees, made logs and dug them into the floor of the loch, reaching up to just below the surface of the water. The flat tops of the logs were a secret stepping stone path that led back to the island."*

As he spoke, he drew a stick figure of the man running across the line of dots.

*"Only the people in the hut, or crannog, knew the one route across the logs that went to the island. They dug in decoy logs as well to make a maze with some dead ends. If you were a stranger or a very clever bear and didn't know which logs to stand on, you ended up in the water, with spears being thrown at you."*

He added more stick figures, standing on the island, holding spears.

*"Two other things to add here, before you ask,"* said Mr. Marshall, looking pointedly at Cromley.

*"First, the Neolithic people didn't have scuba diving gear, so they must have been very good swimmers, diving down to dig the logs in so that they were secure enough to stand on. Secondly, you're probably wondering why they went to all that bother. Well, some of the other tribes who lived in crannogs decided that it was easier to build a causeway,"* said Mr. Marshall adding a bridge from the shore to the island on the whiteboard. *"But these tribes could be attacked*

*not just by wild animals trying to eat them, but by other Neolithic people, trying to steal the cows that were kept inside the crannog."*

He added "*Mooo*" in a speech bubble above the crannog, to more groans from the class.

So, Davie owed his stepping stones to Mr. Marshall. Although he kept no cows in the Goalkeeper's House, and he wasn't expecting any bears, he hoped his stepping stones would protect him from curious predators of another kind.

In his bare feet, sometimes thigh-deep in the glaur, he patiently built columns of slabs in the mud. He stood on each slab as it slowly sank, then placed another on top until the column was stable and the top slab was just below the surface of the bog. Each of the top slabs he then disguised with chunks of moss, bark and grass divots, to blend in with the rest of the surrounding bog.

Davie memorised the one route across the stones that led to the basement door, stepping carefully left and right, until he could do it almost with his eyes shut. Anyone looking for a way into the back of the house and not put off by his first step into ankle deep mud might discover the first few stepping stones and try to pick their way across. The dead-end routes that Davie laid all led to patches of even deeper glaur, where the mud was slimier, and the smell of putrefaction even stronger.

* * *

Most visitors to the cemetery didn't have relatives buried there. They were tourists on the Red or the more popular Blue Walk; leaflet-guided tours that took them past the Greenock's-Got-Talent names of yesteryear.

There was James Watt, local worthy, engineer, inventor and all-round clever bastard, who improved on the design of the steam engine and contributed to the Industrial Revolution. His cairn looked like it had been constructed from children's building blocks and seemed to compel visitors to stand with one foot on it for photographs, posing like they had just shot a lion.

For most visitors, the highlight of the Blue Walk was the obelisk gravestone of Highland Mary, who was commemorated in poetry and in song by Rabbie Burns, Scotland's national bard. Mary Campbell planned to emigrate to Jamaica with Rabbie, but she died tragically of typhus, aged just twenty-three, before they could leave.

The reality of the relationship was that they had known each other only for a few weeks. This little-known detail took a bit of the shine off the romantic story of the doomed lovers, as did the fact that Rabbie went on to father twelve children by four different women.

The Blue Walk went within two hundred yards of the Goal-keeper's House, passing behind a curtain of trees. It was close enough for Davie to be spotted by stalk-eyed tourists or picked out later in one of their selfies. So, he was extra careful, timing his daytime movement to avoid peak traffic on the Blue Walk.

Highland Mary's story reminded Davie of his time in London. Not the romance and the poetry, but the tragedy and the sadness that followed. He had never written a line of poetry in his life, but if he'd been so inclined, the lines would have been about Sophie. He'd known her much longer than Rabbie had known his Highland Mary, nearly two years longer, and she was gone in just eight weeks.

There was no fancy headstone in a grand cemetery or a shiny

plaque on a park bench for Sophie, just a simple cremation and scattered ashes as she had requested. He had taken a week to get himself sorted, then gone back on the beat. Which was a mistake, as it turned out.

\* \* \*

Most of the headstones in the Greenock Cemetery were standard, upright slabs of sandstone. Over years of rain and casket collapse, some of the four-foot-high stones leaned forward at dangerous angles and others had fallen over completely as the ground beneath subsided. Taller, more imposing markers, the ones that would never lean or fall, marked the last resting places of those who could afford granite and marble.

Ships and anchors on Celtic crosses spoke to the importance of the sea in the town. Those who owned shipping companies or built or owned ships or traded in cargo could all afford memorials that would last, words of rest deeply carved in quality stone, legible even after centuries of rain.

One such timeless stone slab was on the slope above the Goalkeeper's House. The inscription could just be read behind the full-size ship's anchor and chain that lay across it. Ships' captains and some of the wealthier marine engineers had more modest, but equally solid tombstones, pink granite obelisks rising above the rhododendrons surrounding many of the graves.

The largest memorial in the cemetery was also the cemetery's only mausoleum. It stood in a clearing on neatly trimmed grass near the top of the hill, 150 yards west of the crematorium. It had been modelled on a Greek temple and was fronted by two massive Doric columns, and an entrance big enough to ride a horse through.

On one side wall of the structure was the inscription, *"Herein repose the ashes of Dame Frances Caroline Cameron"*. The other side wall had faded, indecipherable letters in red and black spray paint, remnants of gang graffiti, still visible despite rigorous scrubbing and power hosing.

It was a peaceful spot, one of the few places in the cemetery where the river could be seen even during summer. The crematorium car park could also be seen from this vantage point, at least in winter when the surrounding trees had dropped their leaves.

The only regular visitors to the mausoleum were sightseers on the Red Walk and drug dealers.

## WHITE POWDER

Like Davie, dealers were restricted by the opening hours of the cemetery. Nobody except Davie wanted to be locked inside a graveyard at night, especially one that big and with so many stories, whether you believed them or not.

Realistically, the "war on drugs" in Greenock had been lost, long ago. The daily battles involved getting intel and trying to stem the flow, raiding new addresses each week. Someone would see a neighbour who had more visitors than Tesco's, or a queue of punters outside a flat, waiting to deal through a letter box. The curtain twitchers would report, cops would watch, get the paperwork, and do a bust. The following week it was the same punters at a different address. Nobody was winning the war on drugs and there were more battlefields opening up every week. The goal for police was disrupting the flow.

Locals, when asked, would say that the drug problem in Greenock came as a result of shipyards and factories closing in the 1980s, and that it was as inevitable as the tide on the River Clyde. By the time the extent of the drug problem was realised, the tsunami couldn't be stopped.

The town centre was a carnival of human side shows. If you

stood still for more than five minutes, you could be offered drugs, challenged to a fight, asked for money by a stranger, or mistakenly identified as a long-lost buddy by somebody who would eventually ask you for money. The High Street was rammed with people from dawn until dusk. There were regulars and there were travellers.

The same four men idled outside *What Every Woman Wants*, next door to *Safeways*, every day, from where they had been warned off by police for intimidating customers. The *Safeways* supermarket had the longest opening hours of any of the town centre shops selling alcohol. It was good for 8.30am, pick-me-up early morning cider, Buckfast or beer, or for falling in step with anyone vaguely known, exiting the shop with bottles clinking in a bag. It was also a promising spot for steady foot traffic; shoppers who might part with the checkout change in their hands to someone asking for the price of a cup of tea.

"*Restructured civic spaces, offering a more outward looking town centre,*" was promised in the development plan for the town centre. In reality, this meant slapping a glass roof on the main pedestrian precinct through the town and renaming it as the Oak Mall.

With the renovation came increased CCTV. Drug deals done previously in the High Street, or around the back of KFC, once a one-stop-shop for anything you needed, became riskier and rarer. The simplicity of cash and wrap hand-overs in a poorly lit street corners was eclipsed by dealers in cars or on bicycles doing mobile delivery, or taxis that did pick-up and delivery for little more than the usual tip on a fare. Mobile phones brought click-and-collect on an alphabet of drugs from amphetamines to yabba. For those who could wait that long for their fix, there was also the ever-reliable Royal Mail.

Drugs and drug deals, like all good customer-focused businesses, came in sizes and styles to suit; small, medium or large. From tin foil and clingfilm wraps and loose tablets all the way up to shipping containers, sitting at Greenock docks. In between the two extremes was the transport of boxes going to trap houses. These were kilo bricks of heroin that could be carried in the back of a van or the boot of a car to the drop, where the big money changed hands.

The drops were at soulless urban deserts, riverside industrial estates, multistorey car parks on the edge of town or Harthill motorway services on the M8. And Greenock Cemetery had been added to that list. It was another place with no souls, or perhaps many.

* * *

Davie objected. He didn't see himself as a mystical presence, some noble guardian of the defenceless dead against the wicked living come to defile the graveyard, but in his thinking, there was a line to be drawn.

Growing up in the town, the cemetery had been one of the constants in life, even when the shipyards closed and the electronics companies left, taking the jobs with them. Even when the real High Street was replaced by *Poundstretcher*, the *99p Shop* and *What Every Woman Wants*. Davie knew the cemetery as a place of calm and continuity, long before he was old enough to think about it in those terms. It was hallowed ground, not because it was holy but because it was old. It was a place where almost every family in town had a connection, some skin in the game.

Parents took you to visit grandad, then you took your kids to visit your own mother and father. It was real *Lion King*, circle-of-life stuff. The cat got run over or it killed the budgie and children cried and parents found the words to explain about how everything went to heaven, but it only really made sense to children when it was people they had known, buried in the cemetery, not pets in a hole in the garden.

On rare, summer days in Greenock families headed out *en masse* to take the cool breeze of the esplanade by the river or to seek out the shade in the cemetery. The reward for climbing all the way to the highest points was panoramic views over the River Clyde to the Cowal Peninsula. On the way back down the hill, children could read the headstones, trying to spot which one was the oldest or who had lived the longest, or who had the funniest name.

That had changed. Much of the respect for the dead that he had known was gone. Davie had seen drivers sneak into the cemetery at the weekend, parking up at one of the gardeners' taps and hoses, to wash and wax their cars. Soapy streams ran across nearby graves. He'd also seen the drug deals go down at the crematorium and at the mausoleum.

To Davie, Greenock Cemetery still had a noble purpose. It was a bit like the dentist or the chiropodist. You didn't like to think about going, but you were glad it was there when you needed it. And it was where Davie chose to live for now, so he needed the cemetery too. He didn't want to see it go the way of the rest of town, the disintegrated chaos that had led him to leave in the first place. Whole streets, once buzzing with generations of working families, shops and boozers, all turned to shit. Replaced by trap houses, selling drugs through letter boxes, streets awash with litres of Buckfast and cheap cider, and the families who'd once worked together now funding their habits by thieving what little they had from each other, like dogs fighting over a dry bone.

He'd made some token efforts to disrupt the drugs in the cemetery since he had come back. He'd stay hidden at the mausoleum, shaking trees to scare off nervous dealers. When that didn't work, he moved to wedging roofing nails under dealers' tyres at the crematorium car park. Neither strategy stemmed the flow.

\* \* \*

Long before black tar, brown powder or white powder heroin, Greenock, as a town, had past form for mass addiction.

It had its first taste in 1765, and by 1921 the descendants of Greenock-born Abram Lyle and Liverpool dealer Henry Tate had merged their operations to become the largest drug cartel in the world, shipping raw product from the Caribbean to Greenock, where for the next fifty years it was processed and sold to the masses, young and old, hooking them on a habit that lasted a lifetime.

Sugar was eight times more addictive than heroin or cocaine and with just as many street names; sooks, grannie sookers, toffees, boilings, tablet, chews, bonbons, fudge, gobstoppers, MB bars, jubblies, skyrockets, crispies, jap desserts, mivvies and curly wurlies.

The advantage that sugar had over its successor heroin was that there was never a supply problem. Yearnings could always be satisfied. Dealers were everywhere, from static corner shops to mobile grandparents with wraps in their pockets, ready with freebies to keep the customers interested in more.

Tate and Lyle cornered half the British market, then went on to produce sugar syrup, the crack cocaine of the sugar world. The treacle-like syrup from the cane refining process that had usually gone to waste was made into an addictive preserve and sweetener for cooking. "Goldie" was made in small but increasing quantities and stored in wooden casks.

At first it was sold only to sugar refinery employees and local customers, as a wee bonus for workers and neighbours. But word got out, and within a few months the refinery was selling a ton of the stuff a week.

Like the drug trade in later years, dealers adapted quickly. Impractical wooden casks were replaced by Lyle's Golden Syrup dispensers, found on the shelves of grocery stores, for a quick hit that could be taken home in jars and bottles. Goldie could be cut with flour, and baked to make upmarket, higher profit variations of the raw product; cake, biscuits and sweeties.

Goldie evolved into tins of Tate and Lyle Syrup, cheap and widely available. Millions of tins were sold. There was a bizarre picture on every tin of a dead lion with a swarm of bees buzzing around it. Nobody noticed or nobody cared.

The picture had a biblical derivation. Samson killed a lion and left the dead animal at the side of the road. A swarm of bees then made a hive inside the carcass, prompting Samson's lyrical line about sugar, *"Out of the strong, came forth sweetness."* What had once been a mighty beast was reduced to a rotting corpse with bees around it. In Greenock's case, it was more like flies around a shite.

The invisible hand of economics drove the supply to meet

the growing demand and reached a peak with ten refineries producing 700 tons of sugar products a week. Greenock became known as Sugaropolis.

What began as a casual relationship became a pairing for life between the town and sugar. Cravings for the white powder that was sugar were kept alive by faithful generations, who passed on the dependence by using it to shape their children's behaviour. If a baby was old enough to suck a dummy teat to keep it quiet, it was old enough to suck a sugar dummy teat to get its first hit. Where parental persuasion, shouting and arse-skelping failed, every child had his or her price in sugared sweeties to do what parents asked.

Early sugar habits lasted a Greenock child into adolescence, where the longings could be satisfied by an easy weaning from sweeties to rites-of-passage alcohol and the beginning of a more serious effort to build on the foundations that had been established for the obesity, heart disease and high blood pressure that would give Greenockians seven years less life expectancy than people in some third world countries.

In London, Tate and Lyle was Cockney rhyming slang for style. In Greenock it was the name for the come-hither, burnt-sugar, candy-floss-caramel smell, wafting across half the town. Free advertising for a product that nobody thought much about until they had a first taste.

The epitaph of Dundee, Greenock's east coast counterpart, had been 'jute, jam and journalism'. Greenock's own catchy alliteration had been ships, steam and sugar. Now both places were famous for the three 'Ds'; deprivation, drinks and drugs. Wasn't it a long way down?

In the cemetery there were a few older graves where the deceased were proudly recorded as "Sugar Refiners", and many,

many more graves where the product of their labours had cut a life short.

Drugs, the modern-day version, and the deaths they caused were to play a role in Davie's time in the cemetery, but his first encounter with death came much earlier in his life.

# – 8 –

## HOME IS THE SAILOR

Although hundreds of dead people had passed through the gates of Greenock cemetery, only a few people had gone in alive and come out dead. Besides the murdered Scott Birrell, Davie Perdue knew of just one other from personal experience.

No doubt, many deaths inside the cemetery had gone unreported. There had been mourners suffering grief-induced heart attacks and strokes at gravesides over the years, or relatives keeling over in the crematorium as the organ struck up that guaranteed tearjerker, *Abide With Me*. But none of these deaths, piling grief on grief, made the size of newspaper headlines as that of Davie's first death as a cop.

The details he remembered especially well. He'd been just a year in the job, freshly graduated. One of the lots of the rookie cop was *locus protection*, being an automatic choice as the police presence to stand guard at a crime scene for as long as it took for "proper" investigators to get there.

A wet Saturday in November turned into an even wetter Sunday morning as Davie stood, collar up, trying to find shelter from the pelting rain under a tree, waiting for the police SOCO and the undertaker to turn up and take over.

Francis Niven, that was the boy's name. Davie learned later that Francis never asked to join the gang. He had hung about with them for lack of anything else to do, nicking stuff to eat from the shops, climbing onto garage roofs to paint the gang tag on walls, and having face offs with other gangs, more noise than fight. The gang had asked Frances to join, and he said yes. It was only then the Burdy Boys told Francis about the initiation. If they'd told him beforehand, he would have told them to fuck right off probably, but by then he was committed.

Walk through the cemetery to show that you're hard enough to be in the Burdy Boys. Sounded easy, right? But walk through the cemetery at night? That was a different story. The Burdy Boys had finessed the details of the gang initiation and how it was to be done, passed down through generations of big brothers.

Francis first had to get in and hide before the gates were locked. Then he had to make it from the main gate all the way to the crematorium and back, in the dark. The crematorium was chosen as the end point of the challenge because it had an outside light.

Francis could choose any path, since they would all be just as dark. No torches or matches allowed, and he was searched before he went in to make sure. All he carried was a claw hammer and a bag of galvanised roofing nails.

To prove that he'd gone all the way to the crematorium, he had to bang a nail into a tree every few hundred yards and finish with two nails on the tree nearest to the crematorium. The Burdy Boys would check the nails the next day. The final part of the initiation was climbing the massive cast iron gates to get out, to be met by the rest of the gang and welcomed, if he completed the initiation, as a full gang member.

On the Saturday night in question, it was pissing down and dark before 6pm.

On Saturdays, 15-year-old Francis, potential hard man of the Burdy Boys, was allowed out until 10pm by his parents, so there was plenty time for him to get there and back before his bedtime. The gang watched him disappear into hiding in the trees by the gate, the bag of roofing nails weighing down his anorak on the left, the shaft of the hammer stuck up his sleeve and the hammer head in his right hand. The extra weight gave him a lolloping walk that made him look more suspicious than if he had been walking with the hammer held above his head. He hid until it was full dark.

From the trail of the nails hammered into the trees, police pieced together Francis' movements. He had started at the gate, going onto a minor path first, to avoid the risk of being seen by passers-by outside the gate. When he was far enough from streetlights, he moved onto the paved road that took cars to the crematorium, coming off it only as far as necessary to find a tree by touch and nail it. But that was easier said than done as he moved further into the cemetery, where there was more tree cover and it became darker than the inside of a cow's arse.

Eight o'clock became nine and Francis had not returned to the front gate. The alarm went up at half past nine when a reluctant Burdy Boy was sent to Francis' house. There was a cover story for the parents about the gang messing about inside the cemetery and Francis getting lost, but the lies unravelled quickly when Francis' mother phoned the cops.

When they eventually found someone to open the gates, the cop in the car who drove up to the crematorium with lights on beam didn't spot Francis, and his partner following on foot, going side to side, couldn't find him with his torch. It was another two hours before a dog handler and a general-purpose dog was free to join in the search.

PC James Bell and his German Shepherd, Clyde, took just twenty minutes to do their job. Francis was soaking wet, huddled at the foot of a weeping beech tree, hidden from view by the tent-like broad crown canopy of its branches. He was three hundred yards short of the crematorium, with just a handful of nails left in the bag by his side.

The pathologist recorded cause as, *"Sudden death with likely cardiac pathology."* Francis had a pre-existing heart condition that nobody knew about. When PC James Bell got to him, slumped by the tree, he shook him by the shoulder, thinking he was unconscious, drunk or both. It was only then that he saw that Francis was held in his sitting position only by one of the roofing nails that he had hammered through his thin coat and into the weeping beech tree.

The police reported Francis' sudden death to the Procurator Fiscal, but the inquiry went no further after interviews with members of the Burdy Boys. The most likely scenario was that Francis had hammered in the nail and started to walk away, watching anxiously for shapes in the dark shadows. He had felt a tug, mistook it for a hand from one of the graves pulling him back, and the shock had triggered his heart attack. The pathologist also reported that Francis had been doubly incontinent at or near the moment of death, adding strength to this interpretation of events.

Francis Niven's death had affected Davie because it was his first dead body as a cop. It was one that he could still picture in detail. The small body slumped, as if asleep, six feet from where Davie stood, shivering from the cold rain running down the back of his neck. The smells from Francis' body were still strong despite the wind, whipping the branches above Davie's head. Every time he attended a fatal in the years to come, the memory of Francis came back.

Maybe it was some unwitting desire to return to beginnings, somewhere familiar to reset and restart, that had drawn Davie back to the cemetery when he first returned to Greenock from London, dazed, with all he owned in a police duty kit bag. His only plan coming up on the train had been to avoid anyone he knew, for a few days at least.

It was early on that March morning when he came out of Greenock West station. Turning left would take him to the town centre and people he didn't want to meet, so he turned in the opposite direction and started walking, no destination in mind. The cemetery gates were swinging open as he looked up. He maintained his steady pace as he walked through, focusing on stretching his legs after the cramped overnight journey. The walking was a good distractor. Keeping it simple, he could concentrate on swapping his bag from one hand to the other every 500 steps, instead of thinking about where he was going or where he would sleep that night, or the night after that, or the next week.

*"Home is the Sailor, Home from Sea."*

The first time he read it on the gravestone, Davie thought about all the things he'd liked about Greenock. There weren't that many, but he did miss some things when he got to London.

*"You don't know what you've got 'til it's gone."* Joni Mitchell had been lamenting the loss of the environment. Davie supposed that Joni had never missed tattie scones, a pint of heavy, tablet made with condensed milk or a macaroon bar, but when he left

Scotland all his favourite things took on new significance, feeling like essentials that he'd forgotten to pack. Some of the other jocks that he met in the Met had these rare Scottish delicacies sent from home, like Red Cross parcels.

*"Home is the Sailor".* The epitaph was on the gravestone marking some of the men who had died in Sir Gabriel Wood's Mariners' Asylum, a retirement home. It had given Davie a warm feeling. But that had been on that first morning when he was still thinking that he'd be around for just a few days, until he figured out what he was going to do with the rest of his life and moved on.

Following the paths that wound around the graves, Davie had walked all the way up the hill to the golf course wall three times, picking different routes each time as he came back down. He remembered his grandfather telling him that the cemetery was as big as Edinburgh Zoo, and almost as steep. The cemetery was in the centre of a town, not quite a zoo but big enough and with enough plant life to sustain populations of roe deer, foxes, bats, sparrowhawks and woodpeckers.

As Davie descended the hill for the third time, he spotted an old track off to one side, overgrown with trees that had linked branches to cover the space between them. It led him to the original, bricked-up entrance at Bow Road and that was when he saw the Goalkeeper's House for the first time.

When he found the cellar doors and the sanctuary of the basement, his thoughts about existential choices and what he was going to do with the rest of his week and the rest of his life got in the queue behind the more prosaic needs of how to get in, stay warm, fed and hidden. Putting off the big decisions became easier, for a while at least.

* * *

Francis Niven's young death by the tree that wet night all those years ago left its mark on Davie. Although he had no personal connection to Francis, the pointless, avoidable death that was far too soon for the young boy affected him deeply. Just starting out in his police career, he wondered how many more deaths like this one he'd have to deal with; sad tragedies over which he had no control.

Davie had spoken in the following days to the station cop who'd been sent to do the death knock at Francis' home that night. Francis' mother and father had collapsed like bundles of clothes onto the family sofa, the cop told him, but his younger brother, barely in his teens, had to be restrained, as he fought to get out of the door and go hunting for the Burdy Boys to vent his grief on them.

Francis Niven and Scott Birrell: two deaths with different outcomes for Davie Perdue. Francis' death in the cemetery that night changed Davie's way of thinking about death. The murder of Scott Birrell in the same cemetery all those years later called for less thinking, more action. It forced him to abandon the careful routine he had established at the Goalkeeper's House and go on the run, for a while at least.

# – 9 –

## MIND THE GAP

Davie bailed out of Greenock temporarily, to avoid being recognized as the man in the E-fit posters.

He slept until the bus reached Buchanan bus station. There, he got off, keeping his head low and walked down the hill, past Queen Street and on, feeling the muscles in his neck relax in the anonymity of the crowds of Glasgow shoppers.

On his way through the busy pedestrian thoroughfare, he passed the statues of two great men that he admired. Donald Dewar, the politician, proof that being lanky and specky in Scotland need not be an impediment to greatness, and the Duke of Wellington, a man known in history for his courage in battle and in Glasgow for never being seen in public without a traffic cone on his head.

He arrived at Glasgow Central Rail Station without thinking about it, his legs taking him on a route they knew well. He stopped to sit on one of the few free seats in the station to consider his next move. Looking around, he saw how little the place had changed since he'd last been there, nearly four years ago, putting it all behind him, on his way to Euston Station and a new life in the Met. But there were differences.

The information on destinations and train times was electronic now, rather than the overhead clickety-clack boards he remembered. There were new coffee booths near every platform, selling so many types of coffee – ristretto, doppio, galao, affogato – that Davie wondered if the variations had been named after the Italian seven dwarfs.

What was the same, even after all those years, were the waves of people, funnelling to and from platforms, most moving as if they were being chased. On the platforms, passengers strung themselves out, the canny travellers positioning themselves from experience exactly where the train doors would open.

People at the automatic ticket machines cursed and looked around for anyone in a uniform to complain to, one hand on the machine that had just eaten their money, just in case anyone else thought about using it. Uniformed Scotrail staff walked circuitous routes around the station, avoiding automatic ticket machines.

The guy with the crumpled suit and the story about having lost his wallet and needing just £6.50 to get home to Dunoon worked his way along the row of seats where Davie sat, bypassing him without a second glance.

In the middle of the main concourse, a nub of people stood together, all looking in different directions, like meerkats on guard. Passengers rushing to and from trains flowed around the group like a stream around a rock. Only locals knew that this spot on the concourse was the Meeting Place. There were no signs on poles or markings on the station floor. Friends, lovers, drinking buddies and those who got lost or separated had met under the four-faced clock, suspended from the station ceiling, for nearly a hundred years.

Davie's great uncle Charlie was killed in the Second World War and as a boy his mother had told him how the clock chimed on the hour for all the people who left from Glasgow Central Station and never made it back.

Most of the station concourse was on a slope. Passengers heading for trains on the furthest platforms trudged up the hill, walking slower, as if reluctant to leave Glasgow, and those who had just arrived rolled down, as if speeding home.

As Davie watched the flow of people going for trains, a young guy, mid-teens, caught his eye. He was leaning against the one remaining bank of public phones in the station, his baseball cap pulled low on his forehead, sneaking glances towards a platform further up the concourse. His behaviour triggered Davie's cop-intuition for things that didn't look right.

As the crowd thinned, Davie saw the guy shift from one foot to the other, hiking his bag further up his shoulder, as if getting ready to go. Davie watched, more curious now, waiting for him to make his move. Was he looking for a mark in the crowd, someone to bump into and lift a wallet or purse, or was he just timing his run to the ticket barrier to get on the train without paying?

Davie had watched pickpockets, individuals and gangs, work crowds in London. Apart from the gang that had lifted his own wallet on a short trip with Sophie to Naples, the London gangs were the best he'd seen. The distraction, the lift, passing the wallet off, all done in less than thirty seconds. Slick as oil on glass, and difficult to spot even on camera, unless you knew the signs and the moves before they happened.

When the guy with the baseball cap did start moving, everything Davie had been thinking changed. The guy walked on his toes, his knees turned in and his arms held out at his side for balance. His pace towards the barrier at the train platform was slow but steady, as his backpack swung left and right. He had his ticket grasped tightly between two fingers and showed it at the barrier as he moved onto the platform.

Davie felt ashamed. He had the guy down as a sleazeball lowlife and he had been way off. He didn't know if he felt worse because his cop instincts had let him down badly or because the guy had a disability, probably some kind of cerebral palsy. Maybe he was losing his touch for observation, he thought, too long out of the Met, or maybe too long out of living around other people.

As he returned his gaze to the main concourse, he was distracted by a shout on the platform.

*"There's our wee spassy pal! We thought we had lost you there."*

The guy Davie been watching had gone just beyond the barrier, hiding behind a steel pillar, baseball cap once again pulled down. Three young lads, Davie guessed at seventeen, were coming down the platform towards him. Davie switched into cop mode again.

The boy in front was carrying an open can of Tenants Super, supported underneath by two fingers and hidden behind his wrist. He was wearing grey joggers with a matching top and a pair of white trainers straight out of the box; a box for which, Davie guessed, he didn't have a receipt. His two, smaller mates lagged behind, both dressed in polo shirts and the same grey, tracky bottoms.

Davie heard the leader of the group say, *"Now ye wernae trying to gie us the slip there, were ye, doing a runner on yer old mates?"*

Then the three boys were grouped around the guy with

the baseball cap, talking to him too quietly for Davie to make out. The two smaller boys hung back slightly, looking around, anxious to check if anybody was watching or listening, while the leader moved in closer. Davie saw a baseball cap appear suddenly in the leader's hand before it flew in the air onto the rail tracks, just as the train approached. Davie's view was obscured for a few seconds by passengers moving on the platform as the train drew to a halt, and when he had a line of sight again, Tenants Super was being poured from the can into the guy's backpack.

Davie scanned the platform to see if anyone was seeing what was happening, but if anyone was, it was something they had decided to ignore, intent instead on being in the best starting position when the train doors opened. Davie stood up then, hoping his legs would decide for him if he should jump in and do something, to save the guy from more humiliation, or if he should just ignore it, head off in the other direction to do what he'd come to do in the station.

As a man with a suitcase big enough to carry a body wheeled it through the extra wide swing barrier, Davie slipped through behind him, unseen by the ticket checker. The train had disgorged a flood of incoming passengers and Davie bobbed about, trying to see what was happening at the doors in the nearest carriage. The two smaller guys were either side of the guy with the now-dripping backpack, making like they were helping him onto the train, their good deed for the day. He either didn't or couldn't protest as they held him by the arms and planted him in a seat.

The leader of the group watched approvingly, still on the platform. As passengers ran to beat the doors closing, he started jumping on, then off the train, egged on by his mates.

"*Go on Billy, one more, one more!*"

"*Fast as fuck, me. Never been caught,*" he said as he jumped back onto the platform a third time.

The guard on the platform waved at him frantically and then blew his whistle, signalling him to get on the train, just before the beeping door-closing alarm started. The guy in the joggers turned towards the guard on the platform and gave him the finger, before turning to jump on the train.

He had one foot on the platform and one on the train as the doors started to close, then both his feet were suddenly in the air, and he was flying backwards. Davie yanked him by the collar of his sweatshirt and planted him on his arse on the platform. His can of beer went spinning off behind him.

"*What the fuck...*"

Davie took a step back, then leaned down and helped him to his feet.

"*Now that was a close one,*" Davie said calmly.

"*If I wisnae here, you would have been jammed in that door, and maybe dragged down the platform.*"

"*If you wernae here, ya prick, I'd be on the fucking train!*" he shouted at Davie. "*What do ye think you're doing, pulling me off?*"

Davie stood his ground as the guy moved closer to him.

"*Ah well, I have to disagree with you there,*" he said quietly.

"*Ye see, what most people don't realise is that train doors are not like doors in a lift. They might look the same, but the train doors don't open again if there's something stuck in them, and...*"

The guy in joggers was now nose-to-nose with Davie.

"*Now I've missed my train and the next one's no for another fucking hour!*" he said.

*"Well, at least you're alive to get the next train,"* Davie continued, in the same tone, sounding like he was a minister delivering *Thought for the Day.*

*"I'm sorry you're no grateful that I saved your life, but maybe you will be when you calm down and get a chance to think it over later."*

They stood facing each other up close for a beat as the train pulled away. Davie smiled.

The guy in the joggers was waiting, fists clenched by his side. This was the point at which somebody either took a swing to start the fight, or ran. Neither was happening and he was a bit confused.

The smelly dosser in front of him was too weird to predict. He was old, definitely, maybe too old to fight, but heavy looking about the arms and neck. And he could be a mental case, or he might be carrying, a blade in his pocket. Too risky to take him on. He winced and took a small step back.

In a louder voice, for the benefit of the small group now watching from the platform across the tracks, he said, *"Fuck's sake. You smell like a rubbish bin pal. I would kick your fucking head in for what you did there, but I'd mess up my nice clean trainers."*

With one of his nice clean trainers, he booted over a rubbish bin as he stomped up the other end of the platform.

Davie watched him go, then headed back to the barrier. The platform guard there looked at him, shook his head and opened the gate to let him through.

As Davie walked back down the station concourse, he counted the money in the wallet he'd taken from the grey joggers' pocket, then dropped the empty wallet into the first bin he came to. Watching a lot of pickpockets didn't make you a good pickpocket, but you learned the basics.

It wasn't justice, and it wasn't a deterrent. The tanked-up ned would just as likely do the same thing tomorrow and the day after, to show that he was more powerful than at least somebody, and to show off to his mates. Davie knew that. And the guy with cerebral palsy wouldn't be spared from further hassle on the train home. But without the alpha-bully, his two mates might be less brave on a crowded train, this time at least.

It brought back memories, not good ones, of being a cop with the Met. It was always one step forward and then two back, nibbling away at the edge, while the massive, greedy core of crime grew, relentlessly, feeding on whatever was available, whether it was drugs, money or people for sale, with the petty and more serious violence associated with each. Some days Davie went home suspecting that he had made no difference, and other days he went home knowing that he had not.

# – 10 –

## GUISING

*"You need soap and a towel there, pal?"*

It was more a comment on Davie's appearance than a question by the attendant.

Davie had walked the length of the echoing cathedral that was Glasgow Central to the station toilets.

The cost of a shower was £5, which included soap gel and a towel, and any debris left in the shower by the previous user. Davie got into the cubicle, stripped off and then stood holding his clothes, puzzling over where to put them in the wet room so that they didn't get as wet as him. He pushed his bundle into a corner, then tried to shield them from the stream of hot water with his body. There was no limit on the water you could use in the shower, but it shut off every twenty seconds and he had to hold one hand on the push button to keep the water flowing.

The scissors from Boots the Chemist in the station had also cost him £4, and the disposable razor pack took another £2 of his cash. He used the money he had just acquired, but he needed to get more soon. His priority then, however, was to change his appearance from the person of interest in a murder case to that of just another homeless man on the streets of Glasgow.

He started with the scissors on his hair, hacking off chunks and trying to rinse them down the drainage hole in the shower. It was like scything down long grass before a lawn mower could do its job. The *Bic* razors were sharp enough straight out of the packet, but he needed two of them to give himself a scalping, after soaping up his head. Even bald, his head had a five o'clock stubble shadow like coal dust.

The beard was more of a problem. Leave it as it was, and he might still be recognised with a hat on; shave it all off and he might look too well-groomed to be homeless. He took the scissors and chopped his beard from its unruly, fee-fi-fo-fum style to a more wiry, Che Guevara hedge, still scruffy enough to signal that he was living on the street. Looking in the mirror, his head looked smaller and his beard looked bigger, but that was a form of disguise too he thought, right?

Next, he went around the Glasgow Central Station exits at Gordon, Union and Hope Street, asking for the information he needed and coming up blank. People he spoke to glanced once and then blanked him, or asked him for money in exchange for information he suspected they didn't have.

Finally, he found somebody willing to share without conditions, a man who could tell him everything he needed to know, and more. He was sitting in a sleeping bag coat under the Hielanman's Umbrella, as the glass Central Bridge outside the station was known. John was the name he gave.

As soon as Davie stopped to talk to him, John stood up to demonstrate his all-in-one, which was clearly a prized possession.

*"It's a cross between Scott of the Antarctic and being in a sack race, see,"* he said.

He spoke fast, with no prisoners taken if you didn't get it

first time. Despite being born and raised just twenty miles away, Davie had to lean in close to tune in to John's strong accent and follow what he was being told.

"*This bit,*" John said, taking his feet out of the padded pocket and pointing, "*just folds up into the back of the jacket and, presto, you've got a warm bum all day too! I've got to keep an eye on this coat around here,*" he continued, without a pause, looking pointedly at the next doorway along, where a younger man sat on a pile of blankets, his sleeping dog beside him.

"*Not many of these bad boys aboot, see,*" he said, pointing again to his bag-coat. "*I was just in the right place at the right time to get it.*"

Davie heard John draw a rasping breath, saw his chance, and dived in. "*And where could I find one of these fine coats, or something like it, if I was looking?*" he said, wrapping his arms around his shoulders as the bitter wind whipped through under the bridge.

"*Ah well now, there's a few places you could try, see, but I doubt you'll find one as good as this,*" John said, drawing another rattling breath and looking up over Davie's shoulder, as if reading what was available from a list.

"*First off, there's that Unity in the Community bunch, who are good, don't get me wrong. But you need a referral from the social work or a doctor to go there, and I don't think you've got time for that. You look like you need some clathes right now before you freeze to death. Am I right?*" John paused for another breath and then went on without waiting for an answer.

"*Then there's the Sally Ann. They've got a place just the other side of the river. They're all called Lieutenant this and Sergeant Major that, calling you 'Brother' all the time when you don't know them from Adam. Strange bunch of tin shakers, if you ask me. Cannae tell the men and women apart sometimes, all marching for Jesus and blowing trumpets.*

*There's tea and rolls and clathes right enough for the likes of us, but only if go down on your knees and sing for it. Something dodgy about Christians in uniforms if you ask me, eh?*

*Onward into battle? I mean, what's that all about?"*

"Well, that might be OK..." Davie started to interrupt, but John was back in his stride again.

*"Then of course, there's the real Holy Joes, you know, feeding the hungry and thirsty, clothing the naked, bring us your poor huddled masses, saving souls, all that stuff. If you go there, you might get something to wear, but they end up feeling better than you do. And then there's the weird and the wonderful crews..."*

Davie tuned out as John went on with the list of who might help and how much of his soul they might ask for in return. He looked off, further down the road, thinking that he should move soon and find a place to sleep before it was fully dark.

*"...and there's new outfits springing up all the time, of course. You could pretend to be a refugee to get something. Didnae work for me, but who knows? You could put on an accent and chance it, but that's no right either, is it?"*

John drew his bag-coat closer around him. He laughed quietly.

*"The latest crew I saw were giving away suits. Suits? I mean to us, in Glasgow? They were called Dress for Success,"* he laughed again.

*"Success? That boat has well and truly sailed for the likes of you and me a long time ago, I think, eh?"*

Davie was on the point of interrupting and backing off, thanking John for his time, and for the demo of the sleeping coat, when John said, *"There's one more you could try though, since you're here tonight."*

He looked up and down the road, as if deciding which way to send Davie.

*"They're nothing fancy mind, just basic stuff. 'Help the Homeless', that's the name. Does what it says on the tin. They're all right. You don't need to pray and shout hallelujah there and you might get something to keep you warm tonight if you're fast enough."* John waved his hand vaguely towards Renfield Street.

*"They meet up tonight behind the Argos shop, or at least they used to...."*

*"Which Argos is that, John? Where is it?"* Davie interrupted, now feeling his body temperature getting to the point where it was going to be a long way back to feeling warm.

*"Just the back of Argyle Street Station. You'll see where they've set up. All the good stuff goes fast, mind. I think some people go there to nab it and then sell it on market stalls to make money. Shameful that is, when there's homeless people going cold. I think..."*

*"Many thanks John. I'll get going now and check it out. You take care of yourself, and that great coat of yours,"* Davie said, smiling as he backed away, holding up both hands in farewell. He could still hear John continue with more recommendations as he reached the corner.

\* \* \*

*"Never Look Down on Anybody Unless You're Helping Him Up. Jesse Jackson."*

A dog-eared banner that had been roughly laminated using

multiple strips of *Sellotape* was pinned to the front of the main table. It was 6.30 and almost fully dark before Davie got there. As he approached, a woman emerged from beneath the folding table, dragging out a battered cardboard box. Brushing herself down, she looked up at the sky, then started to take folded clothes from the box and fill remaining spaces along the length of the tables.

Davie looked across at the other folding tables set up on the opposite side of the lane. Half a dozen people queued beside a water boiler and stacks of paper cups, and there was a longer queue by a massive stainless-steel pot of steaming soup.

"*Hello there,*" said the woman behind the clothing tables, before she went down for another box. She continued speaking from under the table.

"*I'm glad it stayed dry, because it takes us forever to get all the covers and clips on these stalls when it rains. I'm just topping up the tables here. I'll be with you in just a minute.*"

Davie looked again at the clothes on the tables, not sure whether she was expecting a reply. She straightened up again and brushed her hands down her apron.

"*Now,*" she said. "*My name's Mavis. Tell me what is it you were after tonight?*" she said, smiling.

"*Well, anything to keep the cold out,*" Davie said, returning her smile and looking along the table but seeing very little that fitted his description.

Mavis looked him up and down quickly, with a practised eye.

"*Ah, now, you're probably thinking coat, standing there, shivering without one,*" she said.

"*Most people would. What you* should *be thinking before you think coat is to think hat.*"

Not as catchy as, *"Never Look Down on Anybody Unless You're Helping Him Up"*, Davie thought, but it did sound like another wise proverb. He wondered whether Jesse Jackson might have had anything to say about hats.

Mavis continued to spread out clothes on the table and said, *"Your head's like a chimney see, and all the heat just goes straight up and out."*

*"Now let's see that beanie hat you've got on."*

Davie slipped off this hat and handed it across.

Mavis rubbed the material between her fingers, then bent and rummaged under the table again.

*"Now it looks OK, but try one of these,"* she said, producing with a flourish what looked to Davie like three different sized tea cosies. The first was plain black, knitted in something that resembled boat rope, and the other two looked like the knitters had been watching some fascinating TV show and forgot to stop plain and purling until it was too late.

*"Ah, I see you're admiring the slouchy toques there,"* Mavis said.

*"Very popular with the younger men who come here, they are. David Beckham and all the TV celebrities wear them. The extra length at the back keeps all your hair in...,"* she glanced up at Davie's newly shaved head and then changed tack, *"...and keeps your neck warm as well."*

She laid the three hats out on the table for Davie to try on, continuing to speak as she did so.

*"You see, some people will knit for us at Help the Homeless and hand stuff in to put on the stall. Their hearts are in the right place, don't get me wrong,"* she said, *"but just because people are homeless, it doesn't mean they'll take anything that's given them. People tend to forget that. We've had pink and orange fluffy hats that blind*

*people wouldn't wear, homeless or not, and jumpers with sleeves that are different colours or different lengths..."*

*"The black one would be fine for me, I think, Mavis,"* Davie said, pointing to the boat rope hat that he had put on his head. It was thicker than what he had and, more importantly, different from what he had been wearing in any police description that was circulating currently.

After some more chat about the benefits of a good hat and a decent pair of shoes, Mavis of *Help the Homeless* produced two coats in Davie's size from yet another box under the table. Davie started to wonder how much more was down there. It was like Dr Who's Tardis.

*"I like to keep the big stuff out of sight because, well..."* she started to say and then trailed off. Davie put on a green, padded jacket with a hood and few small holes, most of them carefully patched. It was urban outdoor, rather than Arctic adventurer and it was no sleeping bag coat, but he started to feel warmer as soon as he pulled it on.

As he modelled the coat and hat for Mavis and thanked her again, he heard the sliding door of a van close on the street behind him. Mavis looked over his shoulder, the smile from her face gone.

Two men walked slowly to the table, and without acknowledging Mavis or Davie started lifting and checking the jumpers, trousers and shirts that were laid out, tossing the clothes back onto the table in crumpled bundles. Mavis moved to the centre of the table.

*"Hello gentlemen,"* she said, *"back for some more clothes for your friends, is it?"*

The older of the two men had short-cut grey hair and a broad forehead. He was wearing jeans and a jacket that might have been leather, stretched across wide shoulders. The younger one was taller and thinner, bleached hair sticking out from a blue hoodie, pulled tight around his head. Although his clothes and his twitching movement suggested that he was much younger, his face did not. He had the complexion of a corpse and his eyes hung like a pair of dog's balls.

The older man kept sifting through the clothes for a moment and then looked up at Mavis.

*"That's right, yeah,"* he said.

He continued lifting the clothes folded on the stall, shaking them out, working left to right. He handed a few items to the other man, who put them on a small heap at a space he had cleared on the table.

*"Got any good stuff?"* the older man asked, without looking up.

*"Well, that depends on who needs it,"* said Mavis, following him along the table, refolding the discarded clothes.

Davie stood back and to one side. He noticed that Mavis' hands were trembling.

The younger man stepped forward then, lifting off his hood. He spoke with a nasal twang, that came from somewhere between Galveston, East Texas and Shettleston, East Glasgow. Watching too much TV, listening to too much country and western or both, Davie concluded.

*"Well now, our less fortunate homeless friends on the other side of the city are not able to make the trip here tonight, unfortunately, so they've sent us to find whatever we can to keep them dry and warm through the cold nights ahead,"* he said.

*"I'm sure you can appreciate that we both want only what's best*

*for them."* He cocked his head to the side and smiled through stained teeth.

Mavis kept her head down, still folding as she spoke.

*"Maybe if you brought some of your homeless friends with you next time in your van there, it would be easier to find out what they liked and what fitted them?"* she said quietly.

The older man's head jerked up suddenly from the clothes.

*"And maybe it would be easier if you just put on the table what you've got under the table, so we can pick what we need and be on our way,"* he said, lips tightly pursed.

Davie took a step towards the table, and Mavis give him an imperceptible shake of the head, warning him off.

He kept coming.

*"What sort of stuff are you looking for?"* he said, pleasantly, speaking to the man in the jacket that might be leather. The younger man spun around to face him.

*"Nothing that you would miss, friend,"* he said looking Davie up and down.

*"I think you should just run along and get yourself a nice cup of tea and some soup over there and keep out of this. It doesnae concern you,"* he continued in an accent that was suddenly no longer from anywhere near Texas.

Davie shrugged.

After a pause, he said, *"Well maybe it does,"* his voice rising. *"Because if there is really good stuff going free, better than these rags on the table, then maybe I've got as much right to it as you do."*

Mavis looked up, alarmed, as Davie's voice got even louder.

*"I came here looking for a decent coat and all I've ended up with is this crappy, ex-army cast off,"* he said, sticking his finger through a small hole on the sleeve.

*"Me and these other folk,"* he continued, pointing to the men and women in the tea and soup queues, *"we're no gonne be fobbed off with cast off rubbish, see, if there's better gear that we don't know about, hidden away."* He was shouting as he finished.

The peroxide blond in the hoodie moved towards Davie, leading with his chin, his hands at his side.

*"There's just two things I want you to do now, friend,"* he said in a whisper, *"and that's shut up and fuck off."*

As he came closer to Davie, he was distracted by movement behind him. Half the ragged queue for soup and most of those queueing for tea were walking slowly toward the clothing table, like a scene from a zombie movie, some drawn by Davie's shouting, some by the prospect of better clothes than those they were wearing. As the crowd pushed forward, the older man saw them too and grabbed hoodie by the arm. They got clear just before they were corralled against the table by the advancing mob.

*"Now, now, no need to push,"* Mavis said in her schoolteacher's voice, *"there's plenty of good stuff here for anybody that really needs it."*

The people at the front started to inspect what was on the table, while others bent down, trying to see what treasures were kept in Mavis's secret stash.

*"We'll be back,"* hoodie shouted, over his shoulder as he was led back to the van.

*"Yes, yes, welcome anytime,"* Mavis said under her breath, as she dug out a washed out, cable knit jumper from beneath the table for an older man who looked like he might really need it.

She looked over to Davie as he walked off and gave him a quick wave and a thumbs up.

\* \* \*

At the end of October each year, Scottish children yet to fully develop the embarrassment emotion dress up and go knocking on neighbours' doors for money and sweets. The origin of the Halloween tradition was that by disguising themselves as evil spirits, guisers would be safe from recognition and harm from any real wandering dead demons, also known to wear disguises.

Davie wasn't tormented by any demons, other than his own. With his makeshift disguise of a shaved head, straggly beard, padded jacket and thick black tea cosy, he relaxed a bit. Still somewhere to find for the night, but no longer recognisable as one of Greenock's most wanted.

Davie Perdue, created anew.

# – 11 –

## MISPERS

After checking a couple of the homeless hostels, Davie decided that his chances of getting a bed for the night near the centre of town were slim, and the likelihood of sleep in that bed even slimmer. The drop in temperature had brought a rush of street sleepers in search of a roof.

In the few nights that he had not made it back to Greenock and the Goalkeeper's House, Davie had paid for a night in a Glasgow hostel. There were places to go and places to avoid. Night shelters were free, but Davie learned the hard way that if you were not desperate when you walked in the door, you would feel that way very soon. A bed in hostels for the homeless had to be paid for, either through housing benefit in advance or in cash, which Davie still had. So, hostels were better than night shelters, but that didn't make them a good place for a sleep. Davie's first night away from his cemetery basement had taught him that.

Glasgow Council had decided just that year to close all of its warehouse-sized hostels. Within five minutes of signing into the 250-bedded James Duncan House in Bell Street, Davie realised why.

The most obvious and audible sign that the night would be

a long one was the clamour of shouting coming from the street at the back-facing windows of the building. The shouting was always followed closely by the thump of feet running along the corridors above and then downstairs. A drug dealer, or more likely several, had set up shop in the hostel. Orders for £5 or £10 bags would be shouted up from the street, then runners would deliver and collect the cash.

This went on all night, addicted sex workers replacing the daytime addicts as darkness fell. The sound of orders and deliveries competed with the background bedlam in the hostel. Men with mental health problems, alcoholism, drug addictions or combinations of the three, talked to themselves in rooms and shouted at anyone who interrupted. Older men and younger men without mental health problems found things to argue about, just because they had nothing in common, and even the few men who were sleeping shared their nightmares loudly. With so many men crammed into the rooms, there was a perpetual racket, shouted complaints about the racket, followed by even more racket.

Davie needed somewhere to lay his head, but not at any price, so James Duncan House was off his list, no matter how cold it was.

At the first place he went to that night, Home Mission, there was a fight between two men at the front door, with the other, queueing homeless men spilling onto the road and stopping the traffic. It was an argument about who had been there first, from what Davie could make out from the swearing he could hear between the punching and kicking.

There were no vacancies at another Glasgow Council hostel, a bit further out of town, a fact not appreciated by the man who was repeatedly trying to put his foot through the sandwich board sign outside, reading, *'FULL – PLEASE CALL THIS NUMBER...'*

By the time Davie got to his third choice of accommodation, at the Salvation Army hostel, there was a cutting wind blowing down all the north-south aligned streets in the city centre. Even his padded jacket and his rope beanie were not enough to prevent him shivering after just ten minutes of standing still in the queue.

His late arrival in Glasgow put him behind a long line of homeless who had already been to other hostels. Davie judged the number of people waiting outside the Salvation Army hostel and decided that any action he took would be better than waiting in the cold for another hour, only to find out that this hostel was also full.

\* \* \*

Union Place was a narrow cul-de-sac, close to Glasgow Central Station, where he'd showered and shaved his head earlier. A massive set of rusting metal doors at the end of the cobbled lane was the only sign that traffic or pedestrians had ever used it. All the other doors in the lane had been sealed or bricked up, and broken or blackened windows stretched to five stories on each side. From the end of the lane, the roar of three galvanised air ducts high on one wall bounced off the brickwork, the sound venting at the end of the lane, drowning out conversations of people passing on Gordon Street.

Littered knee-deep in discarded bottles, paper and cans, and too narrow for street sweeping lorries, Union Place was described in one of the tourist street guides as, *'one of Glasgow's most honkin' lanes.'* Because of its east-west orientation and its height and length, it also had the earliest sunset and the latest sunrise of any street in the city centre. After the day Davie had just had, the hidden depths of Union Place suited him just fine.

He walked into the near darkness until he was out of sight, then found enough fast-food cardboard to keep him off the cold cobbles and a few more layers to cover his feet and legs. His new jacket and hat were good insulation now that he was out of the wind and he managed to get some sleep, about an hour in every two, awoken only by the periodic roar of the pipes. It was not five star, but being homeless had taught Davie the true value of shelter, just as being hungry for the first time that he could remember had taught him the true value of good food.

In his darkest hours in London, after he'd resigned from the Met with no purpose other than not to go back to work, he would sit about in his flat for long hours until he saw the streetlights come on outside his window.

The shadow of that black dog came back to him again briefly, sitting in the dark of Union Place. He willed himself back to sleep through the night, fighting the thought that where he was sleeping and what had become of his life were both the same dead end.

\* \* \*

Davie stayed up in Glasgow for the next two days, hoping that interest in Greenock's person of interest would fade, and the spotlight would move on. He did a morning of *Big Issue* sales and some thinking, then went looking for some decent grub.

His favourite Glasgow café was Luigi's, but only when Luigi wasn't there. The place had been a 1960s café, and mostly still was. New coffeehouses and tearooms were opening in the city centre as fast as high- and low-end fashion shops were closing or relocating to impersonal shopping malls in the hinterland. After the loss of industry and employment from Glasgow, the city centre began to die, and heated, dry shopping malls became an attractive lure. Most shoppers spent more time travelling in the free buses than in the shopping malls when they got there, but window shopping in heated malls became a cheap family alternative to dragging bored children around cold city centre streets.

Shopfitters in what remained of the cities commercial centre eateries were being contracted to create retro interiors with uncomfortable seating and farm implements or bicycles hanging on the walls. Luigi's was an exception; vintage, rather than retro, with no shopfitters involved.

The Formica tables were still screwed to the floor, the walls were washable, and the chairs were as unforgiving as they had been for 30 years. The only concession to modernisation was a new-fangled coffee machine, to cater for the 'younger crew', as Luigi called them. There was salt, pepper and vinegar on all tables, and bottles of *Irn Bru* could be added as the *vin de la maison* on request.

Luigi's did sit-in fish teas, and that's what Davie went for. He found a seat near the back of the busy café and waited for one of Luigi's daughters or nieces to take his order.

The table opposite him was occupied by a man who could have been twenty-five or thirty-five, dressed in a lime green T-shirt and tight black jeans with more pockets than anybody could ever use. He had two phones in front of him and was spinning one of them on the Formica top as it sprung into life, the *Grande Valse* Nokia ringtone loud enough to drown out the background music, which was Luigi's choice of bossa nova covers.

Green T-shirt man picked up the phone, frowned at the number, put the phone to his ear, but said nothing.

*"Fuck's sake,"* he said after a pause, *"I telt ye no to phone me on this number. This is for business."*

There was another pause, before he said in an even louder voice, *"Well, it might no be the business you want me to be in, but it's what I'm doing now, until my other job opportunity comes through, right, so don't phone me on this number, and don't fucking phone me at all at this time in the morning, when I'm just up."*

With that, he ended the call and slammed the phone back on the table, mumbling and getting to his feet. He lifted the other phone, pushed a few buttons and music started up. With many of the frequencies of the song stripped out by the cheap phone, the sound was a tinny but loud percussive thumping, competing with Luigi's bossa nova. To Davie's ear, it sounded like a recording of somebody in a suit of armour falling down a flight of stairs. The guy next to him stood, stuffed the phone into one of his many zip pockets, muffling the sound. Then he moved to the back of the café, put both hands on the wall and started some stretching exercise routine, still mumbling.

He'd been there before Davie arrived, so when the waitress came, Davie nodded towards the other table. She raised her eyebrows and shook her head. Green T-shirt wasn't ordering anything, it seemed.

*"Fish tea with bread and butter please,"* Davie said, without looking at the laminated menu.

While Davie waited, green T-shirt's other phone, the one still on the table, started to vibrate, dancing across the smooth surface. He came back quickly and picked it up, the muffled music still going in his pocket.

This time he said, *"Hello?"*

The caller said something, and green T-shirt replied, *"OK. I can get you that gear for half eleven. Usual place."* He finished the call, replaced the phone and walked back to continue his exercises at the wall.

Davie turned his head to watch him, and when he turned back, Luigi was standing at his table.

*"What are you doing here?"* Luigi said, having to shout to be heard above the competing music.

*"I've told you before. I can't have you in here."* People at other tables turned to see what was happening.

Davie knew how this ended.

Luigi's nieces, Luigi's cousins, everybody else who worked there, even Luigi's brother would serve Davie, quietly and without a fuss. But not Luigi.

*"This place is for my paying customers."*

Davie didn't reply, but this didn't stop Luigi continuing as if he had.

*"It's no a shelter for smelly vagabondos."*

Davie was already on his feet. He could hear the green T-shirt's Nokia ringtone blast out again as he reached the door.

\* \* \*

After finding a carry out stall that did serve vagabondos and a quiet corner to eat his chicken gyro, Davie took on another pile of *Big Issues* from the collection point, and moved about his familiar spots until he'd shifted them all.

He sought out pitches in doorways, where he could stand in the sunshine, sheltered from the wind, and moved to another as each of his spots fell into shade.

The temperature rose a few degrees over the two days and the wind fell back a bit. As the sun went down, Davie worked his way back to Union Place, rummaging through a few skips for extra bits for his bedding that might soften his street mattress for the night.

A few of the supermarkets in town still chucked out-of-date food that couldn't be donated to charities, because of food standard rules. Being in the right alleyway at the right time was a combination of street knowhow and luck. Getting there too soon got you chased by the lorry drivers and supermarket staff taking deliveries; getting there just a few minutes too late left you with the fag-end of what was going in the galvanised steel wheelie bins, because others had beaten you to the good stuff. Those few minutes were the difference between perfectly edible bread, with cheese or bananas to go on it, and inedible wet sops and mouldy fruit.

Davie bought his food when he was in Greenock. He could pick the times and smaller, quiet places without drawing suspicion. When he was in Glasgow, he avoided supermarkets. Around the city centre they were busy 24/7. Homeless people with folding cash in hand drew looks and suspicion at checkouts, and unwanted followers when they came out. There were also cameras inside the supermarkets. Nobody reviewing the footage just yet for his face, Davie calculated, but why take the risk? And even though he could afford to buy decent food, where could he go to eat it?

So, Davie went to the back of the Glasgow supermarkets rather than the front, learning how to time his runs and get enough to get by. The combinations that he ended up with were not always the approved serving suggestions on the packaging. Out of date, peanut butter or jam wrapped in anything was good; bread, pizza or day-old rolls were best, but even smeared on apples or rolled up in lettuce that still had some life in it was tasty, when you were hungry.

\* \* \*

Next day, as the Glasgow bus reached the outskirts of Greenock, Davie cleared a circle from the condensation on the window to check for the person-of-interest posters. He'd been checking day-old newspapers in Glasgow, scanning pages for something that would get him off the hook and let him relax. Something definitive, like a new development in the murder enquiry or an arrest, or a new suspect, pressured into coming forward following all the publicity.

As the bus neared the town centre, he at first thought he saw even more of the white, A4 laminated appeals than before, on lampposts and in shop windows. Davie ran his hand over his beard and bald head, wondering what else he could do to change his appearance, or where else he could go.

When he got to the bus station and started his head-down walk back to the Goalkeeper's House however, he saw that the posters were in the same places but with a different face.

The circus had moved on.

\* \* \*

*Strathclyde Police. Missing person. Appeal for information.*

James Quigley

Last seen on the afternoon of Friday 25th April leaving his home
address in Finnart Street, Greenock.

James is 69, described as white, 5ft 5 inches tall, of stocky
build with thinning grey hair. He was wearing a dark overcoat,
light-coloured trousers and a flat cap.

*Do you know anything that may assist Strathclyde Police?*
*Please phone...*

The thin, pale face looking out from the poster was turning
towards the camera. He was wearing a suit jacket, shirt and tie.
The photograph looked like it had been taken at some family
celebration. Other faces in the shot had been blurred out and
there was a table of drinks in the background.

One of the first shocks for Davie in London was how many
people were reported missing every day across the city. On
average, it was about a hundred every week. He had read that
number a few times to make sure it was correct. He was put out
on searches for a few such cases in his time at Peckham and that
was how he learned that the statistics didn't tell the whole story.
Most of the missing didn't make it onto posters as smiling faces
because they were found quickly, alive. Only a few were gone
forever.

There was a distinction between lost and disappeared. Both were terms for missing persons, whereabouts unknown, being sought by someone who cared. Lost was lost, whereabouts currently unknown. Disappeared, however, was a red flag for police, alerting them that there may be something more sinister, possibly involving other people.

Somebody went out to the shops for milk or rolls or cigarettes and never came back. The last person in a group of walkers on a path didn't appear around the next corner. A CCTV image showed a face passing one street security camera but not the next. A car was found in a remote spot, empty, door open. These were disappearances.

There was an unspoken hierarchy of urgency in the Met, and in other police forces too, when it came to mispers. There were written protocols and risk assessment checklists to be completed to assess priority, but most cops carried a shortened version in his head.

Emergency services were always stretched. Like medics during war or a big city Accident and Emergency Department on a Saturday night, the police had a triage system to find at least some of those who went missing before the outcome was injury or death.

Category 1 was children reported missing. This boiled down to children who had wandered off or had been taken. There were also children who thought that they were adults without understanding the consequences, which put them in the sights of paedophiles and other abusers seeking prey. For category 1, police rolled out the Full Monty of resources in the crucial first 24 hours, putting paid and unpaid feet on the ground, using road checks, sniffer dogs, eyes in the air, and full media publicity.

Older teenagers with previous form and adults known to the police were included in category 2. The response, realistically, was background checks for runner indicators, possible addresses, checking train and bus CCTV, and phoning around likely bolt holes.

Somewhere between categories 2 and 3 were old people who had gone missing, either by choice or through befuddlement. Among themselves, the cops called these "silver alerts". The questions to be asked were the same as for other categories. Was the person vulnerable and what were the risks? Although the vulnerability and the risk might be just as high as for cases in category 1, even with the best of intentions, the police and the public response was more muted for category two and a half.

The 'correct' resources were allocated to deal with such cases. This meant what was available, and that in turn meant not much, because there was so little slack in the system.

Davie knew that the posters he was seeing about the missing James Quigley would stay up for two weeks, maybe three, before being replaced with whatever case bubbled to the top of police priorities and public consciousness next; most likely the latest Greenock murder.

The shock of a child going missing, but even more, the *mystery* of such a disappearance fuelled any searches, keeping interest alive much longer. For an old person, there was less mystery, and far more imaginable possibilities.

In Greenock, people could picture a confused old biddie wandering off, falling into the Clyde or a ditch somewhere. There was little to be done, because sending out mass search parties for the poor old soul wasn't going to change the outcome.

When Davie rescued a copy of the previous day's *Greenock*

*Reporter* from a bin at the bus station, there was a little more detail on the disappearance of James Quigley.

*Police this afternoon issued a fresh plea for help to trace James Quigley, 69, amid a major search operation.*

*The new appeal comes after officers were seen scouring woodland in the town and Coastguard crews were involved in a search of the shoreline and pierhead yesterday.*

*Householders are asked to check their garages, and any sheds and outbuildings. Mr. Quigley was last seen on the afternoon of Friday 25 April, leaving his home address in Finnart Street.*

*Nothing was missing from his flat apart from his brown overcoat, his hat and his wallet.*

*He is described as 5' 5" tall, of stocky build with thinning grey hair.*

*Inspector Paul Thompson said:* "James has some health issues and there are growing concerns for his welfare. Please get in touch if you have any relevant information, no matter how trivial it may seem."

The mention of the Coastguard crews in the police statement was a tell for Davie, as it would be for many other *Reporter* readers. Like similar press release staples – *"Police are not looking for anyone else,"* or, *"No other vehicles were involved and no one else was injured,"* – there was information behind what was reported.

Non-reportable information was provided to the media on the understanding that it was for guidance only and not for publication or broadcast. The extra information could be used as further context for the basic coded statement. So, *"Police are not looking for anyone else,"* might mean that there was a suspect, or that it was a case of self-harm. *"No other vehicles were involved,"* might mean that the driver had come off the road at speed and hit a tree. *"Coastguard crews were involved,"* meant that James Quigley was more likely to be in the water than in some neighbour's shed.

The only remaining unknown was whether he slipped or had jumped into the river.

Despite the sanctuary of the Clyde being never more than half a mile away for anyone in town thinking about ending their life, death by drowning was a rare method of suicide in Greenock. Hanging or poisoning was much preferred which, to Davie at least, seemed like a tough and uncertain way to go. A rope, plastic bag, a handful of pills or some combination of these could still have you waking up in hospital, feeling worse than you did before. Walking or jumping into the Clyde was cold, yes, but if you held your nerve, a quick and bloodless death was guaranteed.

At one time there had been a spate of drownings in Greenock; twenty-one in a single year. This produced local alarm, shouty newspaper headlines and even questions to the Home Secretary in Parliament. But that had been way back in 1940 and none of the twenty-one deaths were suicides. The drownings were all harbour workers tripping and falling into the Clyde during the wartime blackout. In modern times, harbour drownings were rare, by accident or by suicide, but the death rate in Greenock continued to make headlines in Scotland and internationally.

On slow news days, local journalists would dig through back issues and periodically write too-clever articles about the rate of suicides, aimed at building their own portfolio, rather than increasing understanding about why so many people took their own lives.

By coincidence, or perhaps not, the same issue of the *Greenock Reporter* featuring the police appeal on *James Quigley* also had a piece entitled, "*Unexpected Grief: Greenock's Unenviable Record*". Davie read the first paragraph before folding the paper and tipping it in a bin on his way back to the cemetery.

"*Greenock and Greenland share more than a harsh climate and a common prefix in their names. Greenock is the town with the highest rate of suicides in Scotland, and Greenland is the country with the world's highest prevalence. The sky-high rate of felones-de-se on the world's largest island is put down to some combination of poverty, alcoholism, depression and dysfunctional homes. Greenock, of course, has all of these diseases of despair in spades...*"

The police continued to look for James Quigley and to pursue, albeit with less intensity, the E-fit that was Davie Perdue.

But the police were not the only force patrolling the streets of Greenock.

# – 12 –

## ALROY THE PROTECTOR

All the best ones were taken.

Names that included the words shadow, phantom, moon, knight, hawk, captain, tiger or any of the other big cats; all gone. The names of superheroes with real superpowers had been claimed by Marvel Comics and the second string, street superheroes of major cities had taken the rest.

Wolverine, Spider-Man, Thor, Hulk, and Captain America, battled evil, first on the pages of comic books then on the big screen, while flesh and blood figures like Masked Maniac, Dark Guardian, Phoenix Jones, Knight Warrior and Black Mercer were patrolling city streets around the world, striking fear into the hearts of real criminals, wherever and whenever they could find them.

Most street superheroes were out late at night, dressed in masks and stab proof vests, actively searching for crime to confront or victims to rescue. Other public guardians, like Alroy, did it a bit differently.

They were protectors, serving the public by being the extra eyes and ears of the police. It was an equally valuable if less visible, less glamourous role. Protectors were crime fighters, but they were not vigilantes. He hated that word. It made him think of crowds with torches and farming tools, storming Frankenstein's castle.

Like his fellow real-life street superheroes, Menganno in Argentina or Captain Australia in Brisbane or the Dark Avenger in Vancouver, Alroy was ready, if it came to it, to step up and put his body on the line for others. Of course he was. No self-respecting street superhero would think twice about the dangers of doing the right thing and doing it right. When he had made the decision and the commitment to become Alroy the Protector, he did so knowing well the risks of a beating or a stabbing that came with the job. His preference, however, would be to report, rather than fight.

He didn't go looking for trouble, but he did go to spots on his patch where he knew help might be needed. He understood that he could be a target if criminals redirected their frustration and fury when he stood in front of them, protecting their intended victims.

Pain was part of the job too, because as Alroy the Protector, he was also a shield.

Using physical force was a last resort, but if violence was inevitable, he would take the blows to save the innocents, and sometimes the oblivious; those not even aware of the danger they were in. If hand-to-hand clashes between good and evil could be avoided, he was for that too, which was why he kept the Greenock Police Station and Crime Stoppers on speed dial, as well as the phone numbers of Neighbourhood Watch Greenock West, Beats 63 and 64, which was his patch.

He didn't have a car to patrol his area, and if asked he would have said that it had been shot up in the line of duty, as had happened to Shadow, one of his real-life superheroes.

So, he was limited to keeping a vigil on foot, walking miles and keeping him fit for the job.

Alroy the Protector lived everyday by the creed of the real-life superhero.

*Always operate within the constraints of the law, even when provoked.*

*Prevent criminal activity where possible and stop it personally when it was ongoing.*

*Use persuasion, threat if necessary and as a last resort administer no punishment to criminals beyond incapacitation.*

*Above all else, trust your gut.*

Alroy could recite the creed from memory and did when he was patrolling. He was especially sensitive to the final part of the creed because he was conscious that his outfit tried but failed to hide the muffin top that crept over his tight jogging bottoms. The tight-fitting tactical vest he wore under his red cycling top helped, but there was still a roll of gut hanging out. On the streets, as Alroy the Protector, he disguised it by doing his superhero knuckles-on-hips pose as often as possible.

A year ago, when he was still plain Ruairidh, he'd put together the outfit, even before he had decided on the name. After a few drawings, he modelled his kit loosely on that of Deathstroke the Terminator, one of Ruairidh's favourite villains from DC comics. The baddies always had a more menacing look than any of the good guys in Ruairidh's experience, and menacing was what he was going for, in a costume at least. He liked the dark side look. For the name however, he wanted something well on the light side, something that made it clear what he was about.

Ruairidh the Redeemer, Ruairidh the Rock, Rough Justice Ruairidh and even Ruairidh the Radge all made it to his short list, but they all had the same problem; his name. For all of his twenty-three years, through school and in work at the supermarket, he'd had to spell it out to almost everyone he met. Even then, most got it wrong.

People called him Roddy a lot, and most often Rory. There was one teacher who had insisted on calling him Rahoorie, and other children in his class who called him rhubarb. As a crime fighter, part of the job was striking fear into the hearts of would-be criminals, by building a reputation that made them think twice before going out on the prowl, or had them looking over their shoulder if they did. If nobody could say or spell his name correctly, he was going to be at a disadvantage, right off. Police reports, newspaper reports and word on the street would be a jumble of different names, most of them wrong. If criminals couldn't pronounce his name, they wouldn't fear him.

His mother, God rest her soul, was to blame. Holding him on the day he was born, she decided immediately on a name to match what she saw. Two weeks later she had walked proudly to the Municipal Buildings to register him as Rory Logan Mackay, giving him her maiden name as an extra.

A week later she was back at the Registrar, after her cousin in the Western Isles had phoned to congratulate her and to enlighten her on the Gaelic spelling for her red-haired king. From that day, he was known by the colour of his hair. Ruairidh; four vowels, four consonants and much confusion.

He often wished his mother had not gone back to the Registrar to change his name or that she had compromised and called him Rory or Rooney or even Erik the Red. With any of those names his life would have been easier.

Like the character in the Johnny Cash song, he'd had to

toughen up fast, living his life as A Boy Named Roo. He'd faced up to bullies calling him Winnie the Roo, Irn Bru Heid, Swan Vesta, Gingeroo and at Xmas, Rudy the Red Nosed Reindeer. He stood up for himself and fought back when he could.

But it wasn't just his hair that made him different. He tried to fit in, to be just like all the boys around him, copying what they did even when he didn't understand why he was doing it. It just made him stand out more.

His father didn't help much.

*"The laddie's bothered with his nerves."* He'd say it to anybody who asked and to many who didn't, with or without Ruairidh in earshot, like he was commenting on the unusual colour of his son's hair. With that throw away phrase, his father dismissed why Ruairidh was different from other young children, and made him stand out even more.

Later, when Ruairidh was older, his father's explanation changed to, *"He's sick with his nerves,"* an equally vague explanation for Ruairidh's differences.

When Ruairidh finally admitted, after three months of misery, that he was being ragged at school by older boys because of his name and his hair, his dad responded without looking away from the football match he was watching on TV.

*"The record shows I took the blows. And did it my way."*

The wisdom of Frank Sinatra, when Ruairidh was standing behind his father's chair, his hair still wet and stinking from having his head dunked in a toilet pan at school again that day. Thanks a lot dad.

But now, all these years later, the song came back to him. He'd had his fill, his share of losing. And now, as tears subside, he found it all so amusing. The dismissive drunken words of his father, who still sat in the same chair, had a new resonance for Ruairidh, and for Alroy the Protector.

Alroy had been his mother's cousin's second suggestion for a name. Like Ruairidh, it was also Gaelic and something to do with red. He had taken time to decide on his crime fighting name, then even more time trying to make his mind up about whether 'the' should be in capitals. He wrote down both versions to compare, picturing how each would look in a newspaper headline. Alroy the Protector looked just fine.

Written down, Alroy The Protector looked more super-heroish, but it might suggest that he was the *only* Protector, which wasn't true. Those old enough might remember the original Protectors of pre-Marvel comic days; Nightmask, Gravestone, Prince Zardi, Iron Skull, The Eye and Miss Fury. So Ruairidh Logan Mackay became Alroy the Protector.

He finished off the black jogging bottoms, stab proof vest and red cycling top with a Guy Fawkes facemask. The mask kept his identity a secret, while still allowing his distinctive carrot top to be seen and known by criminals. After a couple of false starts, he had taken scissors to cut off the chin and mouth of the face mask, so that the criminals could hear him as well as see him. As a final touch, he added a pair of wire mesh gardening gloves to the costume and red, Kevlar sleeves, which cost a day's wages and reached to his elbows.

*"Self-defence is the best goal,"* was also part of the real-life superhero creed.

The first time that he looked at himself in the mirror fully kitted out, he knew that Alroy the Protector was ready for the streets. But were the streets ready for him?

He prepared himself. It was all right to be called names in the course of duty, he reckoned, and even names that hurt and made him feel like a complete clown, if by being there he still got the job done, no matter what was said.

"*Prevent criminal activity where possible and stop it personally when it was ongoing.*"

It was part of the creed.

# – 13 –

## THE GRAVEYARD SHIFT

Anybody who wanted the night shift usually got it. There were regular vacancies. People applied, believing it would suit them, found out quickly that it didn't and moved on. The core night shift crew however, were old hands who'd been doing it for years.

The number one reason for working at night was that you didn't have to take shit from customers and managers. There were fewer pointless staff meetings also, and nobody looking over your shoulder to check that you were doing what you were paid for. A fringe benefit was the chance of a quick powernap in the storeroom while somebody covered for you. But some night workers at the Tesco Greenock branch had other reasons too.

Jessie Mae Holmes had swapped from day shift because of her situation at home. The reason she gave to her co-workers, to save explaining things, was a different one. She was sick and tired of customers asking the same, stupid questions every day, she said. It was like being trapped in Groundhog Day. Being asked every day by strangers when her shift was over, reminding her of how many long, boring hours she still had to work.

For Joe McMahon, it didn't matter much when he slept. He

didn't plan beyond the next fortnight in his chaotic life. Tesco, day or night shifts, provided a source of income for his drinking when he felt like it and betting on horses, which was most days. An added attraction of moving to the night shift, a liking that he would never admit to others, was the comfort and warmth of the Tesco night worker fleeces.

It was easier, too, for lesser stars to shine, or to at least have their existence acknowledged on the night shift. The loners and outsiders who would be ignored by their fellow workers on a bustling day shift were obliged to step up and fill the silences at night, because there were so few of them.

Ruairidh knew that most people in the town thought that being a shelf stacker in the supermarket was a job for losers and dummies; strong backed nobodies who couldn't do anything else.

He thought about it differently.

If nobody put boxes on the roll cages in the storage room and nobody took the cages from the storage room and nobody put food from the boxes onto the shelves and nobody made sure the shopfloor was shipshape to save people from slipping, then nobody would be able to shop in Tesco safely and nobody would be able to buy food to eat.

So, Ruairidh knew it was an important job, even if nobody else thought so.

It was a job that didn't need a lot of talking, which also suited him just fine. You were told what was needed and you just got on with it. You didn't need to be told if you had done the job right because you could see it, and so could everyone else in the shop. Clean floors and straight shelves, all filled. One glance down any aisle told you whether a good job had been done.

Ruairidh had started as a part-time *Festive Colleague (Nights)*, when Tesco took on extra staff to bridge the gap between shopping aisles packed with customers and staff holiday requests. He was kept on after Christmas as a *Replenishment Colleague (Nights)*, then increased his hours to become a *Night Replenishment, Supermarket Assistant*. He was now a *Replenishment Associate (Nights)*. It was the same job with different titles, unloading and shelving the same roll cages of toilet rolls or tuna and keeping the aisles spotless.

The *Replenishment Associate (Nights)* hours started as 21.00–07.00, then changed to 22.00–06.00, four nights a week. Then it was three nights on, three nights off, repeating. When the store needed more flexibility, Ruairidh went to full time hours, spread across seven nights including weekends and those hours could be anytime between 21.00–07.00.

This could mean four hours before midnight one day, then four hours after midnight the next. It was a nightmare for staff with places to go, people to see, or children to get to school. But for Ruairidh all it meant was changing his patrol time, when he ate and the time his alarm went off.

*"This is a job for doers, with no day being the same. We look for warm, reliable, team-players, who are flexible, amenable and can work at pace."*

That was what Tesco Associates signed up for. For most night staff, those who just wanted a wage, the chopping and changing work hours to optimise Tesco operations was a test of endurance; some kind of stamina and loyalty test to see who really, really wanted to work at night. Only the strong survived to remain on the graveyard shift.

So, Ruairidh Mackay put in the hours, did the job well and

got paid. All that suited him fine. And the night shifts also suited Alroy the Protector.

Occasionally he wondered what it would be like to work days, chatting with customers, joking, even going to the pub with other workers after a long shift. But he had accepted his lot. For him, there was little chat on a night shift, other than what he could overhear from others. There were small posses of staff who gathered in the staff room or at the end of aisles to blether quietly, but he knew that as one of the last night workers to be taken on, all these cliques were well established before he started. He settled for friendly "hellos" and "see-you-laters" from most of the staff.

*  *  *

One of the other night shift workers, Alex Mabon, spoke even less that Ruairidh. He would give a short, jerky nod of the head to acknowledge any greetings from other workers when they started on shift, then keep his head down, doing his work with zero chat. He sat at a table by himself during his breaks.

Listening to music was not allowed while working. Despite this, Alex would bury his ear buds deep and have the wires trailing down under his shirt at the beginning of each shift. He took them out only if the shift manager was about, which was rarely.

Tesco had a buddy system for heavy lifting and moving jobs in the long hours of the night shift, and when they were both on shift, Ruairidh was always paired with Alex.

After two months, Ruairidh still didn't know what kind of music kept Alex distracted through the night hours. He didn't even know if it was music. Alex never showed any signs of nodding, moving his body or feet in time, nor tunelessly sing-alongs. For all Ruairidh knew it could be some all-night radio station, the collected speeches of Adolf Hitler, a reading from the Bible or just white noise. What he did know was that if he asked, Alex wouldn't tell him.

To begin with, everything else that Ruairidh knew about Alex came from other workers. When Ruairidh started on the job, he heard whispers and not-so-quiet jibes directed at Alex when he was out of earshot. People talked about the two holidays Alex had spent in the 'big hoose'.

While other workers found this funny, it scared Ruairidh. He knew the big hoose was Glasgow's Barlinnie Prison. The Bar-L was Scotland's Alcatraz, where only the really bad men were sent.

What had Alex done? Ruairidh couldn't ask. He spent the time he was with him, lifting or moving stuff together in the first few weeks of his nightshifts, studying Alex's hands. Were they the hands of a burglar, a pickpocket, or a safecracker? Surely not the long fingers that had been around somebody's neck? Alex's hands were quick with a Stanley knife too, Ruairidh noted, when it came to slashing open the stretch wrap on pallets or boxes in the storeroom. When the boxes were rolled out to the shelves and emptied, the same two strong hands reduced the cardboard to flatpack in a flash, ready for recycling.

It was the not knowing that spooked Ruairidh most. He made sure to keep himself at arms-length from Alex when they were working together and avoided being in the store-room when it was just him and Alex, making up excuses about needing a pee, or going to check on stock on a shelf. He knew that Tesco wouldn't have employed a strangler, even an ex-strangler, even on the nightshift, but stranger things had happened in Greenock.

Avoiding Alex came to a head one night when they were in the storeroom together, trying to manoeuvre a roll cage full of tinned tomatoes. The food crates from the warehouse had come in badly packed. One of the wheels on the cage had collapsed and it needed them both to be at that corner, supporting, so that the cage could be rolled out to the shop floor on three wheels.

Ruairidh was trying to keep his usual distance, at least one arm's length from Alex's hands of death, but this also kept him too far from the faulty corner. Without the strength of both men on the corner of the roll cage, it kept digging in, scraping gouges into the storeroom floor, pitching the tomatoes forward, adding more weight to the faulty corner.

After the fourth attempt, Alex stepped away from the cage and slowly removed his ear buds. He looked through the wire of the cage at Ruairidh.

*"OK, what is it? You got a weird phobia or something? Being too close to people bothers you? You cannae stand how I smell? You think I'm gonne jump on you or something? Is that it?"*

It was the most Ruairidh had ever heard Alex say.

*"I keep going forward and you keep moving backward, like we're chasing each other around the...".* He stopped, mid-sentence, sucking his lips together.

After a pause, he looked down at the floor and said, *"This cage is going nowhere if we don't both hold up the same corner."*

The surprise of hearing Alex speak shocked Ruairidh into action. Without saying anything in reply, he moved into range of the deadly hands, grabbed the corner of the cage and together they wheeled the disabled trolley of tomatoes out onto the shop floor.

Following the trolley incident, there was more chat. In neutral, staccato bursts at first. *"How's it going?"*, *"Delivery just came in,"* *"We need to move those boxes."*

Then testing the ground, exchanging information.

*"Which cage you want to do first?"*, *"You see the state of aisle five when that case of beetroot smashed?"*, *"I'll stack the high shelves, you stack the low, then swap over halfway, right?"*

\* \* \*

When there was more chat and they got to asking about what shifts they were each on and who would be taking the first break, Alex felt like a dam might burst. He wanted to speak to other human beings at work so much, yes, but Julie the Occupational Therapist and memories from his two previous jobs were both screaming at him in alarm, like the robot from *Lost in Space*, *"Stop! Stop! Danger Will Robinson, Danger!"*

He made the decision to talk to Ruairidh, but to limit it to that.

*"Yeah, yeah, just one chat, just one drink,"* the voice in his head mocked.

He told himself that he was an older and wiser Alex, who would not repeat the same mistakes of the past.

*"Yeah, yeah, never again,"* the voice continued.

He could keep a lid on it at work and he could disconnect the over-productive thought factory that was his brain from his mouth before it got out of control.

*"Well let's see how that works out for you, shall we?"* the voice bounced back.

Alex knew that both he and Ruairidh stood out, even among the odd bod, flotsam and jetsam recruited on the Tesco nightshift. Alex, because he ignored everybody with his head-down-earphones-in isolation, and Ruairidh because everybody ignored him.

Alex's old Highland granny might have called Ruairidh "unco slow" or she might have said that he was a man with a "strong weakness." Other people were less poetic or kind. One of the shift supervisors called Ruairidh Irn Bru Head to his face and crueller names to get a laugh when Ruairidh wasn't around to hear it. Other staff said, *"One sandwich short of a picnic,"* and *"Not the brightest crayon in the box,"* or *"One card short of a deck."* Alex had heard them all and worse, used by staff describing patients during his time in the big hoose.

One of the first things that Alex explained carefully to Ruairidh when they did start talking was that there was more than one big hoose. There was Glasgow's Barlinnie Prison, yes, but there was also Greenock's very own Ravenscraig Psychiatric Hospital. Ruairidh was relieved to hear that Alex had spent time in only one of these.

Alex was happy to tell Ruairidh about other patients in the big hoose and the slap-arse crazy things they did, but he was vague about how he himself had ended up in the hospital, and how he got out. Ruairidh got Alex's story in pieces, with gaps.

Classed as one of the hospital's 'never-any-bother' patients soon after his second admission, Alex had been given jobs in the grounds, then the kitchens. After some kind of recovery, when he stopped talking gibberish that nobody understood but him, he had been discharged.

Bored after a few weeks at home, he had volunteered to go

back to the hospital to help out in the Occupational Therapy Department.

Longer term patients sat about, knitting, painting, and making cards, Alex said. His job was to lay out the stuff in the morning, keep patients going with wool and craft supplies and help the OT, Julie, tidy up at the end of the day. He was also there to supply a bit of banter, to keep patients entertained, or at least smiling.

Julie would direct him to sit with different patients, and he would pepper them with questions, stories and generally fill the silences, making the long days go a bit easier, for the patients and for him. He was good at that. Only occasionally did Julie have to ask him to reign it in a bit, when he got on a roll and went off on some tangent that left everyone else's understanding trailing behind.

Then one morning Julie brought in the advert for the part-time job at Tesco, told Alex he should go for it, helped him with the application and gave him a reference. The Tesco manager had his doubts because of Alex's history, but he was an old friend of Julie's and he agreed to take him on a trial period.

Having seen Alex discharged and re-admitted once already, Julie was blunt. She had been therapeutically tactful before, encouraging him to talk, then telling Alex that he was a bit loquacious, explaining what it meant only after he'd taken it as a compliment. She sat down with him at the end of one shift and gave it to him straight. The time for sugar-coated euphemisms was past. She told him to keep his chat to a minimum in the interview and at work if he wanted to make an impression and keep the job if he got it.

*"If you go off on a ramble, like you sometimes do here, you'll*

*not be there long. They all know that you've been in here,"* she said.

*"Turn up on time and show them that you can do the work. That's all they're looking for."*

Alex understood.

Her final piece of advice stuck with him. *"Speak to nobody, unless you're asked a question. That's the easiest way for you to keep this job."*

That became his mantra later, backed up with the earphones, playing his same favourite songs to run interference on the wild thoughts trying to build up any head of steam in his head.

He was nervous. He'd been there before. Holding down a job, then being taken aside by the boss, told that he was making people "uneasy" – whatever that meant – with all his crazy talk, asked to tone it down, then asked to leave, back to the big hoose, some more therapy, then another job. Rinse and repeat.

Doing the work at Tesco wasn't a problem. Alex picked up all the variations of the storeroom and shopfloor routines fast. One of the other staff had been given the grand sounding task of 'onboarding' Alex to Tesco during his first week, but the staff member left him to it after just two days. There was a finite number of ways in which lorries could deliver, boxes could be unpacked, and shelves stacked and cleaned.

But not speaking? That was hard, really hard. There were so many conversations in the shop and in the staff room that Alex wanted to jump into, because he knew stuff that others should too. There were so many replies he had that everybody would find interesting or funny, and questions that he not just wanted, but needed to ask. His head was like a dam, ready to burst. But it didn't. He held it together, held his tongue. *"Speak to nobody, unless you're asked a question."* A couple of times when it became almost too much, he put his hand up to hold his lips together, disguising it as a cough.

It did get easier to stay quiet after the first few nights. He began to treat it like moving the boxes and filling the shelves. Not speaking was part of the job. Put on the uniform and shut up. Simple.

At the end of the trial, the manager told Alex that he would like to keep him on, at least a bit longer. It was a cheap way for Tesco to use his labour. Then the full-time night shift post came up.

Alex rehearsed his answers to the questions that he knew he would be asked in interview. *"Why do you want to work in Tesco?"* (*"Tesco is a good employer and I have the skills that you expect of your staff."*); *"Why should we employ you at Tesco?"* (*"I would be a good addition to the night shift team. I have shown that I can do the work as part of a team."*)

His replies were short, as Julie had advised when he went back to see her. His answers were also enough to give him the advantage over the only other candidate interviewed, an older man who had left a job with Lidl, without a reference. His answers had been less impressive.

*"Why do you want to work in Tesco?"* (*"Well, to be honest, there's fuck all else available around here for somebody my age. Excuse my French, by the way."*); *"Why should we employ you at Tesco?"* (*"I have a lot of trouble sleeping at night, so I think the graveyard shift would suit me."*)

What Alex didn't say at interview was that he preferred working in the shop when there were no customers. It was one of the things that he and Ruairidh had in common. That, and being able to graft and never complain about the work to be done, even when he was knackered.

# – 14 –

## TO THE RESCUE

Ruairidh could do the job at Tesco's. He was smart enough for that at least.

There were times off the job though, when he wondered if he just plain stupid, not able to keep up with what was going on around him.

He watched some TV programmes at home and got confused, losing the plot after ten minutes, trying to figure out who was who and why they were shouting at each other. He couldn't get back on board with what was happening, no matter how hard he tried. It was only now and then, but he felt so dumb, like the people were speaking another language that he would never understand.

At other times, it was the opposite. He thought he could see what everyone else was missing, predicting what would happen next and then watching slack jawed as it did, and everyone else looked surprised. It happened on his TV programmes, and it happened in Tesco's.

He could see fights coming at work. Somebody would bad-mouth somebody else, then the person who'd been slagged off got to hear about it, from somebody who, *"should have kept her big mouth shut,"* usually. Then something else would be brought up about what somebody else said before, and at the beginning of the next shift two workers would be face-to-face in the back storeroom, both shouting at the same time, flecks of saliva flying everywhere under the overhead lights, like a flare up at a weigh-in before a big-time boxing match.

Why did no one else see that coming, he wondered? He might not be able to leap tall buildings or run through walls or become invisible like real superheroes, but Ruairidh believed that he had powers that were unique to him. And when he thought about it, that was all he had ever wanted, as Ruairidh or as Alroy the Protector; to be good at one thing, something only he could do.

The superheroes with the greatest powers were usually baddies. That was a fact in his Marvel comics. Ruairidh had seen rare appearances of the barrel chested Übermensch, a Nazi super-agent who was as strong as Superman. But good always overcame evil, no matter who had the greater powers.

As Alroy the Protector, he tried to put his great powers of observation and prediction to best use in protecting others, resorting only to showing himself or to physical combat if there was no alternative.

\* \* \*

He had a regular route that he patrolled on Neighbourhood Watch Greenock West, Beats 63 and 64, moving from one spot to the next, watching, listening and staying hidden. He worked his Alroy the Protector shifts around his Tesco shifts and his nights off. Most nights nothing happened. Alroy the Protector was not called upon to protect.

People poured out of the pubs or parties late at night, making a bit of noise, before drifting off home or for taxis and buses. Sometimes, if the weather was bad and nobody was out, he'd knock off early and go home. Standing shivering in his costume in the shadows in one of his shop doorways or hiding in a tenement close on those quiet nights, he'd try to convince himself that just his presence on the streets had made trouble less likely.

On his nights off from Tesco's, it was easier to organise his time. He could choose his hours for darkness patrols. On the nights that he was working, it took more planning. His hours were full time across the week, but they could be anytime between 21.00–07.00 and he'd know just a week in advance what slice of those hours he had to be in the supermarket. He could slip out of the house early with a bag containing his gear, get changed somewhere quiet, get in a couple of hours on patrol, then change back, hide the bag and be at Tesco's on time for his shift. Or if he was working earlier in the night, he would take the bag, stash it, do the shift, then his patrol.

If his dad woke when he came home, he'd tell him that he'd got a flyer from work at Tesco because he and Alex had got through the shelfing extra fast. That was on the few occasions that his dad was interested enough to ask.

His greatest moment as Alroy the Protector came early in his career, as it did for most superheroes. He saved a woman from being mugged, raped or murdered.

That one night had justified all the time he had spent sneaking about in the rain and cold, hiding, getting changed in secret, and all the money he'd spent on his costume. All the nights lying to his dad that he was on Tesco night shift had been the right thing to do. Any doubts he had about giving up even his nights off to patrol the streets were suddenly gone. He knew on that one night he had fought for justice, and that he was a real street superhero, doing the right thing and doing it *right*.

The problem was that the fight for justice had gone disappointingly downhill from then. There had been nothing since that night on Dempster Street that came close, nothing as triumphant, nothing that he had so much trouble keeping to himself, bursting with pride to let somebody else in on his bravery in the face of real danger. Playing it over and over in his head had kept him going, kept him vigilant, during the long, cold hours when nothing was happening. Knowing that he could be a street superhero also kept him believing when things went wrong. And they did go wrong.

Twice since, he'd come out of the shadows to save women from slaps or punches or worse. Both times it had been a man and a woman screaming at each other. Both times it had ended badly, for him.

That first time, the man had the woman pinned against a wall by the throat, and the second time the couple were taking drunken swings at each other, while a pram with a baby in it rolled off down the street. When Alroy the Protector turned up, the same thing happened both times, so similar that he wondered later if it could have been the same couple.

Alroy the Protector had stepped up, come to the women's rescue. Knuckles on hips, his first tactic the loud shout, *"Whoa, whoa, whoa! Just stop!"* to refocus attention on him, although the red cycling top and cut off Guy Fawkes mask had already done that.

*"Stop that now. Police have been called,"* was the next part of

his script, learned from clips of street superhero videos. If he was forced to, he could do the double palm push to the chest or chin and, as a very last resort, the rear naked choke hold that he learned from watching *WWF Superstars of Wrestling*.

The shout was enough to stop the fighting both times and he was glad about the success of that at least. Then the questions started, and he wasn't prepared for that.

When his dad was drunk, he would ask Ruairidh questions that had no answers.

*"What time do you call this"* or, *"When are you gonne get a real job son?"* or, *"Do you think your mother would be proud of how you turned out?"*

Both times, when he'd stopped the couples fighting, they had frozen for just a beat, like statues, before their loathing for each other evaporated and they had turned on him, with the same kind of questions.

*"Whit's any of this got to dae with you, Batman? You like watching people doing stuff, do ye?"* was the response of the first man, and, *"Why don't you fuck off back to where you were hiding and mind your own fucking business?"* was the second, before both women had piled on, egging their partners to do something about, *"That nosey peeping-tom bastard,"* or, *"That paedo perv,"* in the second case, after Alroy had run to stop the baby and the pram rolling off into the main road before trying to stop the fight.

He had rehearsed what to shout, and what to do next. Although he was confident about the two-handed, straight arm push, having practised it on his mattress, stood against his bedroom wall and on a pile of empty boxes in Tesco storeroom, he had never clamped anyone or anything around the throat.

Breaking up the fighting couples didn't seem the right time to try out the push or the choke hold.

He had stopped the violence both times, and prevented street crimes, which he felt good about. That was in the superhero creed. But he had had to back off and run away both times too, which was not.

Why were the two women not grateful when he turned up and saved them? He never understood why the couples turned on him. What was he missing? Was it one of those special man and woman secrets that he would never understand?

He thought about Jessie on the Tesco nightshift. She would turn up for work with a cut lip or wearing too much make up to cover a bruise, talking about, *"Being slapped about a bit by that bastard,"* like it was nothing, like it was something that just happened now and then if you had a real boyfriend or a husband in the house. Like it was the price to be paid for having a dog that would bite you if you crossed it, and sometimes even if you didn't. You wouldn't report the dog for biting, because then it might get taken away. And you would never think of biting it back.

To Ruairidh, it was another man and woman mystery. He knew that he wasn't smart enough to solve it by himself, but he was smart enough not to ask Jessie about it.

Alroy the Protector remained faithful to the creed, jumping in if he saw late night couples fighting on his patch. But he had learned what to expect. There would be no,

*"Thanks for saving me, whoever you are,"* or, *"Wow! Are you a real superhero?"* like he'd imagined before it all began.

What he got was, *"Fuck off,"* or, *"Who the fuck are you supposed to be?"* or, *"Where's the party, ya fat muppet,"* or, *"Beat it pal, before I shove that stupid mask right up yer arse."*

So, on the coldest nights and the slowest times, Alroy sustained himself by reliving his greatest glory, the memory of his Dempster Street heroics. He ran it as a tape loop in his head, keeping it fresh, drilling himself to remember the details so that they didn't fade.

\* \* \*

He'd been in the right place. That had been crucial preparation for what happened. It gave him a boost, to know that one of the spots he'd picked on his beat had been well chosen.

From the space between a garden wall and the 5th Greenock Boy Scout Hut he was invisible. He caught snippets of conversation from the people leaving the Norseman Bar at one end of the street and the rougher crowd from the Green Oak coming up the hill in the opposite direction. From his vantage point, he could see along the street in both directions and across the road to the Mount Kirk, which stood at the gates of the path leading up to the Murdieston Dam, the local reservoir.

As the pubs cleared out, the noise of conversations faded, until there was just the sound of footsteps from stragglers heading for home. Ruairidh passed the time by trying to guess who the footsteps belonged to before seeing if he was right when the person walked past his hiding place. There were old men in leather soles, slapping the pavement, young men in near-silent trainers, high heel clicks and shoes that creaked like doors. There was a pair of shoes with metal toe and heel segs that Ruairidh could hear clip clopping from way off before the wearer appeared around the corner.

He was getting ready to give up and move to the next spot on his round when he heard an unusual tread in the distance.

It was a slow moving, uneven 'click-thump, click-thump'. He stayed hidden and silent as a young woman passed. He knew she was young from the clothes she was wearing, but he had no idea how young. He was rubbish at guessing people's ages, always had been. As she crossed the street going towards the gates into the park and the Murdieston Dam, he saw the broken heel that she was carrying in one hand. The short cut through the park saved a walk all the way down the hill at the end of Dempster Street, then a long haul up again on Brachelston Street, although Ruairidh guessed she had opted for the path through the park to avoid the embarrassment of hobbling, rather than the longer distance.

Just as he was about to step out from his hiding place and move on, he heard the soft crunch of grit underfoot as someone else stepped off the pavement close by, to cross the street. Ruairidh froze, then took one silent step backwards. He saw an untucked, light-coloured shirt, dark jeans and what looked like cowboy boots from behind. The figure sped up as he went through the gate behind the limping woman who had disappeared into the shadows of the park.

Ruairidh waited another beat, undecided. Then Alroy the Protector and the creed of the superhero kicked in. When something just didn't seem right, "*Above all else, trust your gut.*"

Self-consciously pulling the waist band of his jogging bottoms up over his paunch, he started after the pair into the park, telling himself he could just tail them until they had safely reached streetlights at the end of the path. There would be no damage done, no false alarm or awkward apology to be made. He could fade back into the shadows silently, knowing that the woman was safe and that he had trusted his gut and been right to follow the man, just in case. There would be no criminal activity to prevent, and nobody would be any the wiser that he'd been there.

Any light from streetlamps faded after a hundred yards and the man and woman ahead of Alroy were visible only as grey moving shapes on a black background. The limping woman stopped once and swore as she tried unsuccessfully again to slam the heel back onto her shoe and Alroy had to walk faster to make up the distance that the man had gained on her.

He lost sight of them both as they reached a bend in the path, with a high hedge on both sides. Speeding up again, he was suddenly glad that he had kept his old trainers for another few pay days at least. They were burst down one seam and any spring in them had long gone, but they were like an old pair of slippers; comfortable and silent.

When he rounded the bend, it was even darker. He tried to judge the distance of the pair ahead by the sound of the click-thump. He stopped and put one arm out to feel the distance to the hedge and to keep himself in the centre of the path. Conscious that the pair ahead might hear him breathing heavily after the exertion of speeding up, he walked more slowly. All that changed when he heard a sudden hoarse shout ahead, followed by a deeper voice, saying, *"Shut up, bitch."*

Alroy heard feet scuffling on the path and then a louder, raspy scream that stopped as soon as it started. He pushed off one foot, running blindly into the darkness, shouting his stand-ard, *"Whoa, whoa, whoa! Just stop!"*

He almost ran into the pair, struggling on the dark path. As his eyes adjusted, he saw that the man had one arm across the woman's neck and his other hand gripping her ponytail. Alroy stopped in front of them, shouting again, but not as loud, as he was just an arm's length from the man.

*"Stop that now. Police have been called."*

Even in the near darkness, Alroy could see that the woman's eyes were wide with panic. The man was a foot taller, and he was lifting her almost off her feet, pushing her chin up with his arm.

What the man saw at first when he looked around at Alroy was the white of his Guy Fawkes facemask and a faint glow from the red Kevlar sleeves.

*"Who the fuck are you?"* he said, panting heavily with the effort of restraining the woman.

Alroy took a step closer, and the man looked him up and down.

*"I'm Alroy the Protector, and I'm telling you..."*

*"You're telling me nothing superman, or whoever the fuck you're supposed to be. You're gonna keep walking and stop sticking your neb into other people's business, right?"*

Alroy took a step back. This was not how it was supposed to go.

*"Stop that now. Police have been called."*

He said it again, with less conviction.

The man looked at him, now able to see all of Alroy's costume close up.

*"Fuck's sake!"* he muttered.

Releasing the choke hold, but still holding the woman by her ponytail, he moved closer to Alroy. The woman coughed, drawing in deep breaths, straining to stay on her toes.

The man prodded Alroy hard with one finger in the chest as he spoke.

*"I'm only gonna say this once more pal, then I'm gonna kick your stupid head in, right?"*

*"Stop that n..."* Alroy started.

*"Shut. Up. I don't know what you're doing out at this time of night, dressed up like a cartoon, but this is grown-ups time, see. Me and the lady here have got some business to take care of, and it doesn't concern you. Now fuck off like a good boy and leave us alone."*

Alroy took another step back, out of the range of the prodding finger. He was going to be sick. He could taste the bile rising up his throat. He knew that if there had been enough light and he looked down, he would see his heart pounding, pushing out the tight material on his cycling top.

*"Prevent criminal activity where possible and stop it personally when it was ongoing."* He repeated it in his head, over and over in those few seconds. That was the creed. That was the creed. That was the right thing to do. But that was in superhero land, where good always conquered over evil and Alroy the Protector always foiled the villain's plan.

But this was Greenock. The police had not been called. It was dark and they were in the middle of nowhere. Nobody could hear them and nobody else was coming. This guy was going to kick his head in if he said, *"Stop that now,"* one more time.

Looking back, it was the woman's shout that did it. Released from the neck hold, she got enough air in her lungs. Her throat was raw from the choking and the shout was guttural and not loud enough to be heard at any distance. But she was trying.

Alroy took two more steps back to get enough space for his run, then he went for it. The boxes in the storeroom had crumpled when he hit them and the springs in the mattress in his bedroom had been compressed all the way to the wall, but Alroy had never done it wearing his full costume.

His two-handed, straight arm push had quite a different effect on the man. Alroy didn't shout or give any warning. He just ran straight at him, aiming for the centre of his chest, hoping he could strike before the man saw him coming and before he went back to choking the woman.

Thinking about it later, he realised that he must have shut his eyes at the last minute. Yes, it was dark, but he would have seen and remembered *something* about the impact. Maybe it was fear, the thought that it would go all wrong and he would get a beating anyway, before the guy went back to what he was doing before Alroy turned up.

He missed the man's chest by a foot and straight armed him in the throat, with hands clenched with tension inside Alroy the Protector's wire mesh gardening gloves. The effect was instant. The man went from trying to get his arm on the woman's throat again to putting both hands on his own windpipe, wide mouthed and wheezing. He stumbled, tripped over his feet and fell backwards into what Alroy could see, even in the dark, was a particularly dense and jaggy section of the holly hedge behind him.

When he opened his eyes, all Alroy could see of the man was one leg with a cowboy boot on the end sticking out the hedge, bent at the knee, the other foot scrabbling for grip on the path. The rest of his body was either in the hedge or sticking out the other side. The man was making a dry boaking sound, interspersed with higher, yelping as he moved about, impaled on the spines of the holly, trying to free himself.

Alroy moved nervously from one foot to the other,

undecided whether to run or to stand. His arms shivered, and he clenched them across his chest to try to stop the trembling.

He reassured himself that it was in the creed. *"Use persuasion, threat if necessary and as a last resort administer no punishment to criminals beyond incapacitation."*

He looked again at the legs struggling in the hedge. He felt OK. Someone who had done what that man was doing deserved punishment, even beyond incapacitation. If incapacitation meant what he thought it meant.

Alroy turned just in time to see the woman grab her handbag and run flatfooted up the path, leaving both her shoes behind. He didn't expect thanks for what he had done, and he wasn't surprised. She was terrified. Later, he did wonder if she would have reacted differently if he hadn't been in his costume.

He stood still for a moment in the darkness. This was the bit in superhero land where he detained the defeated villain until police turned up and led him off, handcuffed, head down, to face his punishment. He was disappointed to find that trusting his gut told him that now that the woman was safe, he should run away before the cowboy boots got out of the hedge and proceeded to kick his head in.

He thought about running after the woman and returning her shoes and the discarded heel, then decided against it. She'd been chased once that night. That was enough. He retraced his steps, half jogging, half walking as fast as he could to the gate and onto Dempster Street. He slowed, breathing hard, and moved onto the next stop on his patrol, near the town centre, buzzing with what he had done.

Thinking back on how he'd saved that woman always brought him a warm glow, unlike anything else. There were some bits that he would have done differently, better or faster, but his only real regret, the minor one that nagged at him most, was that he didn't have anyone to share it with. Nobody to fist bump at the end of the night, to celebrate a good job, done well.

He couldn't go to the police station. It would be too difficult to explain. There was no man, no woman to back up his story, and the police would be suspicious. What was he was doing in a darkened park at midnight, in or out of costume? Had he been there on other nights? Did he like dressing up and following people at night?

He still thought about phoning it in, but what was there to investigate? A pair of discarded shoes and a few broken branches in a holly bush wouldn't be enough to get a forensics team or anybody else out of bed, on the strength of an anonymous call with no name for the victim or attacker.

He had phoned in a crime in the same park the year before, reporting vandalism and water pollution. That hadn't worked out so well.

He told the police officer on the non-emergency line that someone had rolled or dumped bales of hay into the Murdieston Dam. He didn't see them do it, no, he explained, he wasn't there at the time, no, but the bales were still there, four of them, half submerged in the water.

The officer he spoke to listened until Ruairidh had finished his description of the position of each of the bales, before explaining, very slowly it seemed to Ruairidh, that the bales were not hay but straw, barley straw. They had been put in the water deliberately by the local council, to stop the growth of algae on the water, and there was nothing for him to worry about. He went on to explain to Ruairidh what algae was, before thanking him for his public-spirited concern and then rang off.

So, Alroy didn't report what happened the night that he saved the woman from being mugged, raped or murdered and no reporters ever wrote about the mysterious masked hero, protecting the public from evil on the streets. Ruairidh settled for the satisfaction that he had saved the woman.

Although a fist bump would have been good.

If saving that woman had been the high point of life on the street for Alroy the Protector, then being witness to a murder and failing to live by the creed had been the low point.

He'd been there. He had done nothing at the time or since. He had failed.

# – 15 –

## NOAH VALE

Nina Vale loved all her boys equally.

When they were born, their father had dreams for them, and she had hopes. She had hopes for Ian too. When her husband went to jail for robbing shops with a knife and then disappeared with some Glasgow dinner lady when he was released, she realised that her hopes of building a strong foundation with a hardworking man to set her three boys on their way to a better life than her own had been just a dream.

Nina didn't have much, but she sacrificed a lot. She had no career to give up or money to pass on, but she gave her boys all the time she could, and gave up the social life she once had with and without Ian, so that her boys could have what other boys at school had, the boys with two parents and at least one wage coming in.

Even before Ian went to jail and left with the dinner lady, it was always Nina who had given more thought on how to give her boys the best start, on what little money they had as a family.

One thing that was free was names, and names were important.

It might not make a big difference to where they ended up, but strong names, carefully chosen, could get her boys off to a flyer, early in life. It was something to make them stand out from the rest of the pack. Nina's mother had named her daughter after a character in her all-time favourite movie, *The Gay Falcon*. It was some 1940s Hollywood B movie with George Saunders as a suited detective. In the movie, Nina was his doe-eyed fiancé. The name might have worked in Los Angeles, but a fat load of good having a Hollywood name in Greenock had done Nina.

So, Nina had chosen names for her boys from the most reliable source she knew; The Bible. Proverbs, 22:1 said, "*A good name is to be chosen over great wealth; favour is better than silver and gold.*"

She gave them strong, Old Testament names. Names that came with character, thus ensuring God would be with her boys into adulthood. Her firstborn she had named Noah, and the other two boys were Matthew and Benjamin.

Matthew got shortened to Matt and Benjamin was Ben by the time he got to school, but her firstborn, always the head-strong trailblazer, was never anything except Noah.

In his younger years, some children took to calling him Noni, which he ignored. As a teenager, he decked two older boys who called him 'two-by-two' once too often, a reference to animals going into the Ark. By his early twenties, he was Noah to family and Mr. Vale to those who worked for him.

All Nina really wanted for her boys as they grew up and grew away was that they were healthy, happy and able to pay their own way. Anything more than that was a bonus. She guided them as best she could from what she knew about earning a living, which wasn't much.

"*Get what you can and keep what you have, that's the way to get rich.*"

It was an old Scottish saying that her own mother had drummed into Nina when she was old enough to earn.

Her boys would listen, and then tease her about her wise granny words.

*"Yeah, sure mum, Confucius-he-say, look after the pennies and the pounds will look after themselves. Confucius-he-say, man who cuts himself shaving, loses face. You like all that fortune cookie stuff, don't you?"*

The brothers all stayed healthy. Nina's other two hopes, happiness and wealth, came and went and they all survived teenage trauma and made it to their working years.

There was just a year in age difference between each of her sons, they all had the same father and they had all lived in the same house for most of their lives. So it amazed Nina that they each turned out so differently, despite the shared beginnings.

One brother could be relied upon to be there for the other two, who had both usually just run off behind his back in the meantime. At school, one brother would never fight back, but didn't need to, because his brothers always beat up anybody who hit him. As they grew older, one brother was better at getting money, one was better at keeping it and the other one was good at neither.

Although there was only three years between Noah the oldest and Ben the youngest, they were a generation apart in how they treated money. Noah got it, flaunted what he had, lost it, then repeated the cycle; boom, flash, skint. He worked two weeks on, two weeks off on the oil rigs when he could. These were short-term, well-paid contracts, laid off or sacked, moving to another company. There was big demand then.

The money bought him the status that he hankered after.

Noah was the big man with the best seats at the game on Saturday, buying rounds in the pub before and after, his clothes bought in Glasgow, not Greenock, and hairstyling at a barber's that didn't need a free whisky with every haircut to attract customers through the door.

Ben, by contrast, kept enough cash in his wallet or in his account to do whatever he wanted to do, even if it wasn't much and never as much as Noah. Ben was the only brother who had what came close to a steady job and savings that were in a bank, rather than stuffed in bags and drawers around the house. He sold cars, or more accurately he wore a suit and a name badge that said *Care Sales Executive*, stalked people around a car show-room, writing figures first in pencil then in pen, and occasionally making enough commission to put what was left over at the end of the month into savings.

Matthew followed in his big brothers' footsteps, or tried to. He'd apply for the same roustabout jobs as Noah, make it onto some of the same North Sea rigs, where he would end up with the really crappy jobs – cleaning, housekeeping and relieving other workers during lunch and tea breaks – while Noah had the excitement of working at heights, rigging cranes and operating hoists, trading more on his confidence than on any training.

Was it something about Noah or something about Matthew? If they arrived on the same rig together, two unskilled grunts, the rig manager took one look at them and allocated the type of work the same way, every time.

Matthew would come home from Aberdeen, give some of his wages to his mother, spend some on days and nights out, trying to keep up with Noah's speed of life, and eke out what was left until another job came up, wondering all the while how he could come across more like Noah next time they went offshore.

To Noah, money was important because it showed how successful, how respected he was. With enough money, he could do whatever he wanted. The main point of earning money was to feel free and to be free. When he finished on the rigs, he found a way to make some real money. Earnest money, he called it.

*"The reason that money is flat is because it is designed to be piled up,"* was one of his favourite business maxims.

Matthew told Ben that he shouldn't blame Noah for being rich. And besides, what was so bad about being rich anyway? Wasn't that what they all wanted? Noah was making good money, enough to keep Nina comfortable and give her everything she needed, including feelings of pride in her first-born. Could Matthew or Ben say that? Probably not, unless they pooled what they were making and started living on rations.

After the rigs, the money that Noah earned back in Greenock made Ben even more wary of him. He had a fear of finding out where all the money came from and where it went. As long as he pretended that he didn't know the details, he could still meet with Noah, make small talk, make arrangements for Nina and find some common ground for things to like and things to slag off. But when Noah invited him out to one of his fancy dinner hang-outs, or on a hospitality package at Ibrox Stadium, Ben made excuses, terrified that if he went, whatever he heard couldn't be unheard. Or worse, his ultimate nightmare, that Noah would offer him a job.

He could just hear it.

*"Why keep slogging away trying to shift motors six days a week Ben? You're wasted there,"* Noah would say. *"Come and work with*

*me."* Not for me, but *with* me, which made it even worse. *"You could make twice what you're making on the cars, guaranteed, for half the hours, and you wouldn't have to crawl up the boss's arse every day."*

Ben had played it out in his head with different variations, all ending the same way.

*"You're good at sales and sales is my business too. The only difference is...".*

And that's when Ben would mentally put his fingers in his ears and make the *lalala* sound, to avoid confirming what he knew about Noah's business.

Earnest money, Noah called it. It was money that his customers gave him because they had good faith in what he was selling. There was no contract or written terms and conditions, as with Ben and his car sales, but buyer and seller each understood where they stood. In Ben's business, a dispute or a breach of contract could be arbitrated by some consumer ombudsman. In any sale by Noah, there was no mediation; one of his employees would pay a visit to the buyer, to explain more clearly the conditions of sale.

Like other successful businesses, Noah had competition.

The Vale brothers and the rival Moore family all came from the same part of town, went to the different schools but lived on the same streets. They had all played in the same kickabouts, in the same parks, even if they dreamed of playing for different big teams. None of them had money as teenagers and they all knew the score about the grinding jobs in town that awaited them when they left school; the shipyards in decline or electronics on the rise.

While Noah and his brothers had more differences than

similarities, the Vale and the Moore clans were like members of two different species.

* * *

The last fatal duel in Scotland was in a field at Cardenden, Fife, on August 23rd, 1826. George Morgan, described as a *'carnaptious or crabbit banker'*, had dissed David Landale, a linen merchant, by spreading rumours about his inability to pay back a loan. Landale had in turn complained to Morgan's boss at the bank, which in smalltown 1826 was the equivalent of social media shaming.

A few weeks later, the two men met by chance in Kirkcaldy High Street. Morgan went radge, hit Landsdale with an umbrella about the head, resulting in the formal challenge to a duel. Reputations were at stake, and the duel was never going to be a gentlemen's settlement, where one man intentionally fired wide, while the other shot into the air and honour was satisfied without blood being spilled.

The two men fixed a time and a field, each walked twelve paces, turned and fired. Morgan was killed, shot in the mouth. Decades of bad feeling between the two families followed.

The duel that caused the feud between the Vale and the Moore families of Greenock could be traced back more recently in history, to September 3rd, 1972.

John 'Hank' Moore was drinking in the Rotunda Bar with his then girlfriend, Janet. After knocking over a table of drinks, and twice trying to get the rest of the bar to join him in singing, *The Sash My Father Wore,* he was asked to leave by the barman, Cammie Vale.

At the trial, several witnesses said that what happened next was not a result of Hank being asked to leave, but of Cammie's final shout as he did.

*"And take that fat cow with you."*

Hank Moore went home, continued drinking until closing time, working himself up, and returned with Janet to The Rotunda to challenge Cammie Vale to a modern day duel. He accompanied kicking in the Rotunda's swing doors with his slurred shouting.

*"Come ahead Vale if you think you're hard enough. Let's see if you're still such a big man when you're out from behind that big fancy bar of yours."*

Cammie Vale phoned the police, but before they could arrive, Moore had smashed the glass in the bar door with repeated kicks and the barman had gone outside to prevent further damage. Vale managed to dodge Moore's first drunken swing, but Moore turned quickly and punched the barman square on the side of the face. Vale lifted an elbow to ward off a second blow and caught Moore on the forehead, sending him stumbling backwards. Hank Moore tripped over the kerb and hit the back of his head on a concrete bollard, put there to stop cars parking on the pavement.

The result was a bleed to the brain, death three days later, a charge of culpable homicide, a trial and a four-year sentence for Cammie Vale, followed by years of inter-family feuding, fist fights, knifings and even a firebombing.

Perhaps the family feud would have petered out and the duel at the Rotunda would have been forgotten, if not forgiven, if the descendants of Cammie Vale and Hank Moore had not gone on to be the main competitors to run the town's drug trade.

\* \* \*

Drugs and cash passed hands under the cover of solemn activity at the crematorium. Dealers checked for upcoming funerals and cars drew up discretely at the edge of the crematorium car park, buyers and sellers standing by their cars in black ties, mingling like grieving relatives and friends before handovers, out of sight at the nearby mausoleum.

Noah Vale's last drug deal began in the usual way, with a text message to his Nokia 8210. It was a primitive piece of technology that got the job done. It was impossible to track and small enough to hide if he needed to conceal evidence of his dealing.

The message was short. The quantity coming in had been agreed already, as had the price. A brick, wrapped in plastic and gaffer tape, had been sitting in the Glasgow garden shed of Noah's supplier, watched by the warehouse man for a week. The brick had been cooling off and resting after its long journey by air, sea and road from Afghanistan via Portugal, arriving on the English south coast and then travelling on to London.

Noah's advantage over London and Manchester dealers was the lack of major competition. Greenock was no big city, with shifting sands of gangs, shooting their way to the top of the distribution network and then plummeting to bankrupt obscurity or jail time as fast as snow off a dyke.

Noah saw himself as a slow swimming big fish in a very small pond. He had the Moores to contend with, but that was it, and they were a known quantity.

Noah didn't call himself as a dealer. Dealers were shooting stars. They all went the same way, on a trajectory, up then down. Most ended up as unsmiling police mug shots, dressed in T-shirts with skin fades, careless losers who had taken too many risks, gambled and lost. The rest, the few who weren't busted, got a liking for what they sold and ended up as gaunt white, shivering burnouts rattling for their next fix, any get-rich business plan just an addled memory.

So, Noah was not a dealer. He was a plug. He was a businessman who imported and supplied sought after products. He was never a user and had never been tempted. Seeing up close how cheap drugs reduced people he had known from live human beings to wasted shadows was an effective deterrent for him.

Neither was he a big city operator. He liked to keep it simple, so that everybody knew where they stood with him. On a map, he could draw a line that defined the limits of his empire. It was limited but safe. Although he knew how to expand his business beyond the line, he chose not to.

Those empire building methods might be for sprawls like London or Manchester, but they were not for him. That was where he differed most from big-time, short-term operators. He set his horizon low and achievable. To get there he had a list of dos and don'ts, strictly enforced.

He didn't employ junkies to sell drugs, ever. He didn't sell drugs to children. He didn't touch firearms or other weapons. Finally, he didn't ask his brother or anyone else to do anything that he hadn't done or couldn't do himself.

Noah's approach to enforcement was also as simple as he could make it. Although he didn't sell to children, he treated the people he sold to as if they were children. Maybe once, maybe twice it was necessary to smack a child hard enough to make them understand what was being asked of them. After that they only needed a light smack, a raised hand or a warning word and they would comply, because by then they knew what came next. It worked most of the time for Noah with his customers.

The men who worked for him were all full time unemployed, employed by Noah. Three guys he had known for years and trusted like Matthew, his brother. City gangs, by contrast, had dozens of part timers, dealers and users who would do anything that was asked, anything, for twenty quid. That was how the gangs controlled vast areas of the cities; dope fiends with no loyalty to anything except their next hit.

The temptation to expand and to sell more product and to make more cash was always there. The demand for more and more product was beating on the door with a bigger stick every week. Noah resisted. He was resilient, even when faced with the Moores taking on new customers, new markets, setting lower prices, pulling in more cash with minimal extra effort. Although he knew it wasn't true, it suited Noah to imagine that his customers were a steady population of users, who effectively managed and regulated their heroin use, unlike the dependent and chaotic users who bought from the Moores.

Owen Moore had no brothers. His two older sisters had got the hell out of Dodge as soon as they were old enough to see the well-worn track that would be their teenage years. Skanky, toothless, disappearing boyfriends, then children, prams, and a long, lonely slog into middle age. They had bailed out to London. To do what, didn't matter. It had to be better than what lay ahead for them in Greenock.

Although Owen had no brothers, he did have eight cousins who came and went, mostly in and out of HMP Greenock, serving sentences that were short enough to ensure that Owen could keep his business staffed on a rotational basis. Only three of the cousins had the same surname as Owen, but when working, all eight cousins took on the name Moore. Two of the cousins had the same Christian name and this caused confusion when police were issuing arrest warrants, as Michael James or Paul James were also known as Michael Moore or Paul Moore, and Michael Davies or Paul Davies were also known as Michael Moore or Paul Moore.

To Noah Vale, the Moores – the real ones and the temporary ones – had no code of honour, no qualms, no dos and don'ts to live by. If somebody could stand upright long enough to buy, drugs were for sale. The only additional requirement for a legitimate Moores' customer was cash, and even then, cash-in-kind for services could be negotiated for valuable return customers.

The Moores, led by Owen, were onto every new trick, no matter how grubby. Stories came to Noah of Owen Moore forcing junkie customers who couldn't pay their drug bills into shop lifting so that they could be convicted and jailed, then smuggle Moore's drugs into Greenock Prison as payment in kind. In return, the debts to the Moores were wiped clean and the debtors were even given extra incentives. Those who managed to stuff more than two drug-filled, plastic Kinder eggs up their arse before going into jail got to keep the third Kester plant egg for personal use, or to sell the contents.

Noah had watched the Moores expand their business. Some called it enterprise. He called it sad. He was above all that grubbing about in the dirt for a few extra hundred quid. Sticking with the same suppliers, the same customers and the same, steady income. That was the right way to run a business.

He knew Greenock, and that was Noah's power.

# – 16 –

## THE TWO DIGGERS

*"What do you want to be when you grow up?"*

A simple question, right?

Yet when 14-year-olds are dragged along to a Careers Fair, the most common answer to this question is a shrug of the shoulders or an indifferent, *"Dunno."*

Fair enough. Why would you think about growing up when you were only fourteen?

The teenagers who haven't already skived off on the walk between the school and the Careers Fair, those who manage more than a one-word answer, want to be actors, singers, pop stars, models, beauty therapists or footballers. There's a handful of aspiring firefighters, police officers or teachers, and just one or two doctors and vets, who answer the question quietly, to avoid been overheard and being called "bones" or "medicine man" or "sheep shagger" for weeks back in class.

*"What do you want to* do *when you grow up?"* might be a better question to ask, to separate a job later in life from a teenager's self-worth and identity. But identity is a difficult enough idea to understand for big, grown-up people, let alone 14-year-olds.

Many grown-ups *become* their job, known only by their job title to others and eventually accepting it as who they are; Simon the doctor, Mark the firefighter or Elsie the physiotherapist.

Or Noah Vale the plug or Ruairidh the Replenishment Associate, or Alroy the (part-time) Protector.

Somewhere, at the edge of this confusion over growing up and finding an identity and a role, there are career path cul-de-sacs. The very worst jobs that title holders either don't want to be defined by, or just don't care about. These are the jobs that for years, mothers in the street have pointed out to their children as a warning of what happens if you don't stick in at school. Low paid, smelly and filthy jobs, doing work that everybody agrees need done but nobody wants to do.

Five hundred years ago, it was the gong farmers, digging out and removing human faeces from privies and cesspits. Now, it's the sewerage plant man, dislodging and flushing away your fatbergs and nappies and tampons, or the scaffie man, emptying your stinking bins, or the abattoir operative, disposing of animals' guts and blood, so that the local butcher has juicy steaks to sell you for Sunday lunch.

Or the Bereavement and Environmental Services Operative, digging out your dead relative's grave when nobody is around to see.

\* \* \*

Greenock Cemetery employed two Environmental Services Operatives, Sam McLaughlin and Jamie Bruce, neither of whom had ever dug a new, unallocated grave in the cemetery.

The last burial plot, sold in September 1994, had not yet

been used. There were also some smaller, cremated remains plots sold after this date. Sam and Jamie, the grave diggers, had been called upon to use their tools and their skills only to open up existing graves and pre-paid lairs, so that a relative or a column of relatives could be added to, by prior arrangement.

The cemetery had the same acreage and roughly the same slope as Edinburgh Zoo. Shaped like a fat man reclining on a lounger, it had over fifty sections, numbered and lettered to allow visitors to find a grave. Easier said than done, since no two sections were the same shape and the referencing system, developed *ad hoc* over years rather than planned, had a seemingly random selection of letters of the alphabet, combined with equally baffling number-letter combinations.

Lost souls could be seen, wandering parts of the cemetery, particularly sections S, P, T and 2L. These were not dead spirits, caught between two worlds, seeking release from torment. They were the bewildered living. The overconfident couples who didn't need a map or couldn't read one, or the tired mother and children, trailing behind the father who thought he knew a line-of-sight shortcut back to the main gate. Many families coming to find a grave in the cemetery for the first time left at the end of the day feeling that they had been in an escape room challenge.

Sam and Jamie's work took them from the head of the reclining man (section 4Q) to his feet (section D), always driving or walking up- or downhill. The only longer stretches of flat land in the cemetery were sections that had been terraced for rows of graves over a hundred and fifty years ago.

There were just two sections of the 80 acres that Sam and Jamie were never called upon to work in. One was set aside for the very old and one for the very young.

Sir Gabriel Wood's Mariners' Home was the Greenock Asylum for destitute seamen. Over 350 men who had died there were buried in group plots in sections 2B and 2G, up until 1870. These were men who had no family able to pay for an individual lair. In the southwest of the cemetery, in section N, opposite a side gate, there was an area of common ground. It was here that an unknown number of stillborn babies had been buried, up until the 1950s. Cemetery volunteers, rather than paid workers, maintained the plots in both of these sections of sad, hallowed ground.

* * *

Sam had gone to work for a landscape gardener straight from school. It was a job, it paid, and having his own money was a teenage novelty. He then bounced around construction jobs for a couple of years, labouring on building sites, spending his Friday wages over the weekends at the pub, or on high-priced nightclub drinks. The job at the cemetery came up and he had taken it on as more reliable work with regular hours, as part of his new, dependable, Steady-Eddie Sam resolution.

The epiphany that brought about this change in Sam had been a bad weekend at a Glasgow casino after a Saturday match and drinks. Sam didn't know or care about how much money he had lost until it was too late. The next morning, lying in his bare bedroom, in his parents' house, he realised that he had fewer possessions and less cash than when he left school.

Jamie, eight years older, had been digging graves since he was twenty, travelling by train each morning to the Glasgow Necropolis, where 50,000 souls had been buried, not all with headstones. He had reached the level of Chargehand before leaving that job before he was sacked. He had pushed a co-worker into a newly dug grave. *"Just a wee joke,"* he said at the employment tribunal, but nobody else was laughing.

He applied for the Greenock job without a reference, knowing that there would be few applicants. A job was a job. It was crap hours and conditions, but better than dole money, just. At work, Jamie wore an old pair of motorbike trousers. He had bought the creaky, leather pants with reinforced knees second-hand in a Glasgow charity shop, beating down the price to half of what was being asked by the greedy bastards, he told Sam. The leathers made him sweat like a racehorse in the summer, he said, but they were great the rest of year for all the crawling about they had to do on the job.

Sam and Jamie joked about gravedigging being a dying occupation and they had both taken the chance to register for the national certificate for Cemetery Operatives and Crematorium Technicians, a training that would happen whenever the Council had the money in the budget to spare.

Their motivation for career advancement was simple. Neither of them was driven by a noble desire to help bereaved families say goodbye to their loved ones, or to smooth the passage of the dead into the next life. They wanted the certificates to allow them to work in the cemetery's crematorium, where it was warm and dry all year round.

The crematorium was built in Scandinavian Modernist style, according to the Cemetery Blue Walk guide. The front of the building had welcoming arches over the door, leading to the reception area. Inside, the main ceremony room was a cross between a church and a posh hospital waiting room.

The polished pine, bum-friendly cushioning and thick velvet curtains in muted green were washed over by minor key organ music for most of the day. The business end of the operation was in the back, where Sam and Jamie hoped to be if they ever got the Crematorium Technicians qualification.

A single chimney, partly hidden from view by the front arches, was flanked by aluminium pipes, signalling what went on after the mourners had left. As Crematorium Technicians, Sam and Jamie would be raking out the cremation chamber, putting what was left in the so-called 'Kenwood mixer'; a cremulator that reduced bones to ashes, which could then be buried, scattered or displayed on mantlepieces. The secondary chamber pipes, to filter the fumes from the bodies, needed regular cleaning and the chimney also had to be scrubbed periodically. The primary cremator would heat bodies to 1750 degrees Fahrenheit but still leave a barbeque deposit on the chimney flue.

Sam knew one of the technicians, Phil, an ex-fireman who he'd been to school with. Unless you were standing right beside the door, Phil told him, there was no smell. If you were curious enough to stand that close, the smell was like an oven that had burnt a pork joint.

*"That's the bits I don't fancy,"* said Sam, as he pulled on his wet weather gear, *"and this,"* he said, pulling out a crumpled copy of the job description that Phil had given him.

*"The discrete dispersal of unwitnessed cremated remains in the crematorium grounds."*

*"It cannae be any worse than this,"* Jamie replied, *"putting up with scraping out stuff in there in the warm has to be better than grubbing about, freezing our balls off out here. And I mean, how hard can it be? You just read it out. The only time you'd be outside*

*in the cold on mornings like this is when you have to chuck some ashes on the grass, right? Big deal."*

Sam and Jamie, the Environmental Services Operatives, were occasionally called upon to work with the cemetery gardeners, headed up by old Tom Wilkinson, who still liked to call himself the Cemetery Sexton, despite the fact that the title had been dropped long before he got the job, twenty-five years ago.

Sam didn't mind the walking, up and down the hill, and he enjoyed going back to doing a bit of landscaping with old Tom and the gardeners when it was needed. Jamie, on the other hand, hated taking orders from the old guy, mumbling to Sam under his breath while they worked that Tom wasn't even his boss, and he wouldn't be taking any orders from some doddery geriatric, who should be in the ground rather than digging it.

What Jamie hated even more than taking orders, from anybody, was the never-ending fight against the cemetery's pernicious *Rhododendron ponticum*. The fast-growing thick branches shut out the sunlight to any would-be competitors above ground and the invasive fibrous roots spread a dense carpet below the surface. If the rhododendron had spread to within a few feet of a grave, the gardeners could only saw off roots at ground level at those spots, for fear of pulling up more than roots, which meant that many of the rhodies were left wounded but not dead.

*"It's like painting the Forth Bridge,"* Jamie complained, without fail, every time they took up the tools to tackle a new rhododendron that had rooted, or re-rooted.

*"Even a full-time gardener, doing fuck all else but ripping out these rhodies would be dead and buried long before he'd cleared this place,"* he said, as he swung the heavy-duty mattock again,

sending chunks of rhododendron roots flying in all directions.

*"Now try to dig out the roots intact there, Jamie,"* Tom Wilkinson said quietly, as a piece flew past him. *"The roots will regenerate and then we'll just have more digging to do."*

*"Right you are, Tom,"* Jamie said, smiling at the head gardener as he put aside the mattock. His leather trousers creaked as he knelt to pull at the stubborn roots with his hands.

As soon as Tom was out of sight, Jamie picked up the mattock again and went at the ball root of the plant as if it had attacked him, chopping again and again until there was nothing left except a hole in the ground and an explosion of root fragments in a ten-foot radius.

*"Hope that's to your satisfaction now, ya senile old bastard,"* he muttered, as he threw the mattock to one side and lit up a cigarette.

As another part of their maintenance duties, Sam and Jamie had to work their way around the cemetery, on a schedule from 4Q to section D, clearing weathered headstones which had been claimed by ivy or dwarfed by horsetail. Once a month they also had to clean out the Dame Cameron mausoleum. It was mostly piles of leaves, a bird's nest or two, fag ends, empty beer cans and used condoms that had been chucked in.

They did most jobs together, except when one of them was on holiday. The only task they took in turns was opening the cemetery gates in the morning and closing them after checking that all members of the public had left.

This meant working slightly different shifts depending on the hours of daylight, which they both thought was a pain. The Bereavement Services Manager – *"another arsehole with arms and legs,"* according to Jamie – would remind the two gravediggers at least once a week of their duty, *"to be sensitive to the needs of the people that are bereaved or distressed."*

Jamie understood. He wasn't thick. He didn't need to be told the same thing, every fucking week. No huckling any stragglers out the cemetery gate at the end of the day, so he could get finished on time, and no laughing at work when there were people around. He got it. He wasn't paid enough to take this shit from some jumped up counter lowper every week. The only reason Jamie didn't tell the crematorium manager to piss off to his face was the thought that it might scupper his chances of getting to work in the warmth of the crematorium, sometime in the future.

The final, *"...and other duties..."* part of the grave diggers' job description was to help out at busy times at the other Inverclyde cemeteries. This was usually during winter, when more old people died and the ground was solid with frost, needing more mini backhoe loaders and strong-backed workers to dig the holes.

\* \* \*

The *Funeral Service Journal* (*FSJ*), *"The Industry Bible since 1886"*, was a trade publication with a circulation of 2500, with extra copies going out for advertising mailings.

Published monthly, it was taken on subscription by Inverclyde Council, and distributed to managers in each of the cemeteries. The Bereavement Services Manager at the crematorium would leaf through the *FSJ* to update himself on anything relevant – new regulations, trends in burials and cremations – and then pass it on to his crematorium technician Phil.

After Sam had told Phil about his hopes of becoming a crematorium technician, Phil started to stick old copies of the *FSJ* under the door of Sam and Jamie's gravediggers' howf, a wooden tool shed made wind and waterproof with brick and corrugated iron sheets and equipped with a kettle on dodgy wiring.

The two gravediggers had developed an early morning routine, like an old married couple. Sam would be in first, on time. Jamie would make a point of arriving late each morning. Sam would check the daily job sheet, hang the clipboard on the nail on the wall and then relay the relevant information to Jamie, who stubbornly maintained that he wasn't paid enough to read stuff. By that time, Jamie was on his third cigarette of the day.

*"Never two days the same in this job, eh?"*, was Sam's usual opener, as he hung the clipboard, prompting Jamie's standard reply, *"Aye, same shit though, whatever day it is."* Then they would settle down to their pre-breakfast tea break, before starting work.

Sam flicked through the *FSJ.* He wasn't much interested in the latest trends in direct cremations (*"Go straight to the crematorium, do not pass Go..."*) or the need for families to budget in order to meet rising funeral costs, (*"Planning for those left behind."*) but he did like to check the classifieds.

Sam was a petrolhead. He didn't own a car, but he got a buzz from the ads for secondhand hearses, reading out the ones that had style, which was every one. Classic Daimlers, Austin Princess', Rolls and Mercs for sale every month, all with low mileage and all in magnificent nick.

For morning reading material, Jamie favoured the *Scottish Sun,* for the outrageous and outraging headlines, and for the variation of tits on page three. There was only one publication that Jamie rated above the 20p *Scottish Sun*. When he could get hold of it, he would bring in old copies of *The Digger*, which was journalism of a very different kind.

# – 17 –

## DIGGING THE DIRT

He got the magazine from his brother Graham, who lived in Glasgow, off and on. Graham called himself a sous chef, working in and taking free accommodation in hotels around the country, moving on when somebody noticed that he didn't have much of a grasp of cooking techniques, flavours or menu creation in general.

Despite the name, *The Digger* was not the Environmental Services Operatives' trade magazine.

It was a new publication, not to be found in Safeway Supermarkets or in WH Smith Newsagents. It had been shunned by all Glasgow supermarket and newsagent chains for safety reasons.

It was more difficult to come by than a copy of the *Glasgow Times* in Edinburgh and was sold in select newsagents and garages only. Many of the shopkeepers who stocked the weekly publication had been threatened by the people outed in the magazine. The editor had had his car firebombed and his family threatened, but he continued to dig.

Like the *Scottish Sun*, *The Digger*'s appeal was a combination of looking-through-the-fingers repugnant fascination and reader outrage. There were differences between the two publications, however.

First, the *Scottish Sun* was national outrage, whereas *The Digger* had a hyperlocal focus. Secondly, the *Scottish Sun* reported on crimes and scandals that had a legal verdict, beyond a reasonable doubt, or lawbreaking that had at least come to court.

*"Thugs caged after drugs and murder spree in seaside town,"*

*"Benefits scrounger raked in thousands while going on luxury holidays."*

*The Digger,* on the other hand, had fewer moral qualms about the level of evidence needed before going to print, happy to settle for the balance of probabilities or failing that, hearsay, before firing up public indignation and blood pressures with its capitalised headlines:

*"Organised Crime and Bent Cops Infiltrate the Old Firm."*

*"Smack Dealer's Paedo Past: We Name Names."*

*The Digger's* lawyer was employed full time to keep its editor the right side of being sued for defamation.

The constant supply of headline porn in both the *Scottish Sun* and *The Digger* kept readers gratified with stories of the guilty being identified and judged. Another difference between the two publications was in punishment: The *Scottish Sun* reported on it; *The Digger* called for, and sometimes got it.

The stories behind twenty-four pages of screaming *Digger* headlines were already well known locally before they appeared in print. The stories were avoided by the mainstream media, for fear of legal action or a brick or a bullet through somebody's window.

*"Glasgow Knife Man Plotted Attacks in Home Town and Now He's Doing It In Jail To Anyone Who Disses Him."*

*"Drug Smuggling Cop On The Take Busted."*

Variations of some stories appeared each week, the names different, but the motive and means the same. *'Snitches Get Stitches'* and *'Slash For Cash'* were common themes, with informants attacked by strangers with a drug habit, happy to be in part time employment.

Old copies of the *Funeral Service Journal* in Sam and Jamie's work hut had reported on many deaths and burials. *The Digger* was a magazine said to have *caused* more hospital admissions and deaths than Greenock chip shop heart attacks. Nobody wanted to see their name in *The Digger*. It always brought somebody you didn't want to see to your door.

*"Wait 'til ye hear this one Sam,"* Jamie said, folding his copy of *The Digger*. *"A man who last week had the front of his house daubed with paint after being named in* The Digger *as a paedo was in fact someone with the same name as the man convicted of having sex with four children in 1996."*

*"Poor guy. That's mental,"* Sam replied, without looking up from the photo of the sleek, 1980 Daimler DS420 Limousine in the *FSJ*, the car's paintwork still gleaming even after more than twenty years' service.

*"Or here, look, this one's right up your street,"* Jamie continued, turning the headline to show Sam. *"Murder-linked Gang is Tooling about Glasgow in Fleet of Luxury Cars,"* the shock opener read. Sam did look at up then, but only to see if *The Digger* had named the make of the cars.

*The Digger* took no prisoners in its exposure of gangs, whether they were cops or robbers. It sold itself as a champion of the people, with an editorial policy of fighting for justice for the powerless, those low-incomed, unemployed and baffled masses stuck in the middle, between organised crime and corruption and incompetence in the legal system. It encouraged its pennieless readers to ask just one question: *'Why are so many people rich and why are we so fucking poor?'*

Dismissed by the Scottish mainstream papers as, *"a wee, muckraking crime mag,"* or *"OK! magazine for Glasgow criminals and psychopaths,"* The Digger continued its unabashed reporting regardless.

The focus was Glasgow stories, but the investigative journalism could be extended to other parts of the West of Scotland, to report on who was getting away with the same unreported crimes and barefaced effrontery beyond the city limits.

Long gone were the days when there was anything like a moral code and honour amongst thieves and other villains. All that remained was a short list of nefarious activities that were considered universally vile by criminals and public alike, and it was on these activities that *The Digger* did most of its digging.

Jamie was on a roll with the headlines. He pulled his broken plastic chair closer to Sam's.

*"I just cannot believe this one,"* he said, shaking his head. *"That's just no right, is it?"*

He traced the headline with his finger as he read it out, *"Drug Kingpin's Affair With His Son's Granny."* He opened his hands in disbelief.

*"His granny, Sam, his fucking granny! It says that..."*

*"Maybe we should make a start, eh?"* Sam interrupted, folding his *Funeral Service Journal* and putting it under their makeshift table, a wooden cable drum reel, left the year before by electricians rewiring the crematorium.

Jamie stopped mid-sentence, his mouth still open, still

puzzled by the thought of a coupling between the gangster and his stepmother. He looked at the headline once more then put *The Digger* back in the bag he brought to work. He stood, stretched and farted loudly.

*"Aye, I suppose so,"* he said, *"these holes'll no dig themselves, eh?"*

Jamie picked up the spades and shovels leaning against the wall and tossed them into the trailer outside the hut. Sam followed him out, carrying the mattock and a bag of hand tools.

It was May and there was still a chill in the air. Pockets of mist sat in hollows all around the cemetery, reaching the top of gravestones in the deeper dips in the landscape. Elsewhere, the mist looked like it was rolling downhill, obscuring the paths. All that was needed was the horror movie director to shout, *"Action!"*

*"Let's dae the easier dig first,"* Jamie said, *"to get ourselves warmed up."*

\* \* \*

The Mackies had bought the double-depth plot seven years before George Mackie had a heart attack and died at home on a Saturday night, when Rangers scored a controversial goal for the second time that day, during the *Sportscene* highlights.

Jennie, his wife, outlasted him by sixteen years. Those extra years however, and all the visits to his grave gave her too much time to think about what the worms and other beasties might be doing to George's body deep under the grass. So, she had a change of heart and amended her Will, leaving instructions for cremation, rather than burial. She still wanted to be next to George in death however, and when she finally died at 86 the urn with her ashes was to be interred in the double-depth plot.

Sam and Jamie found the plot, checked the name and dumped the tools beside the grave. Jamie lit up and stood smoking the rest of the fag he'd pinched out when they'd left the hut.

*"This is an easy one,"* he said, pointing down to the Mackies' plot, *"just a wee half-and-half with the coffin and the coffee pot to go on top."*

*"Two in one, eh?"* Sam said.

Jamie looked across the graves on both sides, reluctant to get started as usual. As he had told Sam, many times, they were paid by the hour, not by how fast they worked.

*"I did a muti-storey family plot at the Necropolis once when I first started,"* he said, pointing nowhere in particular. *"It was a big one, a four-coffin job."*

*"Jeez, how deep was that?"* Sam asked, walking around the grave, sizing it up.

*"It was bloody deep, that's how deep it was,"* Jamie replied, laughing. *"We had a backhoe that scooped out the hole and did most of the work, then we had to put in boards and these plastic bunk beds things to support the coffins. When that was done, we still had to go down the big ladder to the bottom, flatten it out and check that it was solid and wisnae filling up with water."*

*"Scary, eh?"* asked Sam.

*"Fucking right it was scary. I'm telling you, when I got to the bottom of that hole, I wished I had a miner's lamp and a fucking canary."*

Jamie finished smoking and flicked the glowing filter on his cigarette into the distance with his middle finger and thumb.

He walked over, marked a spot in the grass in the upper half of the grave, towards the headstone. Without speaking, he started with the spade, scooping out regular clods of wet earth in a circle and piling them neatly. He stood aside and, in a familiar routine, Sam knelt down and went in with the trowel to take the hole down to a two-foot depth; plenty for the urn and a decent amount of covering soil between it and the coffin. They stretched a waterproof sheet across the hole, found some rocks and weighed it down at the corners, ready for the internment ceremony the next day.

Mr. and Mrs. Mackie's plot was adjacent to the monument for the 280 civilians killed in bombing during two nights of the blitz in World War II. The German pilots were aiming for the shipbuilding yards, a strategic target, but a few bombers mistook the reflection of water in Greenock reservoir for the River Clyde. They aimed for buildings near the water and casualties in the tenement blocks around the reservoir were high.

Sam and Jamie walked back and piled their tools back into the trailer then went from the Mackies' plot all the way to the top of the hill to section 4Q, near the golf course wall. It took fifteen minutes to get there, as the second-hand Kioti utility buggy laboured to haul them and the rattling trailer of tools up the steep track.

Sam drove and Jamie complained all the way that the cemetery should provide them with better transport to get around, like they did for those lazy-bastard-gardeners, cutting about all day in their shiny John Deere Gator, waving royally whenever they passed Sam and Jamie.

The second job of the day was at another husband-and-wife grave, but a companion plot this time. The husband's gravestone read, *'Passed Away With Great Dignity and Courage,'* which got Sam wondering what painful and lingering disease had killed poor Mr. Neill.

This job needed some real digging. There were just a few side-by-side spaces like this one, bought in advance by couples. They were more expensive because of the double surface area needed. Neither side-by-side nor double depth plots were common in the cemetery. Families in Greenock tended to avoid thinking about the fact that everybody who's alive now, one day won't be.

The Neill headstone was in a long triple row of graves set on a slight slope with a rare, unobstructed view of the river through a gap in the trees. It was one of the few places in the cemetery where there was enough room to have a regular spacing between graves. The three rows of graves contained coffins had been buried facing true east.

East was the direction from which Christ would arrive in his second coming, according to the New Testament. Everyone in that triple row would be in just the right position to meet him, face-to-face on the day of the Parousia.

Jamie had told Sam about all this Jesus-will-return stuff from his time working at the Glasgow Necropolis. Rows of coffins were planted facing east. Jamie's memories were of digging face-on into the coldest, hand-numbing winds that came howling in from the east. On those days, he said, digging graves was something to be done fast or avoided altogether.

*"It's all bullshit anyway,"* Jamie said as they carried the tools to the grave.

*"If the Son of God did come back, do ye think Glasgow or Greenock would be on his list of top places to visit? I doubt it. He'd make a beeline for some place warm, somewhere with a bit of life, not this shithole."*

Jamie was breathing heavily after the walk up the slope. There was no track or path access to the Neill's plot, and they had to park the buggy below the third row of graves and hike up. The lack of access was also the reason that the grave had to be dug by hand. The mini backhoe was too heavy and might damage adjacent plots.

Jamie looked around and spotted a table tombstone further up the slope where the trees started again. After a quick check for visitors, he walked over, sat on the flat slab and lit up. Sam joined him, sitting upwind to avoid the smoke.

Jamie nodded towards the double plot. *"I wonder how many of them would have preferred to have gone together?"* he said, blowing smoke skyward.

*"What?"* Sam said.

*"Well, you know, when one old biddie goes first, it's usually the man. How many of the women would like to have checked out at the same time, if they could, ye know, double plot, double funeral, half the grief, less expense, all rest in peace, like?"*

*"I don't know. Never thought about it,"* said Sam.

Jamie took another draw on his cigarette.

*"Some of them don't last long, mind. Maybe a few months after the first one goes. It's like the plug's been pulled out the wall, or the batteries run down faster."*

Sam paused for a moment and then said, *"It's called the widowhood effect. I read it in one of those funeral magazines with the fancy hearses."*

*"What the fuck's that?"* Jamie said, turning to him, his nose scrunched up, puzzled.

*"Widowhood effect. One partner dies and it knocks the stuffing out of the other one, so they go faster,"* said Sam.

Jamie scoffed. *"Widowhood effect? Pretty fancy word for*

*snuffing it, is it no?"* he said, stubbing out his cigarette on the tombstone.

Sam looked out towards the river and paused again before he replied.

*"Ma granda had an old collie. Used to be a working sheep dog. Went everywhere with him, did that dog. When granda died, the collie didnae last a month. Sat at the door every day, whining, waiting for him to come home. My granny always said that dog died of a broken heart. Much the same thing, with people I suppose."* Sam stood up and stretched.

*"Aye, maybe,"* Jamie said, standing. *"Except dead dugs make better draft excluders for the door, eh?"* he said, laughing at this own joke.

The ground at the top of the cemetery was stonier and more compacted. When it rained, the water ran off the hard surface and washed down the hill. After they had marked out the patch to be dug with string and wooden pegs, 90x36 inches, Sam and Jamie started at opposite ends of the plot, using spades to cut squares of the thin, weedy turf and stacking them into neat stacks.

After they had laid out the green tarpaulins either side of the plot, Sam started on the heavy work, taking the first swings with the mattock to break the gritty surface along the length of the new grave. Then they got to work with the shovels.

\* \* \*

Sam had learned much since he started working with Jamie. When Jamie had first asked him how old he was, Jamie had scoffed.

*"I'm older than you son, and with age comes great wisdom. Stick wi' me and you might learn a few things that yer pals will no tell ye."*

That was on his first day. Since then, Jamie had shared his pearls of wisdom selflessly, repeating his favourites just in case Sam had missed them first or second or third time around.

There was some useful stuff to be found in the weird world according to Jamie. How to do some jobs, and how to avoid others, what to expect from the bosses, who to talk to, who to avoid, and when to phone in sick. Winnowing out the wheat from the chaff in Jamie's wise words however, was hard work. There was much wisdom that Sam heard that he could have lived without.

Jamie had a set of fundamental 'facts'; a knowledge database, built up over the years. First, there were 'changeable' facts, about which football team in any particular week was in cahoots with the police or the referees' association, or which pub in town gave you a free pint if you knew the right handshake. Then there were 'definite' facts, like how it takes seven years for your stomach to digest chewing gum, or how eating four bananas a day kept you hard all night. Lastly, the real gems; 'known' facts, mostly about what women liked.

*"Guys who know what they want, have tight fundamentals and good game,"* was Jamie's oft repeated favourite, closely followed by, *"Bad Boys with hair in right places and hidden muscles."*

Sam had no idea what some of it meant and didn't ask, for fear of showing his ignorance, or hearing more 'known' facts.. Sometimes there was a two-for-the-price-of-one fact revelation, like how hair and fingernails were still growing in people they had just buried, and how, by the way, shaving your chest made the hair grow back both darker and thicker which, obviously, was also more attractive to women.

Of the many lessons from life that Jamie imparted, the secrets of how to dig a hole was one of the few more basic but valuable. In his time as a landscape gardener after leaving school, Sam had dug plenty, not thinking much about it. To dig a hole, you dug a hole, right?

What he learned from Jamie was that a grave was not just any hole. Oh no...

*"If you go at it like a mad man, you'll be knackered before the hole's deep enough to lie in."*

Hole digging 101; steady pace, that was what was needed.

*"Use the biggest muscle in your body to dig holes, Sam. No, not that one. Keep that one for the ladies,"* Jamie had teased Sam on their first grave together.

*"To get the dirt out the ground, let your legs do the work, no yer back and no yer arms,"* he said, *"unless you want to turn up for work next day aching and bent over like a half-shut knife."*

Jamie had shown Sam how to dig down the first eighteen inches along just half the length of the grave, then turn around and use the leverage that the difference in depth gave you to dig out the other half. That also gave one of them a breather, so that he was fresher to go back into the hole.

There was a legal requirement on how much earth had to be left on top of a coffin. A trained eye, rather than a tape measure was needed to know how much digging had to be done. Jamie claimed to know, to within an inch, when the pile of earth by the grave was just enough.

The earth beneath the crusty surface on the Neills' side-by-side plot was mostly softer clay. It yielded easily to the spade but was heavy to lift out. To get down to four feet took Sam and Jamie over two hours, spelling each other. Then it was time for lunch back in their gravediggers' howf and another chance for Sam to hear more of Jamie's lesser wisdom, while they ate their rolls.

They would both be back next day to fill in the Mackie and Neill graves, as soon as the holy men and relatives had said their goodbyes and drifted off. The piles of earth on the surface would be shovelled back in and mounded up. This would accommodate the earth setting. Within a few months the graves would be back to ground level.

## MEET AT THE MAUSOLEUM

The 8x5 inch block resting in the Glasgow garden shed had been repackaged in London. Its contents had travelled in darkness and on dusty roads from Afghanistan, dodging border inspections, customs agents in ports and sniffer dogs when it reached the UK. It had been a long journey, and the heroin was tired.

Some of its strength had been lost on the crossings from Afghanistan to Portugal to London to Glasgow, then to Greenock. It had been unwrapped, cut and repackaged at some links in the chain, more adulterated, more profit for middlemen. The block that Noah was buying was not what he would choose, it was what he could get.

It was the northern curse. Scotland was at the end of the distribution chain for many goods and services and suffered as a result. Like the once shiny and spotless rolling stock that started life on London railways and ended life as cattle-trucks, taking commuters to lesser Scottish stations, until the trains finally broke down, the once pure heroin was still able to do a job by the time it reached its final destination, but only just.

Despite the disadvantages of being last in the queue for product, Scottish drug users in their thousands all did their utmost to keep the world drug market buoyant. In its weakened state, what they bought was still good for a hit, even after Noah had cut it for a final time with crushed pain killers, or baking soda when times were hard. Noah's loyal but less discerning customers never came back to lodge complaints about the purity or the amount of bulking in the pebbles they bought. Any hit was a good hit when you were rattling for a fix.

Sometimes the brick of brown powder came from Thailand or Iran, travelling overland to Europe through Turkey. The brick's journey was through exotic parts of the world, with placenames that neither Noah Vale nor Owen Moore could pronounce.

That was not a problem. Neither man cared about where the heroin originated. They were interested only in where it came *to* and how much it would cost wholesale. Flippin' chickens, they called it. Selling the contents of the brick, no matter how adulterated, for a higher price than they had paid. That was the business model they both used, and one of the few matters on which they both agreed.

\* \* \*

To reply on his Nokia brick of a phone and set up the handover of cash for the brick at the mausoleum, all Noah needed was an agreed day and a time. He checked the Death Notices in the *Greenock Reporter*. There were hourly slots for cremations between nine in the morning and three in the afternoon.

More names on the columns of Death Notices meant bigger turnover of crowds and more cars at the crematorium, which was better cover. *"Suddenly"* rather than *"peacefully"* in the newspaper

Notices was a car park filler for any single cremation. When someone had passed away *"tragically"* it meant the place would be rammed with mourners and Noah and his Glasgow contact would have to get there early to guarantee parking spaces.

Two-man teams from either side was proper drugs etiquette for a handover. Going mob handed was just bad form, showing lack of trust. Turning up alone was arrogant, giving a message that you were either carrying a weapon or stupid, or both.

Like all Noah's other dealings, he believed that the handover should be kept simple. That was the Noah Vale way of doing business. He trusted his brother Matthew and his three other couriers. Of course he did. They never questioned his decisions. He kept them informed on everything they needed to know about what was happening in the business, good and bad. He paid them well for their trust. However, he trusted no one enough to do the exchange of his money for his drugs. His presence at the handovers was also a sign for the Glasgow boys that all was well; no surprises, same routine as last time, nothing to fash about here. All that routine might be boring, but it kept everybody relaxed.

Noah usually took Jake with him to the meets at the mausoleum. Jake, as solid and dependable as the oak furniture in Nina's sitting room. When Noah's customers had bad debts and a visit was necessary, there was no need for harsh words or violence. The sight of Jake at your door after he had hammered it with a bottom fist to wake you was usually incentive enough to pay up.

Noah's drugs debt list was mercifully short. He extended credit only to his long-term, return customers and even then, only if he knew they had money coming in. Again, it was part of his code. It was good business. Buyers knew where they stood, especially when Jake was knocking on the door.

Noah knew that the Moores laughed at his old school methods. Integrity? They couldn't spell the word. The scumbags would get junkie customers to store drugs or money, then rob or mug the same junkies so that the poor bastards were never out of drug debt. It was an unlimited supply of couriers and mules as slave labour for the Moores.

On the day of the meet at the mausoleum for transfer of the brick, there was a last-minute change. Noah didn't like it, but he didn't have a choice.

The night before the meeting, Jake had been leaving the pub after closing time, got into an altercation with something even harder than himself and lost a tooth.

Walking from the pub and gawping over his shoulder at the last of the drunken women leaving the same pub, sashaying off in the opposite direction, Jake spun around just in time to collide with a lamppost. In his lisping morning phone call to Noah, he told him that he was headed to the dental clinic, to queue with other desperate casualties for hours, his tooth still in a wet crisp bag, in the hope that some trainee dentist could put it back in.

So Noah took Rab with him to the meet instead of Jake. Not as big or as hard as Jake, even if he tried to look it. In Rab's downtime, he watched a lot of Jason Statham and Vinnie Jones movies, or maybe just the same movie too many times. He liked to call himself Noah's "drugs lieutenant" and he had developed a Greenock gunslinger's walk. With only his left arm swinging, his right arm was held stiff by his side, or in his pocket, ready to get quickly to the gun that he never had. Rab thought his practised walk made him look well hard. When Noah saw the walk for the first time, he thought Rab was recovering from a stroke.

"So, we get the light tan brick first Rab, in your hands, before you pass over the shoulder bag, right?"

"Yeah, yeah, I know the deal boss. Hands on before the hand off," said Rab, one hand in pocket.

"Keep hold of the bag until we see the merchandise. I'll do the talking. I'll give you the nod and you just hand over the bag when we're ready, OK?"

Rab nodded, bit his lip and didn't reply.

He knew that he was just as good as Jake, the Incredible Bulk, and smarter than him, which wasn't difficult. They were both lieutenants, so they should both be equal rank in Noah's set up. Yet Noah always spoke to him differently, like he was thick, like he'd just come down the Clyde on a water biscuit.

He had never let Noah down, never questioned his decisions, never asked, "Why Jake and not me?" when there was serious stuff to be moved or money to change hands. But still Noah treated him like he was a laddie on his first day at work, repeating everything twice, asking him if he got it, asking him if he was ready.

He was always ready. Noah might not think so, maybe because Rab looked so laid back, but Rab saw himself as a coiled spring, taking in all that was happening around him, ready to strike like a cobra when it was needed.

Noah and Rab got there early and parked the car. It was a Vauxhall Corsa that Rab had opened with a coat hanger and hot-wired two days before for the purpose. Now there was something else Jake the enforcer would never be able to do for Noah, Rab thought. Jake had hands like spades, only good for pounding doors and heads.

Noah never used his own MG Rover for jobs; too noticeable

and he liked to keep it spotless. The inconspicuous Corsa had been sitting in the railway car park, with three-day parking paid for, just asking to be borrowed and returned. The car would be a bit shorter on petrol but none the worse for the wee run up to the crematorium. And its owner would come back none the wiser after his trip on the train, thinking himself lucky to have left the car open and not have it nicked. All fine, unless some eagle-eyed neb recognised the car at the crematorium, which was unlikely. Rab would take the car back to the station later, wipe it down, stuff the wires back up under the dashboard and walk away, job done.

Two of the Glasgow boys with the brick turned up as the final couples attending the funeral hurried across the car park, bickering out the side of their mouths and trying to look dignified, late for the service. The Glasgow dealers' Ford Sierra circled twice before pulling up at the end of a row. Noah and Rab were already waiting and followed them at a distance to the mausoleum.

*　*　*

The Bereavement Services Manager, Cecil Bertram, was a man with regular habits, at work and at home. At the crematorium, he was first in, last out, every day. That was all part of the job. He had a key to one of the cemetery side gates, which allowed him to be at work by 8.30, making sure that everything was as it should be before the other staff arrived.

Checking funeral timings for the day and any last-minute changes to arrangements on the phone messages was his first order of business. There could be no sense of anything rushed when relatives started to arrive. Unhurried tranquility was paramount. Nominated twice for the Best Crematorium in Scotland Award, Cecil was very aware of the small margins that made the difference between winners and runners up in the bereavement industry. On his office desk, sat the latest, 7th edition of Davies' *Law of Burial and Cremation*, the definitive legal textbook on burial and cremation. It was his personal copy. He didn't have all the regulations committed to memory, but he knew just where to look when any queries arose.

When the purple velvet curtain had been drawn on the last coffin of the day and the cremator and cremulator had done their job on skin, bone and wood, everything was switched off and Cecil was left to do one last walk around before locking up.

Getting just the right ambience for the crematorium, and for the ceremony room in particular, was important. No detail could be overlooked. Cecil had learned all this from long years of experience in the increasingly competitive bereavement industry.

The appropriate décor, yes, was vital for first impressions. Lighting too, had to be planned, not incidental. Wall sconces were best, giving uplight, downlight, and directed lighting that could be adjusted depending on the time of year. The wall sconces were a long funeral tradition, setting the mood, going back to days when they held candles and oil lamps. They were one of the many, subtle influences on mood that mourners did not notice until they were missing.

The atmosphere, or more directly the air in the ceremony room also had to be attended to. Ambient scents and an efficient air freshening system to diffuse the trace aromas were equally important. Just enough to mask any unwanted odours, but not so much to make it obvious. One horrific, chastening experience in his apprenticeship had taught Cecil that body decomposition fluids can permeate porous materials, like coffins, even after the best undertaking practices.

The fact that a car had been left in the car park was not unusual. Cecil had seen many people so affected by grief that they were unable to drive home. Seeing the passenger window open puzzled Cecil, but again, distraught relatives might have stumbled from the car distracted, to be driven home by other mourners. It was only when the Vauxhall Corsa was still in the same spot the following evening that Cecil became concerned enough to act.

From the undertakers, he got the phone numbers of the contact relatives for each of the funerals on the day in question. There were only three undertakers in the town and Cecil knew their numbers from memory. The Co-op and Gloucesters gave out the relevant relatives' contact details without question, but the newer business, a one-man show called B.P. Brophy, was a bit snotty about giving out phone numbers, citing confidentiality and the relatives' privacy to mourn.

Cecil was by nature and by profession a patient man, but not a man to take no for an answer in matters of importance. When Mr. Brophy corrected him a second time in their phone conversation for referring to 'undertakers' rather than 'funeral directors', Cecil gripped a phone a bit tighter but kept his calm.

*"It is unfortunate that you feel unable to supply this information Mr. Brophy for professional reasons, which I fully understand. I'm sure that you are aware of the new Funeral Planning Authority who, I am also sure, will be able to act as arbitrators in this matter and resolve the matter quickly. I'll give them a call when we're finished speaking."*

That did the trick.

Mr. Brophy certainly did not want his new business to be one of the first to come to the attention of the new regulators. So, Cecil Bertram, Bereavement Services Manager, rather than crematorium manager, then did a quick phone around the relevant relatives, asking about the abandoned car, with a worried-about-the-welfare-of-those-who-attended-the-funeral line. Keen to avoid damage to the reputation of the crematorium that police presence might bring, Cecil held off for another 24 hours before doing anything more. When no follow up calls came back about the Corsa, he reluctantly phoned in the car registration to police.

The cops came out the following day, informing Cecil that the car had been reported stolen, likely taken by joy riders. The officers agreed with Cecil that a joy ride to a cemetery seemed a strange way to have fun and assured him that the car would be returned to its rightful owner after any prints had been taken.

End of story, as far as Cecil was concerned.

\* \* \*

To the rest of the Vale family, Noah disappearing for a few days was not unusual, although he did usually give them a heads-up when he went. R&R he called it. When he completed a major buy or sold enough product to take a step back from the business, he would head off, only letting the rest of the family and crew know where he'd been when he got back. Pack a bag, on a train and gone. London usually, sometimes Manchester or Liverpool, where he also had some old contacts.

*"Aye,"* Jake would say to Rab, when Noah went away, *"the boss needs a wee break just like everybody else, a bit of R&R."*

Rab was less understanding.

*"Fuck's sake Jake, he's no away to Blackpool to build sandcastles and ride a donkey on the beach. R&R? He's getting rat-arsed somewhere and riding some whore that he shouldnae. That's his R&R. And when do you and me get to go on holiday from this business, eh?"*

So Noah going away was not unusual. But going away with Rab? That was. Then there was the abandoned, stolen car, the missing brick and the missing cash? All that made his disappearance a real worry, something that had Nina on the phone for hours each day, working through her address book, trying to ferret out anything about where Noah might have gone with Rab without letting her know.

Jake made his own personal enquiries. Around town first, keeping it quiet for a few days. Then Nina upped the ante, getting Matthew to put out feelers to the Moores, much as it pained her to do so, and even getting Benjamin to take a few days away from the car showroom to help in the search for Noah.

When nothing came back after a week, Benjamin, as the only one of the family with a legitimate reputation, was sent to the cops with a story.

His brother had disappeared. He had gone out on an errand and had not returned. He'd been associating with some unsavoury characters lately and his family were concerned that he might have come to some harm.

The cops took the details, knowing that the story was a fairy tale, knowing that it was likely a drug feud that had led to Noah's disappearance. They were obligated to treat the report as a missing person case, until they had evidence that it was not. Benjamin's story said nothing about Rab or a car. In terms of priority, the disappearance was treated by police as somewhere between a category 3 and let-them-sort-it-out-themselves. There would be no posters around town, asking the public for information about Noah.

The cops eventually linked the disappearance with the Vauxhall Corsa. They had taken prints. There was just one set; Noah's. There was no missing person report for Rab, and no prints, since he been wearing his short, black gangster gloves. A size too small, but dead gallus in Rab's eyes.

*The Digger* was more interested than the police, it seemed, in Noah's disappearance.

The 36-point Helvetica Bold headlines gave full voice to local suspicions.

*"Smack Dealer's Disappearance In Drug Feud: We Know Who's Responsible. So Why No Arrests?"*

The seeds of these suspicions had been planted by *The Digger* itself the previous week, the headline based on little more than uneducated guesswork about how Owen Moore might be feeling.

*"Greenock Drug Kingpin Missing: Rival Fears He Is A Dead Man Walking."*

Without any reliable leads, the police investigation was gradually stepped down and, without any new rumours to keep the story alive, *The Digger* moved on to the next scandalous injustices.

A few faded E-fit posters of Davie Perdue could still be seen about town, on sites where they had not yet been plastered over with the pale face of the missing James Quigley, or the latest missing person, Neville Mickelson, another pensioner. Scott Birrell's murder in the cemetery remained unsolved. The abandoned Corsa had sparked another flurry of police interest in the cemetery.

Davie had to work a bit harder to remain invisible.

# – 19 –

## CIRCLING THE DRAIN

On March 9th, 2003 Davie Perdue left his job with the Met. He was never seen again by any of his fellow officers in London or by the few non-police friends that he had met in the capital.

There was no dark shadow of an internal investigation or reports of corruption or misconduct associated with his resignation, as was the case for a number of Met officers resigning or retiring around the same time. In his exit interview, there were no complaints from Davie about the lack of promotion opportunities, or organisational stress caused by poor management and supervision.

In his short letter to the Borough Commander, he mentioned how much he valued the Metropolitan Police and opportunities that he had been given to work with colleagues in fulfilling his public service ambitions. In his resignation letter, he gave, "personal reasons'" as the short explanation for leaving the force. He didn't elaborate on the reasons in his letter or in the exit interview, because he didn't want to relive the pain of writing out all that had happened, and because he knew that it wasn't necessary. By that time, every officer in his Peckham station and most in the Borough of Southwark knew why Davie Perdue was leaving the Met.

Then he simply left and dropped off the radar. He was not a missing person, since nobody was looking for him. Anyone he had known in Greenock had lost contact in the three years he had been in London. His colleagues and friends in London assumed, correctly, that he had gone back to Scotland. His mother was dead before he left to go south, his father was long gone, and he was an only child.

By coincidence, two weeks after Davie left the Met, an enthusiastic committee of 34-year-olds in Greenock was organising a school reunion through the latest internet fad, *Friends Reunited*. It turned out to be a once-in-a-lifetime experience for most of those who attended the event: None of them ever wanted to go through anything like that again.

The organising committee had drawn a blank on their old school pal Davie Perdue's address in London and found no evidence of his online presence on *LinkedIn* or *MySpace*. Up for a detective challenge however, they cast the net wider with *Yahoo* and *Internet Explorer*, eventually finding a newspaper report from the previous year, about a David Perdue who had tragically drowned after jumping off the pier at Southend-on-Sea.

The suicide story was close enough to London to be *the* Davie Perdue, and a juicy bit of you'll-never-guess gossip to share at the school reunion, where memories were short and silences were long.

As people got more drunk at the reunion, the tragedy of Davie's death was also a good conversation distraction for those trying not to comment on how many of their old school chums had put on so much weight or makeup as to be unrecognisable on the night. The news that Davie had taken his own life went quickly from speculative nashgab to accepted knowledge in

Greenock as the story was shared with people who had known him.

So Davie, who was never missing but did not want to be found was, for a time at least, simultaneously last week's news and that week's person of interest.

* * *

He could have rebuilt his life and come back after Sophie's death, maybe. He could have done it. He could have gutted out the worst, darkest days, forced himself through alone, cold turkey, without hugs from strangers and concerned words. It would have taken time and perseverance, but he had plenty of both, and he could have done it. He believed that then and he still believed it.

Even in the worst times when he was in his London flat alone, with no Sophie and no shifts to get up for, popping tranquilisers during the day, instead of his usual sleeping pills to knock him out after a night shift, he could see an end to the pain. Even at his lowest point, lying awake for hours in bed, the same thoughts going round and round, wearing a raw groove in the circuits in his brain, not getting up or eating because it was pointless, when he had a notion about why people took their own lives.

He'd attended four deaths by suicide as a cop, all young men, and each time he'd been baffled. No idea why those men had ended their lives prematurely, with no words to explain it. Men with jobs and families, men who went to the pub or played or watched football at the weekend. Men with good mates.

He understood it more then, or thought he did, curled up in the foetal position, trying to shut out the world. It wasn't because those men wanted to die. That was not the main reason, at least. No, it was because they just wanted the pain to stop. Worse than any physical pain, it was relentless and intractable. The tranquilisers didn't touch the suffering, but he took them in fear of how he might feel or what he might do without them.

The Met did mental health support much the same way that the Met did law enforcement or the Met did prevention of crime. There were systems and processes and standard operating procedures, and what you were required to do as part of these were directives, not guidance for good practice.

There was mental health support for officers who had experienced traumatic stress, job related or otherwise, and there was, potentially at least, no shortage of candidates for this support. Repeated independent surveys to assess trauma management and working conditions regularly came up with 85% plus figures for officers reporting exposure to trauma in the job at some point with around a quarter of these officers experiencing symptoms of PTSD.

If even a fraction of those cops had come forward for help, the system would be swamped and collapse. But of course, this never happened. Cops at the sharp end in London were trauma punchbags. They absorbed the cumulative effects of call outs to fatal RTAs, stabbings, shootings, hangings, drownings, overdoses and even old-fashioned beatings. The official line from the Met in the 2003 annual report was that officers were feeling more encouraged and confident to speak out about stress as a result of trauma. The official line on how much of this horror cops had signed up to, however, was never made clear. Were the scenes that they witnessed daily simply part of the job, part of the price of being one of London's finest and having the respect of the community and the long-term job security?

*"Put on your big boy pants and get on with it,"* or, *"Go hard or go home."*

That was the manly advice given at refreshment breaks and in pubs at the end of shifts from those who kept going when other cops no longer could. This custom and practice in real life policing kept the queue at the door for mental health support in the Met short. Admitting to a lack of resilience for the job was not only showing personal weakness, it was also leaving your equally stressed team short-handed. That would make you unreliable *and* selfish.

If you bowed to stress and took leave, there was the added shame of crossing the line from being one of London's invincibles to being one of the code 612s or section 135s that Met cops were called out to fifty times a week. You could become one of the mental health cases that you pitied or got irritated with because they involved so much paperwork and hanging about A&Es, diverting you from the tackling the haemorrhage of real crime in London. Even if all you were doing was just staving the bleeding.

\* \* \*

After Sophie's death, Davie took five days bereavement leave and some extra time he had in lieu, then dragged himself back. For him, it was long enough to do the necessary with the doctor, the Co-op funeral directors and Sophie's family, and then to wean himself off the tranquillisers at the same time as he was convincing himself that he was ready to go back to work.

But he knew that he was kidding himself only so that he could kid others. He felt hollowed out, the worst kind of imposter, like somebody was about to tap him on the shoulder any minute and say, *"So, who are you pretending to be, a Met police officer?"*

He timed his return to work to fit in with the rota, so that he was back for a set of shifts with his team, six days on and four days off. This suited Davie, eager to fit back into the work routine, away from the reminders of what had been, and it suited his Response team, his stressed colleagues covering his absence with extra shifts. Yes, it suited everybody, but ultimately it benefitted nobody.

In the break room at Paddington, Davie concentrated hard, struggling for the right words when anybody spoke to him.

Sophie's death had been rough, but there was more to come. It was like he had been kicked in the head, punched in the stomach and just as he was getting up, kneed from behind in the balls. All that had happened for real once, when he'd been on a response call and he and his partner had been jumped, outnumbered by a gaggle of bevvied up boys who'd been kicked out of a nightclub. But this pain felt much worse. He was in a fugue for the first six shifts, replying to people like an automaton.

*"Thanks for that. Yes, out-of-the-blue."*

*"Sure. I'll give you call if I need anything."*

*"Good to be back, yeah."*

There was the offer of counselling from Davie's Police Federation rep. He declined, figuring that he had done all the talking, hugging and most of the grieving with Sophie in the eight weeks it took her to die. He had prepared himself, saying everything he wanted to say and listening to Sophie so that when the end came, they were both as ready as they could be. They even joked about having completed all the stages of mourning, getting through the denial, anger, depression and acceptance in record time.

He was ready to come back. That was what Davie told the Police Federation rep, and it was what he forced himself to believe at the time. Counselling wouldn't do it. Sitting down and talking to somebody who asked questions and nodded also worried him a bit. It would be like stirring it all up again when he was trying to keep it tied down, holding it together. He might lose it, burst into tears, let himself down and then be ashamed that he'd let himself down. No point in that, and he'd be further from coming back to work than he ever was.

Sophie, gone in just eight weeks. In that short period, they had learned new words together, every one of them burned into his memory. First there were the tongue twisters that sounded like the answers to some deadly medical crossword clues: ductal adenocarcinoma, epidural metastases. Then there were other, shorter words, delivered to them like bullets from a gun in a small room with comfortable seats: insidious onset, rapid progression, terminal.

The cancer cells that had hidden in Sophie's pancreas had been plotting and multiplying for God knows how long. They had kept a low profile, causing her nothing but indigestion and weight loss until they decided the time was right to branch out and spread to her spine, by which time there was so many of them that no treatment was possible.

* * *

Sophie knew exactly how she wanted to go as soon she found out she was dying.

*"A willow coffin, like the picnic hamper we've got, and a direct cremation. No chapel of rest mumbo jumbo, religious service, no wailing, no pulling out of hair or gnashing of teeth."*

She even picked out the coffin from a glossy brochure. It was a rainbow variation of their plain picnic hamper, her only concession to style.

*"What's the point of paying undertakers for an expensive coffin and then paying again for someone else to set it on fire?"* she said, when Davie had suggested that her family might prefer something more traditional in wood.

So, on the day of the cremation, instead of carrying the wicker willow coffin, Davie, Sophie's family and her mates carried out her instructions. They had a meal and a few toasts and memories in the function suite at the Mish Mash, just around the corner from the flat, while Sophie's coffin went straight from the undertakers to the crematorium, unseen, before her ashes were scattered in a shady spot in the garden of remembrance.

On his first shift back on the street, there were the awkward hugs from some, which both Davie and the huggers were glad to be over. There were wordless hands on the shoulder and pats on the back, which Davie preferred to the attempts to say the right thing, when there was nothing to say that would make him feel any different.

*"How's it going?"*

That was what most people said in the embarrassed silence in those first few days. It was the one he came to dread most.

*"Keep working, that'll take your mind of it."* That came a close second.

Nothing kept his mind off it. His body did what was required, the strength of his police training put the right words in his mouth at the right time when he went back out on calls.

He'd been back three weeks, still operating like an efficient android. He finished shifts, went home, collapsed into bed, slept until the alarm, showered, ate, shopped for food and came back to work. The shifts went by without major incident and Davie convinced himself that since the pain wasn't getting worse, it must be getting better.

\* \* \*

On a sweaty summer's day, the year before, Sophie had dragged Davie onto London's even sweatier Piccadilly line and out to Hyde Park, for the first outing of their wicker picnic hamper. They found a spot near the Serpentine, lounged about on the grass, enjoying the sandwiches and the sun, watching parents chase children into the water, both of them wondering what that might be like.

Then Sophie got bored and insisted on hiring a rowboat to go around the island and under the bridge on the flat-calm lake. Davie wasn't keen, happy to soak up more sun, joking that where he came from boats were for getting from A to B, not from A to A. Sophie got up, saying that she would give him a wave as she went past, bluffing, and that was enough to get him on his feet.

They waited in the queue, overheating, for fifteen minutes, then Sophie snapped at the guy getting them onto the boat, when he tried to help her into the stern, assuming that Davie would be rowing.

Out on the water, it was cooler. Sophie gave Davie a demonstration of efficient rowing, setting a steady rhythm out to the bridge, before Davie very nearly got a lot cooler as they shakily changed positions in the boat and he almost went into the water while taking over the oars. After catching a few crabs, Davie got the hang of it. Rowing? Dead easy.

Sophie leaned back on her bench at the back of the boat and they fell into a peaceful silence as the wooden bow cut through the still water. As Davie looked toward the shore, from somewhere in his childhood came BBC radio on Saturday mornings and *Junior Choice*. *The Teddy Bears' Picnic* played in his head as he watched happy, shoeless people running about.

His dad was gone by then and he would sit with his mum, playing with his toys, the radio on while she knitted or ironed, listening to songs only ever played on *Junior Choice*. Story songs his mum called them, like *The Ugly Duckling, Delaney's Donkey, Nellie the Elephant* and *My Old Man's A Dustman*. Some of the lyrics were still with him, probably taking up valuable space in his head that could have been put to better use, he thought.

He had only the first two verses of his favourite song from *Junior Choice*, and he started singing it then with gusto, two strokes of the oars to a line.

> *When the weather is fine you know that it's time*
> *For messin' about on the river*
> *If you take my advice there's nothing so nice*
> *As messin' about on the river*

Sophie sat up and looked at him puzzled, then looked left and right to see if he was seeing something that she was missing that had triggered his singing. Davie continued with the second verse, nodding his head to the beat of the song and his strokes, in that moment as happy as he could ever remember being.

There was a Scottish version of the song, with large boats and wee boats instead of long boats and short boats, but Davie preferred the original.

*There are long boats and short boats and all kinds of craft*
*And cruisers and keel boats and some with no draught*
*So take off your coat and hop in a boat*
*Go messin' about on the river*

Josh Macrae, who'd had a minor hit with the song, had been Iain Macrae. He was Lanarkshire born but so in awe of 1930s American blues singer Josh White that he took on his name and his accent when singing. Three years after Davie had first sung along with his mother to *Messin' About on the River*, Josh Macrae took his own life, aged forty-four, disillusioned with the river and everything on it.

Davie had never got to suicide as the only option to stop the pain. Killing himself had made it, briefly, to a short list of options when he was at his lowest point in London. What steered him clear was his memories of suicides he'd attended as a cop, and most of all the cases where people had tried and failed, leaving them in a long-term state with more regrets and even more of a burden on the family and friends they believed they were relieving by dying.

Messing about on the river with Sophie. Now, a year on, so much had changed.

It was like the life he'd been living, the boat he'd been rowing across the flat pond, making progress, had been struck by a massive, freak wave that had washed nearly everything over-board, including him. He was still afloat, but only just, adrift, distracting himself every day from Sophie's death with the effort of pulling on the oars in a boat now knee-deep in water.

It wouldn't take much of a swell to sink the boat.

He was on a Friday night shift, on a call out to a street fight in progress, when that final wave struck.

# – 20 –

## MAN OVERBOARD

The Police Complaints Authority was on the way out and the new Independent Police Complaints Commission was just being set up, so there was a delay in the inquiry into the incident involving Davie. It was just an extra month, although it felt a lot longer to Davie, restricted to desk duties.

Because of the publicity the case had attracted, the Met's Communication Dept. recommended that, *"in both police and public interest"* Davie be kept on *"amended"* duties in the meantime, to avoid more headlines and scrutiny by the press, keeping him away from all public contact.

Officers subject to a PCA inquiry were not identified by name. Despite this, a journalist at London's *Evening Standard* had the bit between his teeth, running daily pieces on Davie's case. In the absence of any real developments, the journalist had done follow ups on what had already been published or broadcast elsewhere, keeping his original lede alive with background material and reactions from a supply of the usual London media whores, always available for a quote.

Through his contacts in the police, and officers not above a back hander if nobody was harmed by it, the journalist had Davie's name. He was not able to identity Davie in print while the inquiry was ongoing. Even with this restriction, he stretched the information that he was allowed to publish to the limits, to give his writing more credibility, hinting at his insider knowledge.

*"It is suspected that the officer involved was not originally from London..."*

*"The officer has been with the Met for just three years and is thought to be..."*

To keep him out of sight, Davie was hidden away in the bowels of West End Central station, five miles from his own station at Peckham, as a house mouse, as some of his colleagues called it. He was also kept away from the front desk of West End Central, and the walk-ins, in case the *Evening Standard* journalist or some other hack turned up, hoping for a quote or a photo.

Davie's fellow, station-based officers at the West End station, headquarters of C Division, were a motley crew of the demoted, the disgraced, the not-yet-dead and a few of the walking wounded. It was a world away from what Davie had signed up for, working at the sharp end of the force in the Response team.

Officers who had faced the same PCA inquiry board reviewing Davie's case were either dismissed without notice or retained in a very different, lesser capacity, if their misconduct fell short of gross. Breaching the Met's Standards of Professional Behaviour could be punished by a demotion of several grades. For those who had yet to be promoted in the first place, the measures taken were to take that officer out of operational duties and prevent further damage to the Met's reputation.

Those cops were reassigned or relocated, typically in some backwater, to spend long days in records filing rooms, organising old case reports, producing summary reports that nobody would read, or fetching and carrying for the evidence custodian or forensics. These were police officers who had breached the Standards, maybe only once that had been detected, but seriously. Excessive force in an arrest, cocaine in their systems in a spot test, or demands for sexual favours from an accused in exchange for leniency were the most common pratfalls.

Faced with years of boredom in windowless rooms, their pension still light years away, most of these cops gave up on the battle of wills with the Met and resigned.

A different category of officer, the not-yet-dead with whom Davie was also working, were mostly old sweats, seeing out their time. Nothing was too much bother for these officers, unless of course it involved an effort of any kind.

Cops just one or two years off the full thirty years pensionable service were treated differently by the force. The Equality Act of 1995 placed a duty on employers to make reasonable adjustments to accommodate those with a disability in the workplace. The unwritten police code for old sweats placed a duty of care on fellow officers to smooth their fellow officers' passage to retirement, in the hope and belief that the same consideration would be extended to them when their time came.

And then, finally, in Davie's "other duties" station, were the walking wounded. Officially, they were officers in the final stages of recovery from injuries incurred in the line of duty. Most were officers with genuine injuries, and most had not yet fully recovered. However, postings to the backrooms of the station referred to as "beyond the black stump" were sometimes used to test the mettle of officers who had been spotted playing squash or boarding a plane to Majorca while on sick leave and full pay.

Remarkable and full recoveries were made when recovering cops were faced with weeks in the windowless rooms, doing admin tasks that would bore a robot.

Davie was in the West End station, protected from press and public scrutiny for the duration of the PCA inquiry, until the verdict. After nearly three years as a Response cop, racing to unpredictable and horrific scenes and crimes, he resigned himself to the repetitive, mindless work that he was assigned.

The stress of the ongoing inquiry could be forgotten, if only for an hour, by submerging himself in paperwork and scrolling on screens. Working through piles of evidence discovery requests was guaranteed to put Davie in a zone where only the job in front of him existed. Read the request, check credentials of parties requesting the information, check the file number, instigate the search, copy and submit file, move onto next request. Hours went by as if he'd been in a time slip in the bowels of the building, far from the still prying *Evening Standard*.

In a strange twist, the same journalist who had kept alive the PCA inquiry in the *Evening Standard* over all those weeks had previously done a series of articles on the success of the Met's *Operation Trident*; an operation that had led, indirectly, to Davie being the subject of the PCA inquiry in the first place.

\* \* \*

The late 1990s saw callous and casual violence by new gangs of London's Yardies. Rivals and bystanders in equal numbers were killed and injured by knives, reprisals or, increasingly, shootings. There was fighting for control of the streets, or sometimes over nothing more than perceived dissing of opposing gang members.

The goal was supremacy in the cocaine street trade in Shoreditch, Harlesden or Tottenham, where families started living in back rooms of their homes to avoid the stray bullets flying through street facing windows. Outraged politicians and the disproportionately affected African-Caribbean communities were screaming for action by the Met. Eventually it came.

For a time, some areas of London saw more shootings than the organised crime of Chicago in the 1920s. The crimes committed by the Yardies, operating in gangs, was equally deadly, but anything but organised.

It was a war with different weapons on either side. The Yardies had crack cocaine, Uzis and Ingram Mach 10 "spray and pray" guns. The Met had Crimint.

It was a database of 500 mugshots, details and known associates of villains trafficking and selling. Slowly at first, information came into the Met on anonymous lines from people who'd had enough and decided that it was better to risk being labelled a grass than to have another dead family member. In briefings across the city, cops targeted drug dealing and associated gun crime in planned assaults. The payoff for *Operation Trident* and its simple slogan, *"Stop the guns"* had begun.

Gun crime and homicide, carefully monitored, went down, with each of the police Divisions given a role in supporting the new, dedicated Met unit. Which is where Davie and the other cops at Peckham came in.

* * *

Peckham Police Station had been on the High Street for over a century. It was three stories of Victorian redbrick that looked like a giant Primary school. Davie had been assigned to the station just after the completion of a modernisation project to replace all windows and install a new ventilation system. The improvements were still a regular topic of conversation for some of the older cops, who'd sweated through many summers and shivered through every winter.

Peckham, like all other stations, including those in areas with Yardie activity, was given performance targets by the Metropolitan Police Authority in partnership with the Police Commissioner. The annual plan had set reduction in street crime to ten percent below the level of the previous year, and a targeted disruption of the criminal use of firearms by four percent.

What came down from headquarters as station targets translated into individual performance indicators for Response team officers like Davie.

*"We don't want you forgetting what you normally do,"* the shift officer at Peckham had said at the first briefing, *"just because some bean counter in Scotland Yard wants to see numbers on a spreadsheet doesn't mean you're choosing which criminals to nick in Peckham. You still nick anybody who's dodgy, regardless of colour, creed or how much of a bung he offers you to let him go."*

This got a laugh from the room.

*"And remember, a statistic is not an* improvement,*"* the sergeant continued. *"I've been in this game long enough to know what a real improvement looks like in an officer's performance, and it's not the same as having five gold stars stuck on your report card or your face on the front of the Southwark News."*

Just the week before, Davie's shift of Response officers had had a visit from a detective in the Met's Trident Operational

Command Unit, as part of the Unit's who-we-are tour of London stations. The suited detective was there to tell them how the Trident Unit would assist officers in local police stations investigate shootings and collate intelligence from across the city about suspected gunmen, gun suppliers and gun converters.

One role of Response officers, he explained, was to support *Operation Trident* in driving down gun murders across London and getting crack off the streets. The reaction of most of his uniformed audience was a combination of cross-armed hostility and facial expressions of no-shit-Sherlock-indifference.

Despite the Response team's resistance to being told how to do their job by some fast-track detectives and the shift sergeant's continuing derision of performance improvement targets at briefings, the targets and the Trident Operational Command Unit got some traction. Reports on success in reducing drug related shootings became a standing item at each briefing. When Davie went out on patrol or on a call, the drip, drip constant publicity about guns and crack began to change his focus.

He still arrived at an incident ready to deal with it professionally, and to keep the lid on his shock at what people could do to each other or to themselves. He still began his investigation of each incident as soon as he stepped out the patrol car, even as he was chasing runners or struggling with suspects or comforting victims of death and injury.

After Sophie's death however, when the call out involved a firearm, or even the possibility of a firearm, he became a very different cop.

It was like the flick of a switch. If there had been mention of a gun in the call out, he was immediately conscious of every person on the scene, every vehicle, every open window and door, as he got out of the patrol car. He scanned for possible threats, hidden dangers, to him, his colleagues and the rubberneckers who had been drawn to the street theatre for entertainment. Knowing that these unidentified and imagined shooter dangers at a scene were not real didn't change how his antennae operated at the next gun crime scene. Every time, he was on a constant state of high alert, senses straining. He'd never had a bad experience with guns, never had one pointed at him, never had to face anybody down. The change didn't make sense to him, but he had no control over it.

He dealt with and investigated any call outs with the mention of a firearm in a state of hypervigilance. The main effect was utter exhaustion. For the entire period on the scene, sometimes hours, his heart was racing. He could feel it thumping against his stab vest, going faster than if he was chasing somebody down the street. He was jumpy, turning his head to every new sound until his neck muscles ached. After the call out, Davie would make it to the end of his shift, make it back to his empty flat and collapse on the bed, sometimes still in uniform. Returning from some 999 shouts, he was so drained that he had to ask his partner to drive and he had to keep his window open to avoid nodding off.

His usual partner in the car, Pete Baillie, didn't mention Davie being jittery on the call outs or being out on his feet some nights. Since Davie had come back on duty, Pete felt that he had been walking on eggshells on every shift with his partner.

He and Davie lived in different parts of the city and Pete never got to meet Sophie, despite the number of times that he and Davie had spoken about having a good night out on the town with their partners. He only knew her from Davie's stories before she was ill and from seeing how hard Davie had taken her cancer and her death.

Before Davie was back on duty and back in the car, Pete was so anxious about what to do that he had checked, confidentially, with a mate in Occupational Health. He asked him what to say and what not to say to a person who have suffered a bereavement; somebody who might or might not be Davie. Because Pete didn't have a clue.

He got a few pointers from his mate, which helped. But now, three weeks later, saying the same things over and over – *"I'm so sorry for your loss,"; "I'm here for you, Davie,"; "Just give me a call if you fancy a pint,"* – he was sounding like a parrot, and it felt worse than saying nothing at all.

Davie was still suffering. Pete could see that much.

Suggesting to Davie that he was struggling and needed to get some more help from Occupational Health or some head doctor was the right thing to do, but not the done thing.

Then Pete started thinking about what would happen if he didn't say anything. He'd watched Davie since he came back, and he wasn't the same cop. What if Davie went pop, lost it when they were both out on a call? What then? That would be much worse, for both of them.

How would he feel then about having said nothing?

Would it be worse though than saying to Davie, *"Look mate, I don't think you can handle this job anymore, and I don't want to be out on a call with you when you go loopy."* Because that would be what Davie would hear, no matter what fancy words Pete or somebody in Occupational Health could come up with to soften the blow.

Pete had covered for Davie back at the station when other

cops started to notice his state of near stupor after some call outs. Pete would say, *"That was a tough one boss. Davie and me are knackered,"* or, *"Glad we got out of that in one piece. It takes its toll on you."*

Pete worked at it, covering for Davie, hoping Davie would improve fast enough, get back on track, knowing that to admit that he knew Davie was a faulty part in the machine that was the Response team would be worse for him. Pete tried hard to convince others, but seasoned cops on the team could smell shite.

Regardless of the fact that Davie was one of their own, regardless of how long he'd been a cop or how good a cop he'd been, there was no place on the Response team for somebody who couldn't cut it. If you couldn't be relied upon, one hundred per cent, to have your partner's back, facing a mob or a weapon, when you needed to have your stick out, you should stand down or be stood down. There had been some sympathy in the station, sure, but there was no room for emotion when you were out on the job. Being a weak link in the Response team put everybody in danger. A cop who might go pop anytime was a liability.

There was side-of-the-mouth talk at the coffee machine when Davie and Pete were not around.

*"Came back too soon."*

*"We'll be running about like idiots doing double shifts while he goes off again on loopy time, you watch."*

*"Ticking time bomb..."*

*"He doesn't have both oars in the water."*

Davie's boat, already knee-deep in water, capsized on a Friday night call out.

* * *

They got the call at 11.30, kicking out time for most pubs and kicking off time for those coming out. The frantic caller reported a large group of men fighting in the street outside the Ruby Lounge on the Old Kent Road. Pete and Davie were almost there, blue lighting it on Hyndman Street when they were diverted to a priority response on the nearby Ledbury estate, the neighbourhood war zone. Someone had reported shots fired from a vehicle, near one of the thirteen-storey tower blocks.

Davie was instantly wired, sitting up straighter, gripping the wheel tighter, working out how many windows would overlook the scene when they arrived, calculating the number of potential vantage points and shooters.

He did a rapid three-point turn and headed back out onto the Old Kent Road. He had just turned right onto Commercial Way, lights and siren on, when it happened.

Davie didn't see him until he was in the air. The police car hit Eddie Burton side on.

He had come through a narrow lane, a short cut home, across the pavement, then between two parked cars, straight into the path of the police BMW e39. Davie had slowed from the turn onto Commercial Way and was just accelerating again. Investigators later estimated his speed at 45mph.

The collision sent the bike flying twenty metres straight down Commercial Way and Eddie Burton was thrown at an angle, over a wall and into the side of a garage. He had three fractured vertebrae in his neck, six broken ribs and a broken shoulder blade. A fractured skull was given as the cause of death.

The fight outside the Ruby Lounge turned out to be nothing

more than drunken posing, shouting and shoving. The shots fired on Ledbury Estate had been from a shotgun, fired not from a passing car but from a window high on one of the tower blocks. When arrested, the drunken man said that he liked the echo the blast made, bouncing off the other tower blocks. He was charged with firearms offences. No one was injured in either incident.

* * *

When the verdict came eventually from the PCA inquiry, Davie got it just before the spokesman put out the press release.

*"The investigation has determined that there is no evidence suggesting that the officer's manner of driving fell below the acceptable, required standard for a Metropolitan Police Officer."*

At the inquest earlier, the coroner had recorded a verdict of accidental death on Eddie Burton.

The PCA press release read, *"The officer, who has not been named, was driving at above the speed limit in a built-up area of Peckham, as he was entitled to, on a priority response."*

It went on, *"Mr. Burton was injured as police responded to a report of gunfire in the Ledbury Estate. The police officer involved in the fatal collision with the cyclist therefore has no case to answer for misconduct."*

Toxicology tests on Eddie Burton's blood had found him to be three times over the legal alcohol limit for driving a car. For the sake of his family, the coroner and the PCA report both played this down. Similarly, there was little publicity given to the fact that Eddie Burton was returning home from the pub on a bike with no lights.

In the battle for drug dominance that *Operation Trident* had been set up to tackle, innocent bystanders had been injured or killed in the crossfire. Eddie Burton was added to this list of victims.

\* \* \*

Despite being cleared by the PCA, Davie was not able to return to his Peckham Response Team duties immediately. There were recommendations from the Met's Human Resources that Davie be referred to the Trauma Support Programme, (*"responding to ill-health or injury issues howsoever incurred"*) and that his return to work be phased.

The TSP had a month-long waiting list for referrals, and a phased return to work didn't translate to the rigours of the Response team. The job was all or nothing. A phased return to the Response team was like asking somebody to walk along a rail track for a few miles until they were familiar with how the line looked, and then telling them to jump onto the side of the next speeding train.

The double whammy, of Sophie's death and being responsible, in his head at least, for the death of Eddie Burton, had left Davie at his lowest point, circling the drain, scrabbling for a hand hold.

In happy times and in sad times, there was a lyric in his favourite earworm song for every occasion.

*There's whirlpools and weirs that you mustn't go near
When messin' about on the river*

There was no self-pity in Davie's reaction to events, no endless, 'why-me?' preoccupation with what had happened and no dread of the future. There was only a belief, more strongly rooted by the day, that no matter how much energy Davie put into that future, all his efforts were going to make no difference at all to what came next. His future was not only unpredictable, it was uncontrollable. So why bust a gut trying to change it?

Summoning the energy that he would need to convince Occupational Health, Human Resources, his sergeant, Pete Baillie, and the rest of the Response team that he could bounce back to be the same old reliable Davie was beyond him. He decided not to even try. So, just like his return to work after Sophie's death, following the death of Eddie Burton Davie did what suited the Response team best. He resigned.

No more embarrassed silences, no more comments behind his back, no more questions. He made a clean break. He did half his notice period on sick leave and the other two weeks back in the bowels of West End Central station, moving boxes of records to be digitised. On the days that he turned up for work in the basement, he left early, and following the days that he didn't turn up at all, nobody said a word.

In that final week, the pace of activity in his flat quickened. He worked to midnight each day getting ready. Like Nellie the Elephant, he was packing his trunk to say goodbye to the circus.

Gas and electricity meter readings, signing off with the water company and tenancy notice. What he was taking he limited to what could fit in his duty kit bag. Five plastic sacks of fancy city clothes were ruthlessly bagged and carried to the local charity shop.

Mementoes that could be re-sold went the same way. Photos were binned. He spent an hour phoning around house clearance firms, settling on *Goods and Chattel,* who promised to, *"Remove all contents from properties, leaving them completely clear and tidy, and dispose of the contents ethically,"* which was exactly what he needed.

Finally, he was ready to go, leaving behind some of what he wanted to take and taking with him what he most wanted to leave behind.

Unwanted memories accrued for Davie Perdue.

# – 21 –

## SHRINES TO THE LIVING

Egyptian pharaohs did it before and did it best. Now it was Mexican drugs lords.

Digging your own grave might sound uncool, Owen Moore thought, but if you did it right, it had real class.

Some of the still-empty tombs in the Culiacan cemetery in Mexico had been fitted out with air conditioning and satellite TV, for the comfort of visitors. Like other mausoleums, the grandeur of the buildings said, *"Look at me. This is how rich I was and how much of a legend in my lifetime."*

The press and the Mexican police called the drug lords egotistic psychopaths, which some Cartel leaders took as a compliment. Having the graveyard edifices built *before* they died suited these drug dictators. They could soak up daily adulation from the locals in their home base, then visit their own grave and watch even more people file past the mausoleums, paying due homage.

Owen Moore didn't call himself as a drug lord and he thought a psychopath was something for bikes, but he liked that idea of his tomb being built while he was still alive. He liked that, a lot. Having something fancy built – big but not too tacky – then watching as punters that he'd supplied over the years show him even more respect while he was still around.

As well as building holy monuments to commemorate their lives, the drug lords in Mexico also donated truckloads of black money to the Catholic Church, to buy entry to the good place, because they knew that was the only way they would get in, given sins committed. Payment in advance, to guarantee purification of the soul.

Who made that shit up, Owen wondered? Pay your dues to the church to make amends for all the evil and damage you'd done? It was like that carbon offset crap the tree huggers were plugging, and just as likely to succeed. Owen respected the church as much as anybody in his family and he liked the idea of going to heaven. But giving the church fist loads of money that he'd worked so hard to earn? Not so much.

When he was killing time in Greenock cemetery, waiting for sellers or buyers to turn up, Owen looked around for spots of high ground, places where his mausoleum would be noticed. The best spots were all taken, of course.

The tomb that most punters visited was that of the steam engine man, James Watt, Greenock's Bill Gates. Owen thought it would have been an even bigger and better attraction if they had fitted it up with some pistons that moved, train noises and some buttons and lights that the children could press to keep them amused, like at the museum, while their parents were reading the plaque about James Watt's achievements.

The plaque said that when Watt died, his many fans had planned to build a monument that was 300 feet high. Now *that* would have been a proper jaw dropper, Owen thought. Two hundred years after Watt's death, the monument was at last finished. It was a sad, fifteen-foot-high pile of Lego block stones, donated from around the world. And without any moving parts, to entertain anybody. It was a bit of a disappointment all round.

If Owen got his wish, his tomb would be massive. And it would have columns. That was a must. Winding around the columns would be thick vines of ivy, intricately carved, climbing to the roof. To the tombstone tourists who wandered grave-yards, ivy was a symbol of immortality, fidelity and eternal life. To Owen, ivy was a well-hard plant that gets everywhere and was almost impossible to kill, like him.

As well as picturing the pre-death monument to his life, Owen also amused himself with variations on what would be written on his tombstone, the inscription that people would read and nod in approval, before and after he was gone.

*Owen Moore. A Good Man, Gone to a Gangsta Paradise,* was his current favourite. He liked that, a lot. But that could change, if he came up with something even cooler.

There were no shrines to drug lords in Greenock cemetery, yet. There was just one monument in the cemetery that had been built for someone alive rather than dead, and it was rarely visited.

\* \* \*

Davie had heard all the cemetery stories as a boy, told on sleep overs and camping trips, late at night. Stray, wandering spirits of the dead had been seen kneeling by gravestones or heard moaning from underground. Shadow figures had moved across cemetery paths in front of visitors and disappeared. There was a weeping statue of an angel that turned her head as you walked past, to follow your progress, or opened her stone eyes.

Whispering was heard from Dame Cameron's mausoleum. And of course, the ubiquitous white lady, tragic victim of love gone wrong, had been seen floating and forlorn in darker parts of the cemetery.

They were all great stories and Davie had enjoyed being scared by them. They were embellished with each telling as he got older, growing from simple yarns told to scare each other, to urban myths, sworn on mothers' graves to be true.

*"That definitely happened in the cemetery to somebody my cousin went to school with."*

Blurred photos with cameras, and later phones, had been taken, mostly by ghost hunters or by other supernatural enthusiasts. In his time living in the cemetery Davie had narrowly avoided one group, clad all in black, searching for the lost burial place of a Greenock vampire, supposedly marked by a tiny, black gravestone.

Since he had moved in, Davie was in no doubt that the cemetery had atmosphere. In the right conditions you could see what you wanted to see, if you tried hard enough. Granite gravestones were covered in a blood-coloured moss; a sight that didn't need much imagination to scare the unwary. The spooky, low-lying fog that settled in after a day of rain could make you believe that the mist was the undead rising, especially around older gravestones.

Davie had seen the fog move, on the few mornings when it was warm enough and he was up early, choosing to sit outside without fear of being spotted. Older gravestones were not more haunted, but they were made of granite, which soaked up the previous day's rain and then released the humidity as a cascading mist as the stones heated up. There were also cold spots in the cemetery, places that even on the sunniest days still had a chill. Davie rationalised these as shady areas that never saw the light, rather than anything related to the lingering presence of the long dead. Some days, as he made his way carefully through the graveyard, he felt like something was watching him, tracking his movement. This he put down to the number of places that somebody could be hiding, and the fact that he was creeping about furtively himself, trying to avoid detection.

And there were plenty of strange noises, late at night. Rustling, creaks and knocking that Davie had heard on his way back to his basement in the Goalkeeper's House. Flesh-eating ghouls dragging chains, and corpses banging on coffins trying to get out. Or just trees moving against each other in the wind, depending on what you wanted to hear.

There was only one spot that Davie avoided. For him, this was easy enough as it stood on a mound at the highest point the cemetery, far from any of his secret routes back to the Goalkeeper's House. He'd been up there just once, in his time as a cop, when he and his partner, Alan Bishop, were looking for a missing person. Well, not a real missing person, just a runner. He'd burgled two houses on the Bow Road that night and climbed over the wall to hide in the cemetery when he had been chased by one of the homeowners.

With no dog handlers available on the night, Davie and Alan had followed the burglar, trying to flush him out with torches and shouting. Alan went downhill and started to work his way up and Davie walked up past the crematorium to begin at the top.

\* \* \*

The tempietto was not a great place to hide, but that's where Davie started his search. It was well made, solid workmanship, pre-dating the cemetery. Eight sandstone ashlar columns had weathered well, protecting a circular inner chamber, all of it topped by a mushroomed dome, like a miniature St Paul's Cathedral. Anyone able to stand in the centre of the tempietto would have had spectacular views across the river to the hills in the north, and to the countryside south. But the inside of the tempietto had not been built high enough for anyone to stand.

At the beginning of the 19th century, long before the land was purchased for use as a graveyard, and long before the first turfs were dug to bury Marion Russell, its first resident, the bare top of Caddle Hill caught the eye of local bank manager Alex Thomson. In a time when most dreams could be easily realised with enough cash, he had a stately mansion built, with panoramic views over the town.

Alex Thomson and his wife Margaret had six children. Three of them survived beyond infancy. There were two sons, James and John, born 1826 and 1831 respectively, and a daughter, Margaret Shaw, born in between in 1827. The sons followed their father into banking and fortune.

Margaret Shaw, however, spent all nine years of her life at Caddle Hill House. With the birth of his daughter, Alex Thomson learned that most, but not all, dreams could be realised with enough money.

The first signs that something was wrong were sucking and feeding problems. Mrs. Thomson blamed herself to begin with and then, as she became more tired and frustrated, grew impatient with her baby.

The wet nurse she employed fared no better with feeding

and resorted to a pap boat, where the food was blown down the baby's throat through a hollowed stemmed spoon. As Margaret Shaw grew, Mrs. Thomson found reasons to be with her two sons most of the time. Her daughter was floppy, showed few signs of returning affection and cried for hours without reason. It was the crying that led to the construction of the tempietto.

Alex Thomson saw the dresses his wife once wore with elegance hang like bedsheets on her shoulders as she lost weight. The bags under her eyes became permanent, adding five years to her face. Coming home from the bank, he would find her in bed trying to sleep or sitting, staring at the walls, in the most distant parts of their mansion, trying to get as far as she could from the incessant crying.

Sending the child away to be cared for, out of sight, was unthinkable for the Thomsons. It was not done by someone of Mr. Thomson's station, signifying to society as it would something the parents had done or had failed to do, and ultimately reflecting badly on the bank. A wealthy banker had a reputation to uphold and was expected to support elderly and young family dependents alike, regardless of their infirmities.

The Thomsons had raised James, their firstborn, with forbearance, attending to his needs and accepting sleepless days and nights, shitty nappies and full-throated bawling as part of the parental contract. But Margaret Shaw's crying was different. It would be another 130 years before the rare, genetic mutation affecting Margaret Shaw's brain development, and her larynx in particular, was discovered.

Mrs. Thomson could hear James' crying during his first two years of life and know from the sound and the volume if he was hungry, tired or in pain. Margaret Shaw's cry by contrast had no such variation. It was a constant, high-pitched wailing that sounded like a cat trying to attract attention. It grated on the ear of anyone in the room and the sound seemed capable of passing through thick walls.

By the time Margaret Shaw was two years old, the crying had decreased, although loud noises or unexpected movement could bring it on suddenly. She found random distractions, often obsessing for hours over simple toys or objects around the house. Even at that early age, it was clear to the Thomsons that Margaret Shaw would never attend school like James, or take her father's arm as she walked down the aisle on her wedding day.

The Thomsons compromised, for appearances, which were everything. A tempietto shaped summerhouse was commissioned, designed and built in three months, on a small mound close to the house, at the top of the hill. A tasteful addition to the grounds of Caddle Hill House, as an example of Italian renaissance harmony and order, it was admired by visitors and even featured in the *Greenock Advertiser*.

After breakfast and nappie changing it became part of the resident nurse's duties to push Margaret Shaw in her wheelchair out to the summerhouse, out of earshot, where she could spend some hours enjoying the spectacular views.

Because of her lack of speech and mobility, it was not possible for Margaret Shaw to say if she enjoyed the spectacular views, or to indicate when she had had enough of them. She was also taken to the viewpoint, sometimes with a blanket for warmth, whenever the Thomsons entertained guests. The space inside the tempietto was only large enough for Margaret Shaw and her wheelchair, so the nurse would sit by a window in the house with a line of sight to the tempietto, crocheting or doing some needlework.

This daily arrangement went on for another five years, except on the coldest of mornings, until Margaret Shaw died of a heart defect, one of the common complications of Cri du Chat syndrome.

* * *

PC Davie Perdue had heard the story, and it came back to him that night when he approached the tempietto at the top of the hill, searching for the runaway burglar.

It was bitterly cold, with the wind gusting stronger as he climbed the hill. The moon was out, and he could make out the path and shapes of the gravestones without his torch.

Davie didn't know when the sheet metal screens had been put around the summerhouse, bolted between the columns, but he guessed that it had been done to prevent vandalism and gang tags being sprayed inside.

As he got closer, he saw movement on the far side of the tempietto. He stopped, trying to decide on his best line of approach. If the runaway burglar was up there, Davie didn't want to let him know he'd been seen and sprint off into the dark. Equally, he didn't want to make it up there only to play chase around the circular structure, like some Tom and Jerry cartoon. Where was a sharp toothed, arse-biting Alsatian police dog when you needed one, he thought.

Davie moved off the main path and came up the hill on the blind side, which was in the shadow of the moonlight. He switched his Motorola police radio to silent, ready to flick it back on and let Alan Bishop know when he'd nabbed the runner.

It was the smell that he noticed first. He had climbed to

touching distance of the tempietto silently and was deciding whether to make his run clockwise or anti-clockwise to surprise the burglar when the smell hit him.

It was pungent piss, concentrated and cloying like from someone with a UTI. Maybe all the excitement had been too much for the guy he was chasing, Davie thought, and he'd had to take a piss against the summerhouse just where Davie was standing.

As Davie moved slowly to his left, the smell went with him. It was then that he heard one of the metal sheets rattling. It was on the far side from where he stood. Deciding that he'd delayed long enough for what was going to be more paperwork than serious crime, he made his move. Stepping back from the structure, he planted his feet, drew his side-handled stick and charged clockwise.

In the few seconds it took Davie to go all the way around the summerhouse, nobody could have run away without being seen or heard, and nobody did. There was no sign of the burglar.

Davie stopped, breathing hard and switched on his radio to message Alan. Just as he pressed to transmit his message, there was another rattle on one of the sheet metal screens, this time closer to where he was standing. The Motorola slipped from his grasp and rolled away from him towards the steeper slope.

"*Shit,*" he said, as he dropped to his knees, grasping blindly, and catching the radio by its stubby antenna just in time. He heard the sound just as he got back to his feet.

It was faint and he could only hear it as the wind fell away. It was the high-pitched whimper of a cat, coming from inside the tempietto. He stepped closer. It came again. It was no louder, no more distressed, just the same quiet meow.

He looked upward at the structure, wondering how the cat could have scaled one of the sheer, Ionic columns or the metal sheets and squeezed in through the dome, and why. He put his ear to the nearest sheet metal panel and listened. There was silence for a few seconds, then a higher pitched whimper at the same instant as Davie felt, rather than heard a dull thump on the metal sheet, like someone had thrown something against it, just where he was pressing his ear.

He took off down the steep hill like a deer being chased, his knees jarring as he threw one foot then the other into the darkness without a spot picked out to land. His speed became too much for his legs to cope with and he tucked in his head as he flew into the air, did a full somersault roll and came up, stumbling but still running as he reached the foot of the slope.

He had to scurry about in the grass again to retrieve his hat that had come off and the notebook that had flown out of his pocket during his summersault. Sitting on a gravestone for a minute until his heart stopped racing, he could hear nothing above the gusting wind.

Back on the radio, he tried to keep his voice calm as he told his partner there was nothing to report and that he was heading back downhill.

*"He's probably tucked up in bed while we're out here freezing our balls off,"* said Alan when they met up, halfway down the hill.

*"Yeah, probably jumped that wall, ran straight through the cemetery and out, back onto the road,"* replied Davie, clenching his hands together and keeping them out of sight in case Alan noticed, even although it was dark, how much they were shaking,

They passed a sign as they walked back to the gate and the wall they had climbed.

"*This gate will be closed at dusk. No person shall be in Greenock Cemetery after sunset or before sunrise ….*".

"*Oh, and we must be sure to bust him for that too, as well as the stuff he's nicked from those folks' houses,*" Alan joked, as he looked for a suitable gravestone to hoist himself up onto the wall.

As they drove back, Davie gave Alan an edited version of what had happened at the tempietto.

"*So, I got up there and there's nobody, just some cat that's got itself trapped inside. They're supposed to be smart, right? So if it can get in, it can get back out again, right?*"

Davie said.

"*Oh, I don't know Davie,*" Alan said, smiling.

"*That might be just the sort of job for the water fairies, give them something to do other than sleeping all night at the fire station, or eating fry ups and playing cards.*"

Davie laughed, feeling some of the tension he'd been holding in his shoulders ease off at last.

"*Aye, right enough,*" he said, "*our brave fire fighters might appreciate a 999 call when we get back to the station, to let them know that their invaluable services are required. I know how much they like playing at rescuing animals while the real heroes get on with the serious stuff.*"

Any rivalry between the police and their colleagues in the fire service was competitive banter, mostly. There was black edged humour on both sides, helping to distract or debrief from the stress of emergencies. When they were on joint operations, fire crew and police had each other's backs.

When he finally got to his bed that night, Davie found it all easy to explain. He'd never seen a ghost before, and that was still true. It had been windy, the air whistling through the gaps in the sheeting could have sounded like a cat, and a strong gust of wind could have sent the shudder through the metal just as Davie put his ear to it. All much more likely than the ghost of some trapped girl with no voice trying to get out.

He never had any reason to go back to the tempietto, then, when he'd been a cop, or since, and he was glad about that. There was nearly one person for every day of the year interred in Greenock cemetery, but it was that one spot in the eighty acres, where nobody was buried, that still gave him the jitters.

He was reminded of the tempietto when he got to know Yashin a bit better. Sometimes, Davie would speak to himself before he went to sleep in the basement. Nothing profound, just going over the events of that day, or what he would do the next. Trying to cheer himself up with what had been good or talking about what he needed to do more of.

Yashin was the best kind of listener, never interrupting or criticising. He was a silent counsellor, a reassuring presence in the room, almost invisible in the dark. If he didn't have his eyes open, Davie didn't know if he was there or not, until he heard a familiar, deep throated purr of understanding when Davie had finished speaking, or sometimes a higher pitched trill to let Davie know that he could keep talking while Yashin nipped out for a minute for something to eat.

It was Yashin's various meows in the cellar later that made Davie think back to that night at the tempietto. The sound that he'd heard from the summerhouse on the mound was not whistling airflow. It was no wind blowing through metal sheets. He'd heard it and it was a distressed, high-pitched cat's yowl.

# – 22 –

## A BAD CURRY

The Inuit language has fifty words for snow. This oft repeated myth is both true and false. There is more than one Eskimo-Aleut language, with many variations on words for snow, so the total number is difficult to say with certainty.

People who live in the coldest climate on earth do have more words for the white stuff than other cultures, because vocabulary has evolved to describe the environment and what it is important to know to survive. If you are outside in the Arctic, precise language is important. You do want to have a word that tells you when the snow is safe to walk on and a different word that tells you that you are going to sink, waist-deep in the stuff or fall through ice and drown. Similarly, the vocabulary of inhabitants of the wettest town in Scotland have also adapted their vocabulary to their climate, to avoid drowning.

Greenockians have a range of words for what happens almost two-hundred days a year in the town. On any one of those days, there could be any combination of spitting, smirring, hailing, drizzling, sleeting, sleeshing or pelting.

At the beginning of the week that was to be Davie's last in the Goalkeeper's House, there was a pish-oot.

Three days of persistent, heavy rain left the ground throughout the cemetery saturated. A steady stream ran out the front gates, depositing a wide delta of moss and road chippings onto the pavement outside. Davie's stepping stones to his basement crannog were hidden beneath two inches of muddy water which had been washed down the hill, and with nowhere to go, had dammed against the wall that had been built between the original cemetery gate piers.

As the rain pooled in places and soaked deeper into the soft earth in the cemetery, it weakened seals on some coffins, releasing bubbles of trapped, dead air that could be seen popping in the puddles of muddy water at the surface. If there had been anyone at gravesides, they might have commented on the smell. But there were very few visitors on days like these.

Even the most devoted sons and daughters, those with weekly rituals of renewing gravestone flowers and paying respects, were not up to trudging through puddles and muddy grass to stand in the relentless rain, trying to conjure up fading fond memories of mum or dad. The promise of sweets for enduring the same ordeal was likewise a difficult sell to young children, especially when they had never met Grandpa and he never said much when they visited him.

Cremations went ahead, regardless. They were never postponed, even on days when rain was bouncing four inches off the tarmac, or on days when the sombre cortege of cars snaking up to the crematorium was led by a tractor, with a snow blade on the front and a salt spreader attachment behind.

There were salt bins scattered around the cemetery on the steepest slopes. Shovelling and spreading salt was another job for Sam and Jamie on the coldest mornings. One of the gardeners had been sacked for hiding half bottles of vodka in the salt bins. Well, not for hiding the booze, but for taking secret swigs of the stuff to keep himself going at work.

When he first moved into the basement of the Goalkeeper's House, Davie had wrapped up any cold meat he bought in a plastic bag, and then buried it in the nearest salt bin. It kept it cool, dry and fresh, and prevented any smells in the basement that might attract rats, or make Yashin wonder what he was missing out on.

After the incident with the gardener and his half bottles, the council put locks on the salt bins. From then, Davie only brought back meat that he could eat in one sitting in the basement.

* * *

If it had not been for the chicken curry and the rain, Davie would never have found the hat that changed his future.

Davie's greatest luxury, his one indulgence to remind himself each week that he could, if he chose, go back to a life that other people, most people, lived was his Friday night chicken tikka masala. He didn't have a Monday-Friday job, or a job of any other kind, other than the *Big Issue* sales, but old habits die hard. He still liked to mark the end of the working week. He had done it even when he was on police shifts, going out on the night that was closest to Friday to celebrate having survived another week.

The *Taj Mahal* was a converted shipping container that sat on waste ground near a roundabout leading out of Greenock towards Inverkip. The paved forecourt had once been the site of *Autohand Car Wash*. Davie had visited the car wash when it was in operation in his days as a young cop in Greenock. He couldn't remember if the business went bust after laundering money, dealing drugs or making immigrants work for nothing, but he remembered it was definitely something dodgy.

Davie stood in the line of customers queueing at the barred window of the *Taj Mahal*, ordered and paid for his food, then sat under the canopy of the old car wash until his name was shouted. Merely the smell of the chicken tikka masala when he collected it was one of the highlights of his week.

The staff in the shipping container were always bright and friendly, and it was one of the few places in town that he could exchange cash for goods without those behind the counter looking him up and down before serving him, if they served him at all. In some carry out places, he'd had sniggering or whispering or nodding towards him, and often the same, tired comments.

*"That'll be the pigeons in looking for some bread."*

*"He's likely a jaikey, so I'm no serving him."*

*"Beat it pal. I can smell you from here."*

Section 4A of the cemetery was a short hop over the boundary wall from the *Taj Mahal*. Davie walked along the road until there was a break in the traffic and no drivers to take notice, then hoisted himself and his curry up the ivy and over the wall, carefully keeping the foil trays horizontal. It was ten minutes from the *Taj Mahal* to the Goalkeeper's House, where he could settle down, get something on the radio and savour the flavours in peace.

It all went well until the early hours of the next morning.

*"Having a bad curry,"* was a sometimes euphemism for throwing back ten pints the night before and then throwing up five hours later. For workers on a mid-week night out, the bad curry excuse had been used many times when phoning in to work with a hangover. In Davie's case, there was no alcohol involved,

no employer to call and he was pretty sure that the cause of his spewing out both ends of his body really was a bad curry with some undercooked chicken.

He had enjoyed his tikka masala as usual, and he made it through most of the hours of darkness. The noises that woke him up around 4.30am were the plumbing-like, gurgling sounds coming from his stomach. He tried at first to ignore them, but after half an hour he realised that a volcano was about to erupt.

He just made it out through the top door, hopping across his hidden stepping stones like Indiana Jones being pursued, and behind a tree before his whole body was bucking with projectile vomiting and explosive diarrhoea. The urgency of Davie's exit caused Yashin the cat to race out behind him, looking over his shoulder for whatever might be chasing them both.

Davie dug his nails into the soft bark of the tree as another spasm came. With most of the contents of his stomach in two puddles on the grass, he was left dry heaving, and trying to hold his trousers clear of the green liquid coming out his arse like a sputtering tap. Each time he thought it was over and started to straighten up, there was more. Davie looked, and wondered at the volume of liquid on the grass. It was at least double what had been in the containers he'd carried back from the *Taj Mahal*.

After staying crouched for ten more minutes, holding onto the tree, his stomach and his bowels finally stopped contracting. Davie felt totally spent, like he could just keel over and fall asleep on the spot. He shuffled with his trousers around his ankles to a clean spot and knelt down, pressing his forehead to the cool grass. He looked left and right, getting ready to try standing up. It was from that angle that he saw something that he would otherwise have missed in his usual routine.

In the gloom, it looked like a plant saucer at first, or maybe a lid, something from a tub of weedkiller that the gardeners had used to keep the paths clear. When he looked closer, Davie saw that it was neither. Snagged on the elephant's foot that was the base of an oak tree was a flat cap. It had washed down in the pish-oot that had cut a wide channel through the grass and pebbles on the hill above.

Davie, still unsteady, crawled on all fours over to the base of the tree and picked up the cap. The body of the hat, some kind of tweed material, was saturated, water dripping when Davie lifted it. Inside the cap however, the surface was drier, as if the cap had bumped along the stream, like a coracle caught in the torrent pouring down the hill.

Just the image of the cap as a rounded boat was enough to start the verse in Davie's head then, unbidden.

*When the weather is fine you know that it's time*
*For messin' about on the river*
*If you take my advice there's nothing so nice*
*As messin' about on the river*

The song again from *Junior Choice* and from happy times, being on the Serpentine with Sophie. It was an earworm that he just couldn't shake. Josh Macrae and his guitar would strike up when Davie least expected or wanted it. Any points in the cemetery with a clear view of the Clyde triggered the song, or a glimpse of boats in Greenock harbour or in the shipyards was enough. And when it started, he couldn't press a button and interrupt Josh.

He had to see the song through to the end, or until he ran out of lyrics, which was just as frustrating.

His first thought was that he could dry the cap out. It would be perfect to add to his hipster look of not being the man in the fading E-fit posters, still around town.

Inside the bunnet, the manufacturer's name – *Lochcarron of Scotland* – was still clear, protected in a plastic seal. As he looked closer, he saw another, white label handsewn into the inside at the back of the cap. The once neat writing in blue ballpoint ink had been washed out by the rainwater and only a few letters were legible. Davie made out the initial 'J' at the beginning of the name and the last two letters as 'ey'. He looked back up the hill where the steady stream of rainwater was still coming down, any thoughts about his chicken curry belly or wearing the cap as part of his disguise suddenly gone.

\* \* \*

Davie had made the tough decision to leave London, to get out of the game with no real plan. Living in the cemetery, by accident rather than design, had allowed him time, if nothing else. It was a life on pause. Kneeling there in the wet grass, holding the wet cap with James Quigley's name in it, Davie realised he had another, tougher decision to make. To stay out, or to get back in the game. There could be no middle way for him now.

He could toss the cap back under the tree or even bury it. Problem solved, go back to what he was doing before, living under the radar. Or he could leave the bunnet somewhere in the cemetery where it would be found and pass the buck, gambling on somebody else realising the significance of the missing pensioner's cap, which was unlikely.

His first impulse was to go to the cops. If he'd still been a cop, that's how he'd have advised the person he'd become. Bite the bullet, walk into the Police Station on Rue End Street and hand the cap to the desk sergeant. It was the right thing to do. Except he knew how that played out.

Hours in a wee room with hard chairs, trying to explain how he knew James Quigley was missing in the first place, how he knew the bunnet was Mr. Quigley's, and, oh, by the way, while he was there, would he be happy to answer some questions about the murder of a Mr Scott Birrell in the cemetery and Davie's resemblance to a man police had been seeking as a person of interest in connection with the murder some time ago?

Davie had been a cop, not for long, but for long enough. He knew how it worked. It might take the local cops a week or a month, but they would have him in that wee room at Rue End Street eventually, answering their questions. And that would be the end of his secret presence, his simple life on hold, putting off the hard decisions about what came next, and avoiding gutting out the dark thoughts about how he'd come to this. The only way he didn't end up in the wee room was if he buried the cap, and buried his head in the sand, forgetting that he'd found it.

He'd made decisions since he came back, but none as big as this. Stick or twist? Check or go all in?

Maybe it was time to turn the page. But before he sat on the hard chair in that wee room, answering the questions, he had some questions himself that needed answers.

# – 23 –

## NEWLY CUT DIVOTS

The pish-oot had created one main stream, the flowing water loud enough to be heard above the sound of the rain that was still falling. Tributaries cut bare channels into the grass and joined from left and right. The rain that had already fallen filled every void and space in the soil underneath. The rainwater filled hollows on the surface until it overflowed, running downhill over the saturated ground.

The stream ended at the walled-up gate by the Goalkeeper's House. The swamp around Davie's basement door had expanded to twice its usual surface area. All but one of the weep holes in the wall had been blocked by leaves on the first day of the rain, and now only a trickle of liquid mud flowed out onto Bow Road. The water coming downhill hit the wall, swirled and backed up, drowning more grass, and getting deeper by the hour.

It was on days like this that Davie revisited his older worries about what he had to walk through previously to get into his basement. Was the rain that washed over decomposing bodies in water-logged coffins, bringing downhill the diseases that had killed the coffins' occupants? Were there zombie viruses, anthrax and other deadly spores pooling, lurking in the water outside the Goalkeeper's House or worse, drifting in the air that he was breathing while he slept?

He'd spent a rainy morning in Greenock Library reference section, attracting dirty looks, trying to stay dry and find the answers to these questions.

There was little risk, he discovered, not from diseases of the dead at least. But there were other dangers in the water gathering outside his basement. *Scottish Death Traditions & Customs* took him to *Graves and Graveyards; A History of Undertaking*, and into more details.

The problem, he read, was that attempts to make the dead look at smiling peace and leave relatives with a comforting, lasting image of their loved ones had become, over the years, a greater threat to the living.

Before formaldehyde became the chemical of choice for embalming corpses, arsenic was the main preservative. Davie read with horror that toxic fluids were slowly leaching, unseen, into the soil all over older cemeteries. It got worse. Coffins and bodies would collapse with age, adding ammonia, lead, zinc and copper into the deadly cocktail.

It was only in rare circumstances, however, when heavy rainfall caused gravity and pressure to move the groundwater through spaces between rocks and through coffins with enough force, that the cancer-causing chemicals were being swept downhill, to emerge in surface runoff in places like the Goalkeeper's House.

So, on days when there was a pish-oot, the water around Davie's basement was unlikely to contain any zombie viruses, but you definitely didn't want to drink it or get it on your skin.

* * *

Davie continued uphill. In passing, he read a sign that had been stapled to a tree and kept walking, his focus on the cap that he was still holding tightly in his hand.

*"Cremations will be suspended on Saturday morning while action is taken to destroy cypress trees in the cemetery that have been infected with a root-rotting fungus."*

All it meant to Davie was that it would be workmen and not mourners that he had to dodge if he was out and about in the cemetery on the following day.

He walked on uphill, tracking the path of the stream, like a bedraggled David Livingstone in search of the source of the Nile. There was a series of terraced pools in a line of graves on the slope, where the collapse of disintegrating coffins underground had left depressions in the grass at the surface.

The rainwater ran in rivulets from one pool to the next, overflowing and continuing downhill. After picking his way around the deeper puddles and ankle-deep mud, Davie reached a path transecting the hill. A pipe culvert had been laid under the path to prevent sections of the path being washed out. The protruding pipe was angled upward as it emerged from the path and the rainwater was spouting like a primitive fountain. This was the source of the temporary stream, gaining more force as it moved downhill.

The thick cloud cover above, that was still disgorging rain, combined with the shade of trees around the path to make the gravestones in that area indistinct shapes in the damp gloom.

Over the years, what had begun in the cemetery as a planned layout of selected, signature trees – birch, ash cypress, oak and holly – had developed into a battle between those same trees and their saplings and successive teams of gardeners, as the trees staked their claims. The gardeners had lost that battle years ago and the remaining struggle now was amongst the trees, climbing higher and spreading their branches wider in the competition for sunlight and space.

Two of these competitors near the path were monkey puzzle trees. Greenock Cemetery had the largest number of these trees in any site in Scotland. Why the 100-feet-plus conifers had been planted in the cemetery was a landscaping mystery. They stood out like giants in a children's playground.

Davie's memories of these trees came back to him then, distracting him for a moment from the task in hand.

He had gone, or been taken with his mother and her friend, to visit a relative's grave when he was seven or eight. He had just learned how to whistle, successfully, after more than two years of trying. After a few weeks of admiring his new skill and being asked to guess the title of a large number of similar-sounding whistled tunes, his mum's patience was finally exhausted, and whistling had been banned, in the house at least. The walk in the cemetery seemed to Davie like a real chance to show his mum and her friend what they were missing.

Although he didn't remember any details about the long dead relative they were visiting, the story he was told to shut him up in the cemetery that day had stuck with him. As they passed one of the monkey puzzle trees, his mother's friend had looked up and told Davie that the devil sat high up in these special trees and people had to be quiet when they were walking past or else the devil would hear them and give them bad luck.

It was an effective way to simultaneously silence and terrify a seven-year-old. It worked, for at least for ten minutes. When he'd forgotten about the devil in the tree and started on a recognisable whistled version of *Frere Jacques*, his mother's friend had stopped walking again and told him that whistling in a cemetery was also a way of summoning evil spirits, who might come and get him. His mother didn't have many friends after his father left, and that one was a real crabbit killjoy, he remembered.

The adult Davie looked up at the monkey puzzle trees now, towering over the short row of gravestones to the left of the waterspout by the path, cutting out the light. The grass on the first two graves was flooded, like most of the others in the row, but on the third grave a low mound of earth stood proud of the surface water.

As Davie got closer and his eyes adjusted to the poor light, he saw a line of brown, newly cast divots that ran the length of the grave. The turf had been neatly re-laid and there were deeper depressions at intervals where a boot had stamped the divots back into place. The gravediggers mounded up on new graves, Davie knew, in anticipation of the earth settling and of grave subsidence later. What he was looking at was not mounding up. The surface was too high and the shape was wrong.

Davie bent down to read the inscription on the granite gravestone. In the gloom he could only make out the first line near the top of the rectangular stone, *'In Loving Memory of...'* Kneeling in the wet turf, he peered closer, but it was still too dark. He ran his fingers over the rest of the sandblasted epitaph to feel what his eyes couldn't read. The words at the top of the gravestone were weathered with age, the edges softer and the surface pitted.

He ran his hand over six lines of inscription, trying to find something that he could recognise by touch. He could distinguish letters from numbers, but nothing more than that. There was a gap between the rows of inscription. More than one person was buried there, maybe a family plot. Then, near the bottom of the gravestone, the letters changed suddenly. They were sharply defined, the back of each letter forming a deep 'V' in the stone. There was no moss or wear from weather. Davie ran his fingers across the letters, forming the words on his lips as he did so.

*Daughter-in-Law*
*Jean Anne Quigley*
*12th June 1929 – 14th March 2003*

He finger-read the words on the inscription again to be sure, nicking his finger on one of the sharp edges as he pressed harder, then stood and backed away from the grave slowly. At a push, he might have been able to ignore the flat cap still held in his hand, but the newly cut divots and the inscription changed his choices. Now it was not a case of whether, but when he went to the cops.

Davie turned and found a direct route back downhill. He stopped before the Goalkeeper's House to hide the flat cap in a dry spot, under a table tombstone. In the basement, he put some stuff in his bag and headed to the bus station. He didn't want to be in the cemetery or in Greenock until he could decide what to do next.

More time to think it through, that's what he needed. It wasn't a decision to make when he was soaked and in this agitated state, he convinced himself. He had too many things to do and didn't know which was most important. If he took action immediately it was something he would regret later. He knew that much. And whatever he did next would change how he lived, and where.

As he filled his shoulder bag, he told himself that he wasn't doing a runner, even as he packed what he would take with him if he was.

He took his torch, socks, gloves, hat, spare underwear, foil blanket, zip lock bags for food and his current, dog-eared book. He convinced himself that he was coming back by leaving his Grundig *Concert Boy,* but only after trying to squeeze it into the bag.

As he lifted the hatch to the basement, he was suddenly aware of the road noise being louder and of the sound of voices somewhere in the cemetery. He stopped, lowered the hatch again and looked through the gap he'd left, scanning all around for possible threats.

He checked the nearest group of trees, staying stock still and watching for any movement, any figures waiting for him to show himself before they charged out. His heart was racing. Who else knew about the cap he'd found? Were they watching him now?

He waited a minute longer and convinced himself that he was alone, the only person in that damp, sodden corner of the cemetery. When he moved again, he did so slowly, still watching for hidden dangers, telling himself that there were none; no shooters, no devils in monkey puzzle trees, telling himself that he'd been here before.

# – 24 –

## DECISION MADE

Davie booked in on Friday for two nights to what was properly called the 400 Duke Street Hotel. It was a place still called the Great Eastern Hotel by anybody who stayed there, and also known to local taxi drivers as Heartbreak Hotel. He was away from the cemetery and from Greenock with time to plan his next, maybe his last move.

Designed at the beginning of the 20th century and celebrated as one of the first fireproof buildings in Glasgow, the hotel had a promising start. The reputation of the Great Eastern Hotel peaked early however and had been on a downward spiral ever since. It went from a hotel, housing homeless working men, to a hostel for homeless men without a job, then became a last resort zoo for drunk and disorderly homeless men with petty criminal records that no other hostel would let in the door.

To shake off the reputational association between the hotel and dependents of Tenants Super-Lager, the owners had changed the name of the hotel to 400 Duke Street. This name change was as effective as changing a power plant name following a nuclear disaster. Nobody was fooled and the building continued to be known locally as the Great Eastern.

The accommodation and the management of the building improved over recent years, by health and hygiene necessity. But the Great Eastern Hotel still sounded much grander than it was. The space that Davie rented for the two nights was more of a cubicle with partitions than a room. It was fine for what he needed, and he was surprised how well he slept on the Friday night.

On Saturday morning he moved around his familiar pitches by rote, absently selling an armful of the *Big Issue*. The walking and the routine helped him relax and he was able to focus on the task in hand. What did he really know and what he should do with the information?

There was a connection between the missing James Quigley, his cap and where Davie had found it. He was sure of that. Maybe his first instinct was the right one and he was wasting time, overthinking it? Should he just hand the information over to the police, step back and see what they made of it? All roads led back to the same hitch in that attractive, simple plan. What he knew could not be passed on anonymously. He was inexorably linked to discovery of the cap, and Mrs. Quigley's disturbed grave, where his footprints would be found if anybody looked hard enough. There would be questions and suspicions about what else he knew. And what else he had done.

He had played the game as a boy and had been pretty crap at it, but he tried to think like a chess player now. What lay ahead two moves later if he went for a plan A or a plan B? And what would happen to him as a result, four or six moves later? None of the endgame scenarios he envisaged had him winning or even having many pieces left on the board.

Davie returned his remaining *Big Issue* copies to the base

at noon and walked with some other 'vagabondos' who had finished for the day to the Lodging House Mission on East Campbell Street for a hot lunch and some chat. He spent the afternoon walking along the Clyde pathway across river bridges, alternating banks, killing time, no destination in mind. After concluding that there was no best course of action, he focused on what might be the least worst. By the end of the day all that he had decided for definite was that he was wasting time, shilly-shallying, trying to avoid the inevitable.

He was up early next morning and on his way back to the busiest station in Scotland. He wanted to avoid the queues at the station toilet showers. Sunday morning was a peak time at the showers for disarrayed Saturday night drinkers who had awoken in city centre shop doorways or in the wrong house, covered in vomit stains or worse. A detour to wash off what they could from hair, body and clothes was well worth a fiver, to give them at least some semblance of dignity in the taxi or the bus home, and a slightly less disgusted reception from whoever was waiting there.

Davie felt refreshed after his shower. It was five pounds well spent once again.

Revived and ready to make up for lost time, he had at last settled on what he had to do. Walk into Rue End Street station, ask to speak to someone about the missing Mr. Quigley and tell them what he knew. Everything. That was his decision. It was a relief.

The thought of doing it made him feel righteous. When he'd helped Mavis get rid of the unwanted clothes traders and when he'd hauled the bully off the train, he'd felt public spirited, doing the right thing. This was more. This was closer to what he'd been paid for as a cop; detecting crime, maybe even preventing more.

It had taken him the best part of two days, agonising, deciding on a plan, convincing himself that was the only way forward. Then ten minutes later abandoning it as a terrible idea, starting over, reconsidering his options, again and again, arriving back at the same point.

Reporting what he knew was not risk free. His chess-move calculations told him that plan A could go wrong. There was a chance that the cops would shoo him out of the station with comforting words and money for a cup of tea, or lock him in a cell overnight, until the Monday-Friday detectives or the mental health crisis team could question him about his wild story.

Letting them know as soon as possible that he'd been a cop might buy him some credibility and time. He had his Met warrant card number, 206350, memorised and they could verify that easily enough, even if he looked nothing like the guy in the photo now. Yes, that might buy him some time with the cops to explain details about how he came to know what he did about a missing man, and why he was asking for Mrs. Quigley's grave to be dug up to see if Mr. Quigley was in there with his wife. It was all good, a convincing story in his head. Except he knew that it would sound crazy, totally doolally tap when he said it out loud at the police station.

Walking from the station shower towards the train platforms, he added a third possibility to what would happen in plan A, when he presented himself at Rue End Street. There would be no cup of tea, nor a comfy cell for the night. He would instead be put in a police car with an escort and taken straight to the Big Hoose at Ravenscraig, sectioned as in need of immediate care or control. And if that happened, he might be joining a scramble of other patients, all with explanations as long and as urgent as his own, for why they should not be locked up.

When they checked the Met warrant card number he'd been so keen to give them at the police station, word would come back from London that he was, indeed, an ex-Met cop. Other details might come back too. Like how he had some past form for depression, prescribed horse pills, and time off work. It might be enough to make the cops and the white-coated trick cyclists in the Big Hoose wonder if his wild story was a reoccurrence of his breakdown, his paranoid hypervigilance or something worse.

Of course, when Davie explained to them that he'd been living in Greenock cemetery for months, that would reassure everybody about the balanced state of his mental health.

Aye, right.

There were fewer buses to Greenock on Sundays. A new operator, McGill's, had just taken over the route after the previous company, Arriva, abandoned it as loss-making. The new Sunday timetable was still 'bedding in'; a euphemism for the likelihood of Sunday morning buses being cancelled due to drivers calling in sick after Saturday night drinking.

Having made his big decision to talk until he was believed or locked up, Davie didn't want any further transport delays that might give him time to back out. He checked the dot matrix, rail station platform display, saw that there was a train to Greenock in twenty minutes and made the firm decision that he would be on it.

Ticket in hand, Davie passed the station newsagents on his way to the platform and was then distracted by the smell of frying food coming from one of the cafés.

He glanced again at the platform display, wondering whether the time it took to eat a plateful of bacon, sausage, eggs and beans was going to make any difference to the eventual outcome of his visit to the police station and the rest of his life. Probably not, he decided. He would be too late for breakfast in the cells if he was locked up. This might be his last chance for a feed.

Then Davie smiled for the first time in three days as an old quote from schooldays came to him, *"The condemned man ate a hearty breakfast."*

\* \* \*

He'd lost count of all cafés that had refused to serve him since he'd come back from London and he racked his brain, trying to remember if the station café he was headed for was on that list. There were two similar cafes in the station, and he knew for certain that he'd been turfed out of one of them.

*"None of your type here. You'll put the other customers off,"* the guy behind the counter had said, without looking up at him.

Davie had stood his ground for a minute, then backed out the door as the queue grew. If he'd been a different race or had a disability, he knew that he could have taken the guy on, quoting the law. His money was as good as anybody's. He might have won the argument, although he doubted that he'd have left with a coffee in his hand.

Davie looked down at his appearance before pushing open the door. He was freshly showered but still not dressed for any job interview.

Beggar, crusty minger or more nostalgically, by the older generation, tramp or dosser. Being called the names didn't bother him as much as it did when he'd first come back. How he and others were treated still did.

It was the gap between who others saw and who he was that needled him most. He was still the decent, community-minded person that he'd worked so hard to become, helping those who most needed it when he could. OK, he might not look it at first glance, but inside he was the same trustworthy Davie Perdue who'd left Greenock, the same person who'd worked those years in London and the same person who'd come back. Just because he no longer wore a uniform or had a house to live in didn't mean he'd changed, didn't mean that he was fair game for being ignored or treated like litter on the street, didn't mean that his status had switched from someone who had earned respect to someone who now deserved none.

It was down to first impressions, or as Rabbie Burns had said, *"O wad some pow'r the giftie gie us to see oursels as ithers see us!"* Davie had been granted that power to see what others saw. It happened more than once, usually when he was tired. He'd be walking, head down, and glance up to see another homeless man heading towards him. Then he'd look again and see himself reflected in the glass of a shop window. In the few seconds it took for that glance from others, Davie knew many would have him categorised and dismissed, to be avoided at all costs.

Judging the book by the cover. Everybody did it. Davie had looked at plenty of homeless guys and thanked God that he hadn't got to that state yet, without knowing anything about the person.

The smell of bacon brought him back. He still had his hand on door handle of the café. The train he was headed for was gone. Nothing to lose, he thought. Just as he was about to push open the door, there was the clatter of shutters behind him and lights flashed on as the left luggage and lost property office opened for the day. Davie had an idea.

Taking off his coat, he managed to stuff most of it into his shoulder bag, tying the drawstring around the two sleeves sticking out. He paid and put the ticket in his wallet, as the attendant carried his bag to a shelf, holding it out in front of him as if it might be packed with explosives.

Davie opened the top button on his shirt and adjusted his jumper so that it was at least symmetrical on his shoulders. What would the punters in the café see? Not a homeless man carrying all his possession in a tell-tale bag. At a glance up from their plates, he might be somebody dressed casually, travelling to visit Sunday relatives or headed to some out-of-town sports fixture. Maybe.

From behind the food counter, what would the guy serving see of Davie from the waist up? A rough looking guy in a shirt and jumper with a wallet in his hand? Not a regular, but again, not anybody advertising his homeless status.

*"Bacon, sausage, eggs and beans please,"* Davie said, looking down at his wallet, flicking through redundant and expired cards to keep calm.

There was an agonising pause, before the server said, *"You want white or brown toast with that pal?"*

Davie almost blew it by not replying. He'd been ready to be challenged or asked to leave, like so many times before.

*"Eh...brown toast. Thanks very much,"* he said, speaking quickly.

When Davie didn't move, the guy behind the counter looked up. Davie thought the game was up.

*"OK pal. Just find a seat and somebody will bring it over. Next!"*

The breakfast wasn't the best he'd eaten, but it hit the spot. Showered, fed and resolved, he was ready. He didn't go back for his bag in the left luggage. If they locked him up in the station or in the big hoose as a dangerous loony, they'd take the bag from him anyway. If they laughed him off at the police station as a harmless loony, he could come back for the bag.

\* \* \*

The train was quiet, and Davie was calm as it pulled into Greenock West just before noon. He turned left out of the station, striding off, head down, towards Rue End Street.

Then, after a hundred yards, crossed the road and doubled back.

Before he broke his cover and faced the consequences, he wanted just one more look at Jean Anne Quigley's grave in better light, just to be sure.

What if the rainwater had made it look worse than it was? What if the divots on the grave really were swollen from saturation, rather than being freshly dug? Better to convince himself before trying to convince others that his crazy theory might just be true.

He slipped into the cemetery unseen and made his way back to the grave, following paths that he knew well. The rain had stopped and most of the rainwater had drained downhill. The earth around the grave looked the same. It was newly dug, not just swollen. There were the same rough edges, the same square cut divots and the same mound on top to allow for earth sinking after the burial. Except it was a mound which should have settled long before now.

In a final change of plan, Davie went to collect the one solid piece of evidence he had to support his crazy story. He had planned to keep the flat cap as his trump card, to tell the cops about it during his interview to draw them in, get them more interested, then to produce it with a now-do-you-believe-me flourish when he took them back to the cemetery.

But now he was thinking that he would need everything he had going for him if he was to be believed, if he was to bring the cops back to the cemetery with him in the first place. If he had only one shot at it, he had to make it good. It would be too late if he had to go back to Rue End Street station after he'd been seen off the premises, knocking on the door, shouting and waving a wet cap, or if he was rambling on about the significance of a wet cap after he'd been locked up.

He worked his way around to the low table tombstone where he'd left it. An intersecting canopy of branches and leaves protected the tomb and the ground below from rain, and the cap that Davie believed was James Quigley's had dried out as he'd hoped among the pine needles and dry leaves in the time that Davie had been away.

The grass was still wet though, and there was the sound of steady dripping all around. Rain that had fallen many hours ago finally made its way from the highest branches onto the gravestones below. There was no wind and Davie could hear a murmur of voices somewhere far off. Visitors talking, maybe on one of the guided walks around the cemetery. He turned to head downhill and do what he had been planning for the past three days. In the still air, between the crunch of his footsteps on the gravel, he heard a sound that didn't belong.

In the cemetery at night, he heard what he learned were cats and foxes, screeching to claim territory or in search of a mate. There were owls too, and feral pigeons, adding to the late-night screams, making the place sound like a cross between a B horror movie and a maternity ward. But this was sound was different.

It was not the high-pitched animal screams that he knew. It was a low moan, lasting just a few seconds at a time. It faded, there was a pause and it repeated. It was faint and he stopped walking, straining to hear it again. He turned through 180 degrees, trying to identify the direction of the sound. It was somewhere off the path, further up the hill. He clenched the cap tighter in his hand and kept walking downhill. There would be no more putting it off, no more distractions.

But it was no good. He had to know. Even if it was only a trapped fox or a deer. He'd freed a fawn in the cemetery one night on his way back to the basement. It was whimpering like an injured child, its foot caught in a mesh fence.

Davie pocketed the cap and cut across a row of gravestones, going back uphill, past the Quigley grave. The intervals between the low moans had increased and he stopped again, trying to locate the source. He turned his head left then right, checking which ear the sound hit first. He stood still and listened. All he could hear was the background of raindrops working their way down through the leaves.

Continuing to walk uphill, he crossed over another of the cemetery paths, and saw up ahead the solid gable end of Dame Cameron's mausoleum. There was a dry rustle of movement, followed by another sound, more of a sigh than a moan. Davie looked left and right, searching for other possibilities, before admitting that the sound was coming from inside the mausoleum.

He froze.

He was back instantly to a time he hoped he'd forgotten. That dark night five years ago as a cop, chasing the house breaker up at the tempietto, and hearing the child spirit of Margaret Shaw Thomson, banging on the metal sheeting. She wanted out, to let everyone who'd listen know that she didn't want to be pushed to the tempietto in her wheelchair every day and left for hours, alone, condemned by her disability, a silent prisoner.

Did he really hear Margaret Shaw that night? And now, what about Dame Cameron, entombed in the mausoleum. Did she have unsettled business that she wanted to let others know about too? What would he see if he looked in?

He stopped to calm his breathing and to work out what he was hearing and what he was imagining. He felt cold suddenly.

The sound came again, or did it? Was there anything there? Were the deaths of Sophie and Eddie Burton catching up with him again? Had he invented some fantastic story from the cap in his pocket and some newly cast divots on a grave? Was he losing it again, like he had in London, needing to be back on the horse pills? He stopped, trying to think straight, his heart and his head pounding.

Take a beat, he told himself, take a beat. Something he'd been told many times by his old sergeant as a cop. Something he had learned. There were times when the speed of your reactions was tested. You acted fast to stop things getting worse. There were other times, when a pause could save you from jumping in with both feet and doing something that made things worse, much worse.

It was the stress of finding the cap and the Quigley grave and making the decision, eventually, to do the right thing, even if it meant that his life on hold would be over as a result. All that had him jumpy, imagining things. And now he was confused, hearing noises that were only in his head and making up wild stories about dead spirits trapped in tombs.

The sounds from the mausoleum had stopped.

Davie's breathing had returned almost to normal and he turned to leave, looking over his shoulder. There was no harm having a quick look, now that he'd come all the way up the hill, he told himself. Then he'd be able to laugh about it, forget about it and all the distraction and do what he came back for. He took one deep breath and moved forward.

As he stepped to the side of the mausoleum, looking up at the high roof, he tripped over a grave curb buried in the long grass, inaccessible to the gardeners and their mowers. He fell his full length into the rectangular lair enclosed by the low curb stones, barking his shin on the sharp edge of the granite curb at the foot of the grave as he went down, and landing on his shoulder on the unyielding stone chippings that covered the surface of the grave.

"*Shite!*", he said, louder than he had intended.

He got back to his feet, rubbing his shoulder, which had gone numb, and felt a trickle of blood run down his shin. This was stupid. He was hearing imaginary noises and now he had injured himself chasing shadows. Suddenly all he wanted to do was to get back down the hill, into the police station and get all this over. It was something he had been avoiding for the last three days.

But he was already at the front of the vault. He limped forward onto the massive doorstep, and pulled himself up, to look through the padlocked, cast-iron gates into the darkness inside. He felt the rust flakes come off on his hands as he pulled himself higher on the gates to see the section of the tomb inside where the weak sunlight from behind him was reaching the floor. He could just make out a lumpy bundle lying on top of the inscribed ledgerstone slab, laid into the floor in the centre of the room. Davie was easing himself off the gate when he heard two sounds at the same time. There was a sigh of breath from inside the mausoleum, and from behind him there was a creaking sound of leather on leather. A moment later, the light from behind him suddenly dimmed.

Davie turned to look, but it was already too late. The figure casting the shadow was almost on him, swinging. He'd been waiting, holding his spade high, waiting for Davie to take a step back, distracted by what he had seen inside the mausoleum and unguarded.

# – 25 –

## FAILURE TO LIVE BY THE CREED

Alroy the Protector had failed.

He had bottled it last time and he wouldn't let that happen again, ever. If there was a next time, it would be different. He would be true to the creed, no matter what it cost him.

The day that it happened had started out as a simple recce. It ended with him questioning whether he really had what it took to be a street superhero.

It was daytime and he was out of costume, looking for new spots he could patrol in his Neighbourhood Watch Beats 63 and 64, which included Greenock Cemetery.

He hadn't committed a crime that day, but it tormented him as if he had. What made it worse was not having anyone to tell, to come clean and admit his failure to act. There was no street superhero hotline, advice booth or confessional that he could go to for absolution.

He regretted not having someone to fist bump to celebrate his few successes. That was a yearning that came and went, gnawed at him for a while and was then forgotten. But this feeling, this guilt felt worse, far worse. It was with him every time he pulled on his mask, every time he finished an uneventful night patrol without a chance to make up for it.

Since that day, he'd extended his usual patrolling patches, going further, trying to do better. He was a different Alroy, one who was willing to risk even more for the creed. Before, he'd sustained himself on his success, falling back on the memories of his heroics that one dark night, when he saved a woman from being mugged, raped or murdered. Now, he dwelt on his failure. His was weighed down by what he hadn't done that day and what he should have done if he'd been a real street superhero. He was ashamed. He became more and more desperate to put it right.

For the first time in his street superhero career, he started to go out in daylight as well as during the night. Maybe it was to atone, to increase his chances of a heroic act that would make up for what had happened.

Crime happens in daylight too, he told himself, and he could be there to prevent it. He went in the daylight, in the few hours he had between his Tesco night shifts, his Alroy night shifts and sleep, taking his outfit in a bag, changing out of sight and staying out of sight, but always ready for action.

In daylight, there was too much risk of being seen on patrol, so he'd pick a good, quiet spot, get changed there and watch for anything that didn't look right. Increasingly, he was drawn back to where it happened, when he'd been on his recce that day, looking for Alroy the Protector hiding spots.

He'd seen the man with the tyre iron come around the blind side of the mausoleum where he'd been hiding and smack the other man from behind as he was about to pass over the bag he was holding. The man beside him had shouted, *"Rab..."* but that was as much as he got out, and it didn't help. Rab had taken his hand out of his pocket and was looking towards the shout as the swinging tyre iron hit him. There was dull thud as it connected with the side of his head and Rab, who never saw it coming, went down like a sack of tatties.

That was the point at which Alroy should have sprung into action. *"Prevent criminal activity where possible and stop it personally when it was ongoing."* That was the creed. That was the creed. That was the time for action.

He started to step out to the side of the tree he'd been testing as a good hiding spot, just as the other two men grabbed the man who had shouted to warn Rab and forced him face down onto the grass. Before he could make any sound and before Alroy the Protector or even Ruairidh the redhead could stop further criminal activity personally, the man with the tyre iron threw it to one side, pulled a knife from his pocket and started stabbing the man being held on the ground. Ruairidh saw the knife go into his back, again and again, the stabber twisting it each time. He heard a few grunts from the man being stabbed, muffled by the grass, then only the sound the of the knife. Shunk! Shunk! Shunk!

Ruairidh fell, rather than stepped back behind his tree, frozen. Alroy had deserted him at the sight and sound of real violence. This was not the *Kapow! Splat! Blam!* of his DC comics. Hunched there on the wet grass, he reverted to Ruairidh the shop worker, caught in the wrong place and out of costume.

He had never seen anything so brutal, and it terrified him.

He pressed his back up against the broad tree. There was no superhero planning, no thoughts of leaping back out, knuckles on hips, ready to right the wrongs. His single, bowel-loosening thought was that what had just happened to the two men in less than a minute could just as easily happen to Ruairidh Logan Mackay in the next minute if he made any sound.

So he sat there in the wet grass, biting his hand to stifle his crying, like a frightened wee boy, doing nothing. He listened to the scrape of dead feet as the men dragged first one man then the other from the mausoleum, back towards the car park. He waited another fifteen minutes, cowering, convinced that they'd seen him and were just waiting, silently, for movement, so they could jump him and clean up the loose end.

After stealing a quick look around either side of the tree, he stumbled out, his legs stiff and twitching as he walked, the shock of what he'd seen still flooding his system. He spent another half hour inside the cemetery, taking a winding route back to the front gate to avoid being spotted by any visitors, or by the murderers who might still be lying in wait for him.

After walking about for another hour, he slipped the key in his front door and crept up to his room. His stealth was unnecessary. His father was in his usual chair, his snoring like somebody sawing through a particularly stubborn knot in a piece of wood.

He tried to get some more sleep before his Tesco shift, but it was hopeless.

He had failed to live by the creed and now he was in uncharted water. There was nothing in the DC comic wisdom of *The Flash* or *Green Lantern* or *Nightwing* to guide him. Of course, there wasn't. Since none of them would ever have broken the creed and found themselves in his position. If any of the superheroes knew him as well as he knew them, they would have been disappointed, very disappointed. Almost as disappointed as he was in himself.

Putting his body on the line to protect others, as required by his DC and street superheroes? Failed. Not thinking twice about the dangers of doing the right thing? Failed. Taking the blows to save the innocents? Also failed. Superhero marks out of ten? Zero.

Ruairidh lay in his bed going over the day, and what he *should* have done. He came up with many, increasingly daring, street superhero alternatives to cowering behind the tree, almost peeing himself. All the while, a quiet voice in his head mocked him. *Shoulda, woulda, coulda*, it chanted. The voice repeated, louder, with every new, Alroy-saves-the-day scenario that he thought of.

The butchery he had seen was still fresh. Two men, one battered, one stabbed and then both dragged off, God knows where. He was the only one there to see it. Was there any blood or brains left behind to prove what had happened? Anything he could point to?

If he reported it to the police as Ruairidh, how would it sound? Like he was some saddo who had made it all up to seem important, a Tesco shelf stacker who made up stories about helping police fight crime, hoping to get his name in the papers. He could just see the cops sitting there, exchanging looks as they interviewed him.

*"There might be evidence at the scene of the crime, you say? Aye, sure son. We'll get our best forensic team on it right away, see if we can find the DNA and track down those pesky murderers."*

If he reported what he'd seen as Alroy the Protector, it would be even worse. Even if they did believe him, they might ask how come he knew so much about it, and what the hell he was doing there in the cemetery in the first place, hiding behind a tree? Did he do that a lot? Did he like watching people during the day? What about at night? Just men and women, or children too?

Then he'd have to explain about how he lived by the creed, going out in his costume and patrolling his beat, protecting the weak, preventing crime. And when he thought about saying that out loud, to the cops, it didn't sound nearly as good as when he said it to himself.

Who was going to believe what Alroy the Protector or Ruairidh had seen?

He had bottled it then, and two men had died.

# – 26 –

## BATMAN AND RUAIRIDH

Davie dropped his shoulder and the first blow glanced off his side. There was a dull thud as the flat of the spade made contact with his ribs on its way down, knocking him back. His attacker came forward then, chopping the air with the spade like it was a samurai. Davie was fast enough to draw back from the second blow and the blade hit the ground and cut into the soft earth by his feet.

Then his police muscle memory kicked in.

*"Defence against a club or a baseball bat was ideally done by grabbing the weapon with one hand and grabbing the attacker's wrist firmly with the other."*

Easier said than done, when his shoulder was still aching from his fall, and he could already feel the muscles down his side stiffening from that first blow.

His attacker walked forward again, calmly, pausing to re-adjust his two-handed hold on the spade.

Not a word had been spoken between the two men. Davie looked at the man then, as they paused, taking the chance to size him up. Apart from the movements of the spade, which Davie followed warily, his attention was drawn to his attacker's strange leather trousers, creaking every time he shifted his position. At first, Davie thought they were leather chaps for bronco-riding, and he almost lost concentration, puzzling why a cowboy would be trying to kill him in a cemetery.

The man with the spade took another step forward and as he did, there was the sharp snap of twigs from the other side of the mausoleum.

Alroy made his entrance from behind the large gravestone where he'd been hiding. Davie and his attacker stood frozen and looked at him as he stood there, knuckles on hips.

*"I'm Ruairidh the Protector,"* he announced.

It just came out. He was so shit scared of what had happened before and what he'd just seen that he'd mixed up the names.

Davie and his attacker both looked at him and had the same thought, but it was Jamie who said it out loud.

*"Well buckaroo bugaboo, who the fuck are you?"*

Jamie took one step back looking from Ruairidh to Davie.

*"Are you two eedjits in this together, like some kind of seedy Batman and Robin gay lovers deal?"* he said, shaking his head.

He lowered the spade a bit and sighed.

*"Yous shouldnae be here. Neither of you. You've just fucked this up for me and now I'm gonne have to fuck you both up."*

*"Just stop! Stop that now. Police have been called,"* shouted Alroy the Protector, now fully back in role and on script.

Jamie looked him up and down.

*"You got a phone on that utility belt of yours have you, fatman Batman?"* he said, derisively.

*"And you've already phoned the Gotham City cops, have you?"*

He turned back to Davie, repositioning his feet and his grip on the spade. He spoke to Ruairidh again but kept all of his focus on Davie.

*"I don't think so pal. You haven't phoned anybody because you just got here. Now why don't you just fuck off back to pretend world, before you get hurt?"*

Davie spoke for the first time.

*"I don't know who he is. He's got nothing to do with this,"* he said, moving back, keeping out of range of the spade.

*"It's just me you've got to worry about."*

*"I don't need to worry about anybody ya bawbag,"* said Jamie, his voice rising as he spoke.

*"It's you that should be worried. You're in the wrong place and now I'm gonne have to do something about that."* As he finished speaking, specks of saliva were flying from his mouth.

Davie replied evenly while taking another step backwards.

*"You don't have to do anything,"* he said. *"We can work out whatever's wrong here before anybody gets hurt."*

His attention on Jamie was diverted for a moment, as Ruairidh took a step forward. Davie wondered where the carrot top with the mask and the gardening gloves fitted into the story. Was he a possible ally or just some coincidental sideshow in the wrong place at the wrong time who might get hurt?

He rubbed at his shoulder where he had fallen, trying to get some feeling and mobility back into it for whatever came next. He knew that if the spade landed just one more blow, he was finished. He might be able to block the next strike with his forearm. That would save his head but leave him with a broken arm or worse, and then he'd be knocked to the ground or left defenceless. Either way, it would be easy for the guy with the leathers to move in for the kill.

Jamie starting circling, trying to back Davie against the mausoleum, cutting off his escape route.

*"You talk too much, pal, and now you've seen way too much. I've been watching you, sniffing around the graves down the hill there, sticking your nose where it doesnae belong. Then up here, at the mausoleum, like a dog on a scent. What are you, some kind of graveyard groupie who gets off on dead folk?"*

Davie kept moving to the side, glancing at the long grass for anything that he might trip over, or anything he could use as a weapon.

He spoke again, his voice still calm, much calmer than he felt.

*"I haven't seen anything. I was just walking through the cemetery when I heard the noises up here. If there's somebody injured inside the mausoleum, we need to help them before it's too late. Then we can all go back to what we were doing."*

Jamie laughed, a loud double snort through his nose.

*"Go back to what we were doing? Go back to what we were doing?"* his voice getting louder again.

*"Are you fucking kidding me? How stupid d'ye think I am? I know what you've seen, and I know what you think I've done. And now we're just going on wi' our lives like nothing happened? I don't think so."*

He was almost screaming as he finished, his knuckles white as he gripped the shaft and handle of the spade tighter. He stooped lower, widening his stance.

*"Everybody ends up in a grave. Some sooner, some later, and some soon enough,"* he said, just loud enough for Davie to hear.

Ruairidh was rooted to the spot, looking from one man to the other, frantically trying to catch up. It was like one of his

TV programmes, where he had lost the plot after ten minutes, except this time he'd missed the beginning and he was coming in midway through, trying to figure out who was who and what had happened.

The man with the spade had done something, maybe hit somebody, maybe with the spade. Maybe it was whoever was still making noises inside the mausoleum. He got that. If Ruairidh reached for his phone which was in his back pocket, not his utility belt, he might be next, if the man with the spade didn't kill the rough looking guy first.

He was terrified. Again. Standing in his knuckles-on-hips pose, too scared to move.

It was the same as before, except this time the guy was swinging a spade instead of a tyre iron or a knife, and this time Ruairidh had blown his cover early and it was too late to creep back behind a tree or a gravestone until it was all over, then disappear.

Whatever was going to happen next, only he would see it. And only he could do anything about it and if he did he might get hurt, seriously hurt.

Davie thoughts were racing; skipping between the raised spade, where his attacker was moving, where he was putting his feet, the guy in the costume and what Davie would have done if this had happened when he was on a police call out in London. Bits and pieces of training came back to him.

*"When faced with a baseball bat, a billiard cue or a golf club, if it is not possible to grab the weapon and the attacker's wrist, your feet are sometime your best defence. Heed the moment that you can get away from the situation, and then create distance. In other words, don't try to be a hero."*

Before Jamie could swing the spade again, Davie turned and started sprinting downhill.

The last time he had run anywhere had been in London, six months before. It had been a foot pursuit, weighed down by his stab vest and jiggling equipment accessories, but still fit enough to catch most rabbits, suspects who had legged it. As he took off through the wet trees downhill, the panic that fuelled his legs was the realisation that for the first time in his adult life he was being chased.

As Jamie shifted the spade into one hand and turned to go after Davie, he pointed at Ruairidh with his free hand.

*"And you, superman, had better not tell anybody but God about what you've seen, 'cause otherwise, I'll find you and I will fucking kill you. You can be sure of that."*

# – 27 –

## TO FOLLOW THE DEVIL OR TO FOLLOW JESUS

To follow the devil or to follow Jesus? That's the question all those bible thumpers in the street asked disinterested passers-by, waving copies of *Awake!* and *The Watchtower*. Bit of a loaded question, in Jamie's view.

There was no middle ground, according to them. You were either on one bus or on the other. It was a bit like following the Almighty Glasgow Rangers or following the Almighty Glasgow Celtic. If you rejected one, it meant you were seen as automatically signing up to follow the other one.

Jesus or the devil? That was bullshit. There had to be more to it than that.

Jamie had tried to speak with two of the Christian wackos once. Two, because they were always in pairs, mob handed for God. He was in the High Street, and they were manning a stand that read, *"Do you have questions about God, Eternity and your Soul?"* And, as it happened, Jamie did have a question about just that.

It was about his brother, and it was a question that he really wanted answered back then. He was young and daft at the time and stuff had happened that he didn't understand. Nobody else in his family had been able to give him an answer. The question he had was a simple one.

Although he had a different surname to Francis because their mother had remarried, Jamie always looked up to Francis as his big brother, his real big brother, not his half-brother. Francis was dead at fifteen, pinned to a tree in the cemetery on a wet Saturday night after a stupid gang test went wrong. If Jamie had been able to get past the cop that came to his house that wet night all those years ago, he would have tracked down the Burdy Boys, and squeezed the life out of them, one at a time.

Yes, Jamie's question was a simple one, but nobody could give him a straight answer.

*"What had Francis done to deserve that?"*

So, he had nervously blurted out the question to Mr. and Mrs. Evangelist when he reached their holy stand.

They listened, nodded, and then turned his question into something else. The man had jumped in first. His suit was from the 1970s, with a shirt and tie that might have been worn to catch the eye of passers-by on the other side of the street.

*"What you're asking, I think, young man, is a question asked by many who are suffering like you, and that is, 'How can a God of love send anyone to Hell?'"*

Well, sorry, but no, that was not the question he had asked. Fuck all like it in fact.

They were twisting his words. Nobody had even mentioned Hell up until then.

Then the woman piled on. By that time, Jamie was more confused, and sorry that he had asked anything. Although she was smiling at him, nodding reassuringly, coming closer, what she was saying was scaring him.

*"It is only those who reject Christ who will be sent to Hell. People go to Hell only if they do not repent, only if they don't follow God's perfect plan of salvation."*

That didn't help him. He had gone from being puzzled about why Francis had died, to visions of Francis in Hell. Was that because he had died in a cemetery? Because he was there at night? Because he was responsible for his own death? More questions to scratch at the inside of his young head, but no answers.

Jamie was backing off, as both the bible thumpers closed in on him, telling him about *"unsaved sinners"* and making it very clear, even to a naïve teenager, that he might well be one of them.

Was it from then, he wondered, that far back, that his path was decided? Is that what made up his mind not to follow Jesus and, by default, to follow the team in black instead?

All these years later, he was now wondering whether that could be a good defence if he ever got caught?

*"See, I didn't know what I was doing. It was the devil that made me do it. I'm an unsaved sinner."*

That might work. It might at least get him some easy time in the nuthouse, rather than longer, hard time in jail.

\* \* \*

His first one had been spur of the moment. He had not planned it and Old Nick had definitely not been sitting on one of his shoulders, urging him on.

He'd seen the old guy visiting every day, moping about. It didn't bother Jamie at first. It only got to him after the second week, when he was having to escort the old codger out of the cemetery before he could close the gate and go home.

His wife had died. OK, Jamie got that. It was sad as fuck and the old guy was upset, crying everyday into the same snottery hankie, which was the size of a pillowcase. Jamie had suffered loss too. He knew what it was like. But pining at the graveside for hours on end, like he was Greyfriars Bobby? There comes a point when it's time to move on, even when you're nearly dead yourself and you don't have much to move on to.

It was sometime during that third week that Jamie found himself again walking up the hill to where he knew he would find old Mr. Mickelson standing or kneeling by his wife's grave. He would have to walk him back down the hill at the old man's shuffling pace, then lock the gate, and that meant getting another late finish. More unpaid overtime, when he was only being paid buttons for the hours that he already worked.

It was an act of kindness. That's what he told himself later, and that was what he believed still. Old Mr. Mickelson had nothing to look forward to but years of missing his wife and whatever their life had been, then more years of sitting in an artificial leather highchair, pissing and shitting himself in some desolate care home until he died. That's not what Jamie would want, he decided, when his time came. Much better to have a quick end, not long years of dying by the day.

So, without really thinking about it, he swung the spade he was carrying, hitting the kneeling old man on the back of the head, hard. There was little noise as he went down.

Jamie shocked himself when he did it, but he had no regrets afterwards.

There was nobody about. Jamie dragged the body into the undergrowth, then calmly walked down the hill and locked up for the night. That gave him the uninterrupted time he needed to take the turfs off Mrs. Mickelson's grave, remove enough of the soil that was covering the coffin, spread it around and then add Mr. Mickelson to the family plot. Nobody had paid for a family plot, so it was an extra kindness on his part, he thought.

The soil displaced by Mr. Mickelson's body he scattered at the base of nearby trees, and the grave was far enough from the main paths that the fresh digging wouldn't be noticed before the grass rooted again.

Jamie put his shirt back on and walked home.

He did Mr. Quigley the same way. He'd been grieving for just ten days, but it would have turned into two weeks, then four, Jamie told himself, then six.

Why the police made such a hullaballoo about Mr. Quigley going missing but not about old Mr. Mickelson, Jamie never understood, and of course he never asked. The cops never came near the cemetery looking for either of the missing men.

By the time Jamie decided that Mrs. Bilston should also be helped on her way, he had given up wondering whether he was following the devil, following Jesus, or tuning in to some other radio station.

Each time he did it, he became detached. He could see himself swing the spade, like he was standing nearby, watching it happen. It was like he was playing for both teams at those moments; an angel of death carrying out God's mercy killings but doing it in a way that the devil would approve.

Mrs. Bilston had been trickier for two reasons. First, because she saw him and second because Cecil Bertram, full time Be-reavement Services Manager and part time nosey old bastard, had heard her scream.

Jamie's timing had been off by just two minutes, he calculated later. Cecil must have been almost out the side gate, after lining up all the pencils and papers on his desk before leaving, when he heard the scream.

*"Hello? Who's there? Do you need help?"*

Jamie heard the distant crunch of Cecil's sensible brogues on the path before he heard him shout and realised who it was.

Mrs. Bilston had been kneeling. She'd spun round just as he swung the spade and he'd caught her on the shoulder and side of the face, knocking her to the ground. It was a heavy blow, but not a killshot.

*"Keep the head. Keep the head. Keep the head,"* he repeated to himself as he dragged her silently across the grass and bundled her unconscious body into Dame Cameron's mausoleum. He relocked the gate on the mausoleum and was just clear of it, when Cecil appeared, walking down the path.

*"Oh, it's you Mr. Bruce,"* Cecil said, looking at Jamie and glancing at the spade, now under his arm.

*"I thought I heard someone shout. Sounded more like a scream, actually."*

*"Yes, I was just finishing off for the day, Mr. Bertram. Heard it myself and came up here to find out what was happening,"* Jamie said, looking at the end of the spade to check for any blood.

Behind him, he heard movement. The scraping of the small stones on the floor of the mausoleum. Mrs. Bilston was moving. He looked at Cecil for a reaction, but the other man was looking off to one side and didn't appear to have heard anything.

*"Seemed to come from this direction,"* Jamie said, walking briskly past Cecil and hoping he would follow. After a pause, he did.

Jamie walked down one of the smaller paths, leading Cecil away from the mausoleum, then stopped suddenly.

*"You smell that, Mr. Bertram?"* he said, lifting his chin and sniffing left and right.

Cecil looked at him, then to either side of the path, confused. *"Smell what?"* he said.

*"Fox,"* Jamie said, crouching down on one knee of his motorbike trousers, rubbing his hand on the path and sniffing it.

*"Definitely a fox. I think that's what we both heard."*

Cecil moved to where Jamie was crouched and bent over, sniffing.

*"They scream when they're randy Mr. Bertram, to attract the lady foxes, or is it the foxy ladies?"* Jamie said in a lower voice, chuckling at his own joke.

*"Oh,"* Cecil managed, standing up straight again, *"I think I can smell something now that you've mentioned it. It's a kind of musky odour, isn't it?"*

Cecil bluffed to hide his embarrassment. He couldn't smell anything, and he didn't know whether he was made more uncomfortable by not knowing what a fox smelled like, not knowing that foxes screamed, or by the coarse gravedigger's reference to animal sex.

*"Yeah, you've got it now Mr. Bertram,"* said Jamie, walking him still further from the mausoleum.

*"We've both been fooled by crafty Mr. Fox there."*

*"Yes, I think so, Mr. Bruce. I'm glad that we've sorted that out,"* said Cecil, buttoning his coat and regaining his composure.

*"I'll just walk with you to the main gate so that you can lock up. We can both go out that way tonight,"* he continued, reasserting his role as a manager.

*"Eh... Sure, yeah, we can do that,"* said Jamie.

There was no way around it. He was going to have to leave

Mrs. Bilston overnight and finish the job next day. He couldn't risk coming back in after he'd locked the gates.

She would probably die. He had landed a fair whack, she was old, and she was bleeding from a head wound. Dying would be best for both of them. Or he could finish her off next day when it was quiet. Either way, she was going nowhere that night, and nobody would hear her, locked in the mausoleum.

## 28

## SHIFTING SANDS

Davie moved fast, knowing the layout of the cemetery and driven by the thought that if Jamie got within striking distance and struck him from behind it was over. He had no fancy, police college self-defence moves to pull out of the bag to change that. To his advantage, he had the jump on Jamie by running when he'd been expected to fight, and he had created a bit of distance between them. That was the best he could do. Plus, he was running with a purpose.

If he could make it to the Goalkeeper's House and get inside the basement, he could hold the doors. Not great, and not a long-term solution, but still better that having his skull caved in with a heavy-duty spade in the next ten minutes.

Ruairidh's only movement as he stood staring at Jamie, was the involuntary trembling of his hands, still held on his hips. Jamie had glanced once at the frozen figure, made his decision, and headed off down the hill. The ratty guy getting away was the greater threat. He could come back and deal with the dummy in the costume later, if he moved fast enough.

*"Nah, I couldnae catch a bus,"* was Jamie's stock, joke reply to anybody who asked him, *"All that gravedigging must keep you fit then?"*

But he wasn't running for a bus now. This was a different kind of running. In that moment, Jamie's legs forgot about the twenty cigarettes a day he smoked and the many hours each day that his legs spent sitting down. He was running for his life, or what would be left of it if the nosy, minging bastard made it out of the cemetery and blew the whistle on him.

He threw himself into it, taking giant strides over the wet ground, focused on the target. He was gaining fast as they neared the bottom of the hill and the boarded-up house that stood there. The homeless guy hadn't looked back once. As he emerged from the last of the trees, Jamie took a firmer grip on the spade, calculating when he would be in range and trying to decide whether to bring down his prey with a chop to the back or the legs and then finish him off, or just go for his trademark killshot across the back of the head.

When he was just eight feet behind him, Jamie saw his target do some crazy zig zag hopping across the massive puddle by the cemetery wall. Probably crapping himself, Jamie thought, trying to dodge the blow that he knew was coming. Jamie got the spade above his head, both hands on the shaft, close to the handle, ready to strike.

And that's when things went wrong.

As he put his weight on his front foot to swing the spade, he sank shin-deep into the mud. He brought his trailing foot forward and planted it to get leverage to push himself out, and it went even deeper.

As he struggled, the smell of what he was standing in was on him. There was a thin layer of rainwater and floating soil on top, but as he pulled on one foot, a wet brown slurry with veins of black, permeated with years of fermented decay came to the surface. Jamie gagged as he breathed in the stench, ripe and strong.

Davie's plan, to get inside the basement and hold the door, wasn't going to work. When he got close enough to the Goalkeeper's House, he saw some of the good work that the tree fellers had done the previous day, when he been in Glasgow, dillydallying, putting off making a decision. The trunk of a fungus-infected cypress tree that had been felled lay across both doors to the basement. The tree had cracked one of the wooden doors and he could see by its size, even at a distance, that he wouldn't be able to move it.

In the seconds it took him to realise that he wasn't getting into the basement, he was moving so fast that he was already at the edge of the swirling pool of mud and rainwater. All he had left was Mr. Marshall's history class and what to do when being chased by a sabre-toothed tiger or a nine-foot bear.

He could hear Jamie behind him, panting with exertion, or maybe with the excitement of the kill. If he turned to look, it might be five seconds that he lost and regretted. Without pausing he skidded rather than stepped his way across the hidden piles of stones, his underwater path, memorised through repetition. He made it to the basement door and clambered onto the trunk of the downed cypress, desperate for any height advantage it might give him. Chopped in the knees then killed, instead of chopped in the back first? Not much of an advantage.

That was when he looked back, and saw Jamie, knee deep in the glaur, sinews on his neck straining as he tried to pull out a foot.

*"Bastard, bastard, bastard!"* he shouted. Which was legally true in Davie's case, but not why Jamie was shouting it.

He jerked his upper body from side to side, trying to free himself. The struggling only allowed the mud vacuum to suck him deeper. Within a few minutes he had one leg submerged to the knee and only the top of the calf on his other leg was above the surface of the smooth mud slurry. He slapped the spade horizontally onto the mud and pushed on the shaft with both hands, trying to lever himself clear. The spade disappeared beneath the mud instantly.

Jamie's shouts of anger turned then to higher pitched screams of frustration and desperation.

*"Help me, ya bastard. Quick! Dae something before I drown here!"*

Davie had not moved from his spot on the fallen tree. He looked at Jamie but did not reply. After three days of rain, how far down would Jamie sink? Davie thought that he knew the answer, but it was a big risk to take.

Just then, Davie caught a waft of the smell that Jamie was stirring up. His frenzied attempt to free himself was churning up more of the mud, releasing long-buried, rotted matter that was mixing with oxygen at the surface, producing fetid gases that even Jamie had never smelled, in all his years as a gravedigger. Jamie gagged twice, then threw up.

He stopped struggling for a moment, looking at what had been a bacon and egg roll mixing with the surface mud. Then, growing desperate, he resorted to launching the upper half of his body back, then forward, frantically trying to prevent it sinking any further. After two minutes of that however, he was reduced to distressed rocking back and forward, as the liquid around him crept up over his thighs.

The shouting had changed to higher pitched whimpers,

more like a dog than a man. He was half-heartedly slapping the water around him, trying to find one of the stepping stones that he now realised Davie had used to do his Jesus act, walking across the surface. To his left and behind him he reached one of the stones, but only succeeded in pulling off the top slab in a pile of five, which sank instantly.

Davie looked at the branches on the felled cypress tree, wondering if any of them could be bent far enough to reach Jamie. Then he saw the thick veins of ivy that had wrapped themselves around the trunk. Could one of those be strong enough to let him pull himself out if Davie threw it to him?

He had watched Jamie struggle, while struggling with his own dilemma, standing up then sitting down again on the trunk of the cypress tree, undecided. If he pulled Jamie out, then what? He wasn't going to thank Davie for saving his life, put his wrists out in front of him and say, *"It's a fair cop, guv."* If Davie worked his way back across the stepping stones and tried to haul him out, getting hauled in was more likely than any rescue. And if he did get out, Jamie would still try to kill Davie to shut him up.

Mr. Marshall, history teacher, had given Davie the idea for the stepping stones, but it was another teacher, Mr. Cram in physics, that Davie had to thank for calculating that Jamie wouldn't drown.

Davie finally climbed down onto the cellar door and took a step forward. Jamie was buried almost to the waistband of his motorbike trousers. He was no longer struggling, and he had stopped sinking.

*"An object will float if it is less dense than the liquid into which it is placed."*

Another piece of totally useless information had stuck somehow and had become significant all these years later in a time of crisis. The density of the mixture of mud and all the toxic crap that was in it was greater than the density of Jamie's body. He had stopped sinking, having reached a stable equilibrium, better known as half-in, half-oot, and more commonly seen when a rotten egg floats in water.

Davie had gambled on physics and won. He had waited it out for ten minutes. If Jamie had sunk further, defying the laws of physics, Davie would have acted and got him out. He would have done it somehow, despite the risk of being pulled in, or pushed back in by Jamie when they were both clear. He couldn't just sit there and watch somebody drown in that mud, no matter the danger to himself.

Now he weighed up his chances of getting past Jamie's grasping hands and getting clear. Whatever happened next, his residence in the basement of the Goalkeeper's House had come to an end.

As he was sizing up his best route past Jamie, the cavalry came riding over the hill.

He saw a flash of red first, out of the corner of his eye. Looking up, he made out three figures coming through the trees. Alroy in his bright cycling top was taking the lead, and two cops with their hats off, were trailing just behind, cursing as they pushed noisily through wet branches. As they got closer, Davie could hear the voices.

*"This way, just down here!"* Alroy shouted.

The cop on his left took another wet branch in the face as it sprang back from Alroy's shoulder as he led the charge.

*"Bloody hell. How much further?"* the cop complained.

To Davie's ears, it was not the sounds of an urgent rescue mission in the prevention of a serious crime. It sounded more like a child urging reluctant parents towards some fairground attraction.

Before they got any closer, Davie took his chance. With Jamie distracted by the approaching voices, he stepped deftly across the stones and out of sight behind trees at the cemetery wall.

In all that followed, everybody knew something, but nobody ever had all the information.

## 29

## CLEAN UP ON AISLE SIX

Neither Alroy in his costume, nor Ruairidh without it, when he was brought back to the station for further questioning, was able to answer all of the questions put to him.

He was able to tell the cops what had happened between the "rough sleeper" – what the cops were calling Davie, based on Ruairidh's description – and the man with the spade at the mausoleum, but not why. He was able to explain how he came to know that Mrs. Bilston was inside the mausoleum and injured, but not how she got there. He did begin by trying to tell them about living by the creed of the street superhero, but he saw quickly that it was like the cops were watching one of his difficult to follow TV programmes. He could tell that they had lost the plot after ten minutes, because they asked him to go back to the beginning, again and again.

Ruairidh was the only witness the police had, to any of the many crimes that may or may not have been committed. The rough sleeper that Ruairidh described resembled the person of interest in the old E-fit poster, still on the board at the police station, but Ruairidh was the only person who claimed to have seen him.

Jamie was 'no commenting' every question. Greenock's Fire Service had managed to dig him out of the fetid mud, after the cops' efforts with a rope around his chest had almost dislocated his shoulders.

He was charged first with the attempted murder of Mrs. Bilston, who had survived her night in the mausoleum and recovered, following two weeks in hospital. Then there was a further charge of killing Mr. Quigley, when the police found his hat near the disturbed grave where Davie had tossed it on his run downhill. Following a systematic check of other recently dug graves in the cemetery, charges in relation to Mr. Mickelson were added.

The following week, *The Digger*'s used its characteristic journalistic licence to shift a few extra copies. The frontpage headline read, *"Mad Gravedigger Who Buried Bodies in Cemetery Trapped By Quicksand."*

The *Greenock Reporter* took a different, local angle and was more conservative in its reporting of the same events. *"Cemetery Murder Suspect Arrested,"* and a subheading which read, *"Street superhero helps solve missing persons mystery."*

In the publicity following the case, Ruairidh was outed as Alroy the Protector and photographed in his costume for the story in the *Greenock Reporter* and a smaller piece in the *Glasgow Herald*. Given the minor role that Ruairidh had played in the apprehension of the cemetery murderer, and how little was known about disappearing Davie, journalists struggled to find enough real content to fill their columns and were reduced to speculation to fill in the blanks. None of the guesses at the full story were close to all that had happened.

As the story lost momentum, there were strained media

comparisons between Alroy the Protector and Marvel Comics superheroes. Police repeated their previous comments on the case, encouraging people to act as the extra eyes and ears for the police, like Alroy, but not to take the law into their own hands, like vigilantes.

When Ruairidh turned up nervously for his first Tesco night shift after Jamie's arrest and the newspaper reports, he had three high fives from workers in the staff room, and a quiet fist bump from Alex. In the days that followed, some of the other night staff took the piss, of course:

*"Gonne leap up and clean the dust off those high shelves Ruairidh?"*

*"I think I saw somebody nick a tin of beans there, superhero. Had you no better get your kit on and fly oot the door after them?"*

*"Clean up needed on aisle six. Who ya gonna call?"*

His father had only two questions for him. He asked Ruairidh how long he'd been playing at Batman and if he was getting paid for it. He also told him that he didn't want any journalists coming to the house, asking questions, unless they were offering him money for an interview. When none did, he lost interest and went back to his old routine.

Ruairidh could take all the ragging, at home and at work. One of the cops told him, after all the interviews were over, that his phone call – on his Motorola T191 – probably saved Mrs. Bilston's life. Another hour in the mausoleum and she would not have made it. Knowing that, the high fives and the fist bump were enough to keep him going as Alroy the Protector, although he did revert to operating at night only.

\* \* \*

In the weeks that followed, major and minor crime in Greenock continued unabated. The *"Mad Gravedigger"* case took up whatever time local detectives could find. Some cases got less attention as a result.

Both his brothers and Jake had made it their mission to find Noah. Without Noah at the helm and without product to sell, the dealing and the Vale family business was collapsing, as the Vales focused all of their efforts on getting information about what had happened to Noah, and Rab, from old customers.

Just because he was still missing after months didn't mean Noah was dead. He was probably just lying low. Noah wasn't the type who could walk out of one life and into another and never look back. His brother Matthew repeated this to anyone who would listen.

If Noah was swanning about in Málaga or Estepona, keeping his tattoos well hidden, he'd be too tempted not to send a wee postcard or a Christmas card home. Nothing to identify him to his brothers or the police, just a picture of some sunny coastal scenery to let them all know what they were missing.

But neither Noah nor Rab would ever be found. On the day they disappeared, the strains of *"The Day Thou Gavest, Lord, is Ended"* had drifted across the crematorium car park as Noah's body was crammed with some difficulty into the boot of the Glasgow dealers' Ford Sierra. Rab had been bundled into the boot of the second car, which had arrived with its driver and his weapons before Noah and Rab. Both cars had been driven at speed out of town and two miles down an unnamed road that dead ended at Marchfield Farm.

The Glasgow dealers had decided that having to deal with the Vales *and* the Moores in Greenock was getting messy. It was one operation too many. They had scored big from the heroin meeting with Noah Vale and Rab. The Glasgow dealers took the shoulder bag of money from Rab and sold the heroin brick it was meant to pay for to the Moores the following week, no questions asked.

For a handful of the cash in Rab's shoulder bag, the farmer at Marchfield turned a blind eye and allowed use of his power tools. The Glasgow dealers chopped up Noah and Rab and fed them to the farmer's 600-pound Berkshire pigs.

Exchange of bricks and money at the mausoleum stopped. It had become too busy. Jamie Bruce's trial had brought more dark tourism to the cemetery and the photos of the mausoleum in the papers had made it a hot spot for selfies. Drug deals were done instead at one of the many deserted 'enterprise zones' on the edge of town, where empty industrial units waited for start-ups, or at garden centre car parks, where the sole focus of other visitors' attention was on the next available parking space.

At Jamie's trial, when asked how he intended to plead to the charges he faced, rather than the traditional *"guilty"* or *"not guilty"*, Jamie blurted out, *"Euthanasia, your honour,"* before his defence lawyer and the judge shut him up.

Sam was cleared of any involvement in Jamie's crimes. He continued to work in the rain, wind and snow for another year with a new gravedigging partner, before taking up a warmer job in the crematorium, having gained his national certificate for Cemetery Operatives and Crematorium Technicians.

Ruairidh and Alex too, were promoted, from their posts as *Replenishment Associates (Nights)*. They were recognised by Tesco as, *"warm, reliable, team-players, who are flexible, amenable and can work at pace."* Translated from the HR job spec, this meant that they turned up, did the job well and never phoned in sick, which made them stand out from the majority of staff on the night shift. Consequently, they were both offered positions as *Tesco Colleagues*, working the day shift. This meant giving up the night premium in their wages, and the warm Tesco night worker fleeces, but it also meant giving up living like vampires, rarely seeing sunshine or other people who lived by day.

Ruairidh and Alex had a brief chat about it, together, then with the day shift manager. The chats they had together were frequent by then, but still seldom long. They agreed that they were both ready to face the day shift and customers, with all that might bring, good and bad. The day shift manager agreed to their request to be put on the same shifts for the first few weeks at least, until they found their feet. That worked out OK.

\* \* \*

By that time Davie was long gone. He was once again a person of interest, and he would also have been a missing person if anyone had known his name.

His hair was growing back. As he looked over his new surroundings, he sang quietly to himself. Despite the painful memories it triggered, it was still one of his favourite songs. It had verses that fitted when he was rowing with Sophie on the Serpentine, and verses that fitted now.

> *There are backwater places all hidden from view*
> *And quaint little islands just awaiting for you*
> *So I'll leave you right now to cast off your bow*
> *Go messin' about on the river*

Printed in Great Britain
by Amazon